BEAST
MADE OF
NIGH

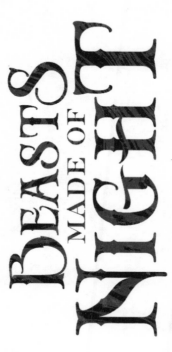

BEASTS MADE OF NIGHT

TOCHI ONYEBUCHI

WITHDRAWN

Fitchburg Public Library
5530 Lacy Road
Fitchburg, WI 53711

RAZORBILL®

An Imprint of Penguin Random House
Penguin.com

RAZORBILL & colophon are a registered trademark of Penguin Random House LLC.

Copyright © 2017 Penguin Random House LLC

Penguin Random House supports copyright. Copyright fuels creativity, encourages diverse voices, promotes free speech, and creates a vibrant culture. Thank you for buying an authorized edition of this book and for complying with copyright laws by not reproducing, scanning, or distributing any part of it in any form without permission. You are supporting writers and allowing Penguin Random House to continue to publish books for every reader.

ISBN 9780448493909

Printed in the United States of America

1 3 5 7 9 10 8 6 4 2

Interior design: Eric Ford

This is a work of fiction. Names, characters, places, and incidents either are the product of the author's imagination or are used fictitiously, and any resemblance to actual persons, living or dead, businesses, companies, events, or locales is entirely coincidental.

For Amber and Mrs. B,
who helped me battle my inisisa.

And for Mom,
who told me one evening, decades ago,
to write. And whose orders I dare not disobey.

Chapter 1

I make sure to sit where they can't see me.

From where I'm perched, tucked just out of sight on a pile of rubble, I have a pretty good view of the other sin-eaters, the aki. They're gathered in the small clearing below, ringed by the rubble of what used to be someone's home.

If they knew I was here, they'd probably get all self-conscious, stop playing, and start trying to talk my ear off. Sky-Fist this and Lightbringer that. Whatever lahala they're calling me these days in the Forum. Seems like barely anyone still remembers my name is Taj.

This group of aki are young, some of them just kids. But there are a few who look close to my age, including one girl with a big, easy smile that catches my eye. They wear jewel studs in their ears, gemstones to remind them of family members or loved ones they abandoned or who abandoned them when their eyes changed and it was clear that they were aki. Others wear coal where gemstones would go. Jewels for the living. Coal for the dead.

I grin as I watch that girl who smiled at me show off for her friends, doing a backflip off a piece of broken balcony. She sticks the landing, her tunic flipping up a bit to expose a patch of light-brown thigh. I catch a glimpse of a fresh black mark wrapped around her leg—a tattoo of a snarling wolf.

Flashing another smile, Wolf Girl holds up her hand to get everyone's attention, and the aki form a circle.

They begin to clap, slowly and in unison, their bodies swaying with the rhythm. Arms wide, then clap. Arms wide, clap. Faster. Faster. Even faster.

Now the aki begin to stomp their feet in rhythm with each clap while they sing a familiar song.

One stone, two stone, three stone, four,
Sound of Arbaa aki knocking at your door.
One stone, two stone, three, four, five,
Khamsa dahia aki set your street on fire.
One stone, two stone, and one makes three,
Aki from Thalatha climbing up your trees.
One stone, one stone, one stone please,
So the pretty aki girl can then see me.

I mouth along, careful not to let out a sound. I can't remember the last time I joined a circle of young aki like this, but I haven't forgotten a single word.

As the last words of the song die down, one of the youngest kids enters the circle and bounces on his feet, twirls, till he's got everyone's attention. Then he really goes at it, bounding to the left of the circle, darting to the right. He spins. Flies through the air. And the little aki around him cheer and clap.

Another girl breaks away and dances toward him, clapping in his face. She matches him leap for leap, and now we have ourselves a fight. The two aki kick and dodge while the circle sings about the kid who steals the pearl and has to leave town, climbing over the massive Wall that surrounds our city of Kos and escaping into the forbidden forest on the other side to whoever is waiting to welcome him home.

I notice most of the aki, except for Wolf Girl, appear to have unmarked skin. But if I look closely, I can spot a small lizard tattooed along the collarbone. A griffin marking one's shoulder blades. Black ink on red skin, brown skin. Most of them are too young to have Eaten much sin, their skin largely unblemished by the animal markings earned by a successful sin-eating. The same markings that label us as pariahs, that earn us nasty looks and shoves in the Forum. These aki are lucky. I tug my sleeves down over my own arms and legs. They're covered with beasts.

I could be inside sleeping like I deserve to, preparing for my next Eating, but it's nice out. Not so dry that the dust'll choke you into a coughing fit in two steps. And not so humid that the air feels heavy.

I even catch myself swinging my legs to the rhythm of the song as it echoes all the way up to where I'm sitting. As I watch the aki laugh and dance, it's easy to forget that some of them are gonna get spit on as soon as they leave our dahia, our neighborhood, and walk through the Forum. Some of them are gonna get kicked, maybe even beaten by the Palace guards walking up and down our streets with their cutlasses and their gloves and their complete and total lack of humor. Here, they're happy and unbothered. Here, *we* are happy and unbothered.

A shadow passes over me.

I flinch, ready to strike, but it's just Bo.

"Don't *do* that, brother; I nearly dusted you," I huff.

But I'm glad to see Bo, even though I know now it's just a matter of time before the other aki notice us. My friend is easily four or five hands taller than most people in the city of Kos. He's hard to miss.

I make room for him, sliding over so he can sit down, too. But Bo just stays standing, his freshly marked arms crossed over his large chest, face as blank and serene as always.

"Taj, we've been called to the Palace," Bo says, then clears his throat to make sure I'm still listening instead of looking at Wolf Girl. I smirk. That means he noticed her, too.

"Jai was called to Eat a sin. He failed."

My smile fades. "So he has Crossed."

"Yes." Bo's voice is quiet but steady. "The inisisa ate him. It's still loose. They need us to take care of it."

I stand up and brush the dust off, ignoring the small shiver that creeps down my spine. I didn't know Jai well, but we'd lift our chins in greeting any time we crossed paths. The aki respected him. And now he's dead. Worse than dead. Eaten.

Already, I'm trying to size up the inisisa, the sin-beast, in my mind. How big is it? How fast?

I check to make sure my daga is snugly tucked into my armband, even though I know it's always there. First thing I do every morning is slip my knife into my armband. I'd feel naked without it.

"Is the Mage already here?" Nobody makes it to the Palace grounds without an escort.

"Yes, he's waiting." Bo lays a heavy hand on my shoulder as I pass him. "Careful, Taj. Jai was good. The inisisa shouldn't have beaten him."

"Did that ruby-licker Mage say how big the inisisa is?" I try to shrug off Bo's grip.

Bo shakes his head. Apparently saying no would be too much effort.

"Well, don't worry, brother." I pat Bo's hand. "If that inisisa even dreams about beating me, I'll wake it up and make it apologize."

I lift Bo's hand off my shoulder and continue making my way into the street, where I find a Mage in a black robe, waiting to take me to my next engagement.

As we make our way to the palace, I run my fingers through my nappy hair. It's starting to grow out, and I like the look, like a massive, cushioned helmet, but it takes way too much effort to maintain. I have to wash it right. And sometimes, when it gets hot and humid, my hair falls all the way down over my ears so I look like a donkey. I don't know—it doesn't seem worth it. But when it's good and upright and all puffed out, I love it.

I hate when they keep me waiting. The more time I'm left alone with my thoughts, the more the nerves start to get to me. I play with my daga, flipping it up and catching it again and again, careful to catch the handle and not the sharp tip. I try to keep from wondering what's waiting for me behind the closed doors.

I'm sitting on a bench on an outdoor balcony, waiting to be called into the Palace where the royal family resides. Even the wealthiest folks can only afford to hire one of us aki to Eat their sins and absolve them maybe once, twice a month. The royal Kaya family calls an aki every few days. Here in Kos, the purest, those most free of sin, rule everything. For the Kayas to maintain power, it's necessary for the royal family to absolve themselves of every little sin, down to the last white lie. For being so supposedly pure of soul, our leaders sure keep us aki busy.

Outside the marble balustrade, there's green everywhere. Green grass that stretches on forever, a few trees, shrubbery that lines stone walkways that curve out on the Palace grounds. I'm so used to the reds and browns and blacks of the Forum that the green almost seems too bright, hurting my eyes. Even the breeze that whistles through this entryway feels like a luxury. We barely get any wind down in the stifling heat of the Forum.

On the balcony, it's just me and some of the Palace guards. Their uniforms are decorated with the royal Kaya crest. The Kaya crest is supposed to be some sort of dragon, but to me, it's always looked like one of those pesky common lizards that are constantly scurrying over walls, popping up in bags of rice, and scaring children.

One of the Palace guards glares at me as I tap a rhythm on the marble floor with my foot. I hold his gaze and grin as wide as I can while twirling my knife around my fingers.

Finally, the door to my left opens and four Palace guards emerge, carrying what is unmistakably Jai's body wrapped in a blanket. His arm hangs over the side, and I can see the markings covering it. Lizards and sparrows tattooed on fingers, a dragon whose wings circle his wrist. For a second, I wonder if his unpurified spirit, his inyo, still walks the Palace halls, preventing him from entering into Infinity. Sins weigh us down, and if you carry them with you past death, the earth and the sky both will reject you. They say that's why the aki poison the ground where they are buried, so that nothing good grows where we're laid. I say plantain trees grow just fine over our dead bodies. Although I'm not into all that superstitious lahala, the Palace still gives me the creeps, and I mutter a quick prayer to the Unnamed, hoping to send Jai's inyo on its way.

Before they put him in the ground, someone's gonna have to cut his throat. He's Crossed but not fully dead, the worst that could happen to us. It would be too cruel to bury him alive.

Jai had never mentioned family before, but I hope he has people, so that they don't just toss him in the shallow pits where they bury our sin-heavy bodies, far from the mines.

Even as I shift my glance away, I see that Jai's skin is blue beneath the tattoos. I know if I were to get up and look into the aki's face, I'd see his eyes glazed over, the color of ice, so unlike their usual brown. The bright stones studding his left ear would be dull as coal now. His face would be frozen in the same expression as when the sin-beast consumed him, sucking out his spirit and leaving only his ruined body behind.

But I won't let myself look, not even to say goodbye to Jai, because that's how the fear sneaks in. As fast as a lizard scampering right into my ears, if I give it that opening. Then it nestles there and grows. It makes me dull and slow, and when it comes time to fight the sin-beast, I won't be able to move as fast as I need to. Maybe that's what happened to Jai. He let himself get scared.

I stare straight ahead as the Palace guards carry Jai's body out of sight. A Mage walks out in a dark robe, and I hide my surprise when I recognize Izu, the head Mage. Back in our slum, we aki joke and call him Big Chief behind his back, but he's stood in the street before with Palace guards while his men ripped us from our families or snuffed us out from our hiding places. Other Mages will call us out for jobs, but Izu is the only one I've ever seen do the recruiting. Very dark coal burns in the chest of a man who can do that kind of work.

It's Mages who have the power to pull sins from people's bodies. The sins take the form of beasts, the inisisa, and the Mages then sit back while we aki risk our lives to kill those monsters.

Izu lifts his chin at me and jerks his head at the door. It's time.

I push myself to my feet and follow Izu as he leads me inside and down the corridor. The doors shut grandly behind us. Everything here needs that extra weight. There isn't a single gesture that isn't laced with self-importance.

My worn shoes track dirt onto the plush red carpet as we walk down an endless hallway. I begin to hear a faint clanging sound that grows steadily louder. By the time we round a corner, the sound is deafening. We approach a door that's nearly bent in half at the middle, bulging from something inside striking it repeatedly. Whatever's inside sounds big. And angry.

I shoulder past the two Palace guards standing at the door, backs as straight as their pikes. A smirk twists my lips when I see their hands trembling where they grip those staffs.

I close my eyes and steady my breathing. There's always the temptation to wonder whose sin I will Eat, whose guilt I'll be taking into my soul and onto my skin. But I can't think about that. Because then I'll start to think about smooth-skinned Kaya princesses and princes. And I'll start to think about how they get to walk around pure and bathed in light, while I have to slip through the muddy Forum, spat on and ridiculed for my markings, proof of crimes I didn't even commit.

But I can't let myself go there. Which is why I don't wonder anymore. I don't ask questions. I'm just here to Eat and get paid.

Suddenly, the clanging noise stops. Izu is at my side, and I look to him for permission. He nods, green eyes glinting beneath his hood. The Palace guards step forward, open the door, and I launch myself into the room, brandishing my blade. I don't even hear the doors close behind me, because the sin-beast rears up and roars in my face.

I stare up at a massive lion, one of the biggest I've seen. The inisisa is formed of shadows so dark that it seems to suck all the light out of the room, even taking the glow from the daga in my hand. Its claws, inky tendrils of black, click against the floor tiles as it settles back on its enormous haunches. Sin made into living, breathing flesh by dark magic.

Let's see how long it takes for me to do what Jai couldn't. I shut my mind down so that it's just me and my body. No room for emotions, for anger or fear or even joy. The beast raises a massive paw and swipes at me.

I duck beneath the first swing. Another paw comes at me and I leap back, but not far enough. Its claws tear at my shirt, the shadows as sharp and lethal as any true claws.

I scramble backward onto the wreckage of what must have been a lavish bed, catching splinters of wood in my palms. The room is a mess. Rugs lie scattered over the floor. There are smears of nearly dried blood everywhere. I'd like to think Jai put up a fight.

The beast rushes after me, and its paw comes up again. I hop just out of reach of its swipe, then launch myself at the beast. I land on its left shoulder and push myself upward so I can scramble onto its back. The lion roars, but I clamp my thighs on either side of its immense neck. It bucks once, twice, trying to throw me off. I plunge my daga into its neck.

The room shakes with the beast's scream, and it bucks again and again, but I hold on tight. I stab and stab and stab. Finally, its legs collapse beneath it, and the beast slumps to the ground. Breathing hard, I jump off its back.

Three and a half minutes. *Uhlah.* No record today.

I dust my hands off and turn to face the dead sin-beast. Slowly, it turns to mist, dissolving bit by bit, limb by limb, until it's a black pool of tar on the marble floor. The inky substance begins swirling, faster and faster, until it rushes toward me.

I hate this part.

I crouch down and open my mouth as the remains of the inisisa swim right down my throat. It burns. I have to close my eyes against it. Every time. And every time it feels like it'll last forever. The sorrow that rakes my skin. The guilt that grips my mind. The cold that pierces my bones and freezes my marrow. And I want to cry out, but my throat is full of sin, and the moment stretches out like a piece of rubber being pulled and pulled and pulled until finally it *snaps*.

And I'm back.

Bits of shadow dribble down the sides of my mouth, and I wipe the rest of the sin away with the back of my hand. I hear echoes of the sin in my mind, but I quickly shake my head to keep them from taking hold. I don't need to know who did what to whom. What's done is done. I'm just here to Eat the sin and get paid. In the beginning, I'd lie on the floor for half an hour after Eating, shivering until my teeth were ready to fall out of my mouth. Now I'm up in less than five minutes.

I walk over to the locked doors and pound on them once, twice, to let Izu and the Palace guards know that I've finished. I Ate the sin, the sin didn't eat me. I did what Jai couldn't do, what no other aki except me could do.

When the doors swing open, I see the fear and horror on the faces of the Palace guards as they take in the room behind me. Only Izu's face remains impassive, looking at me like I'm something disposable. Like a rusting hammer or a nail that'll eventually bend.

I've gotten used to it.

Next to Izu stands a golden-haired princeling that I recognize with surprise as Prince Haris. Probably sixth or seventh in line for the throne, but still royal. I bow my head quickly, but not before catching a glimpse of his cold stare. He must have arrived when I was in there battling the sin-beast. *His* sin-beast.

Coins jingle, there's a flash of gold, then a metal tab is shoved into the palm of my hand. I get a second to look at the marking on it. It's not enough time to tell how much I've been paid, just that I've been shorted. Before I can say anything, the guards are on me and I'm shoved back outside, nearly losing my tab in the process.

I spit a few times to try to forget the taste of the sin in my mouth, then walk down the path to the Palace's front gates, where Bo is waiting to walk me home. A rare smile splits his face, the only sign that he thought I might not return.

By the time I reach Bo and he slaps me on the back in greeting, I feel the tattoo burn itself into existence on my forearm. This lion etched into my skin will be with me forever now, a marker of Prince Haris's sin. Now he can walk around pure and noble and free while I carry the evidence of his crimes in my head and on my body. For a moment, I feel a heaviness. Anguish and despair from the sin wash over me, but I concentrate and push them out of my head like I've been taught to do, like I've been doing since I was nine years old.

With my redeemable tab between my teeth, I fiddle with my hair. I need both hands to fix it, to get it to puff out the right way.

Turns out Jai doesn't have immediate family left, so it's up to us to bury him. A bunch of us aki walk up to a ledge that sticks out from the earthen wall that surrounds the northern Ashara dahia like the rim of a bowl. Just beyond the wall are the mining pits, and even in the heat of midday, I see the men, black as obsidian, working the land. With coal-darkened cloth wrapped around their noses and mouths, the men climb out of the mine shafts or hand up baskets filled with what precious stones they've been able to find. The metallic sound of their hammers banging against stone fills the air. It's a different kind of noisy here than in the Forum.

Stone dwellings dot the base of the bowl, but it's mostly huts and a few shacks with tin roofs. I can barely see the people below, small specks that dart in and out of the huts, but I know that somewhere, a goat roasts over a fire and the women are preparing to dust a young girl's forehead with precious metals to commemorate her coming-of-age. Somewhere, her younger sisters are pounding yams and grumbling about it. Somewhere, in shadowed alleys, stone-sniffers crush rocks and sniff the small bits off the backs of their hands to forget their troubles, just for a moment. Over it all towers the massive statue of Malek, the mythic figure who, long ago, battled the arashi, the demonic monsters that descended from the sky and attacked the dahia. The sculpture is red-brown when the sun's at this angle, and Malek's sword arm is flung back, ready to swing a crushing blow against an invisible enemy. He's looking skyward.

As one of the eldest aki, Bo presides over Jai's burial. After the aki lay Jai down next to his empty grave, it's Bo who cuts Jai's throat, with Jai's own daga, and delivers him from his mind-death. I've got my slammers in my hand and no heart for burials, but I figure I owe it to the aki to at least be around. It doesn't take a miner or farmer to tell where the earth in this part of the dahia has been recently turned. No grave markers signal where aki have been put into the ground, but the grass avoids them. Avoids us.

We bury Jai with his dull stones in his ear.

Inyo flit through the air like black bursts of wind, then vanish, and I feel Jai among them.

Bo begins singing in a loud, clear voice, but I can't catch the words, only the rhythm. He starts the dance, and the other aki join. Jai's inyo dances with them.

The lion on my wrist burns, like all new marks do. I feel a pang in my stomach, and at first I think it's because I'm watching another aki get buried, but then I realize that I haven't eaten all day.

As the burial ends, I scrabble up over the edge of the Ashara wall in search of pepper soup.

Balance is supposed to be the principle that governs us. Sin and sacrifice. Night and day. Death and life. I get to the top of the ridge, and there's a kid standing there with his eyes closed, almost like he's waiting for me.

There's no expression on his face, but there are tearstains on his cheek. His clothes hang off him: a robe full of holes, billowy pants, all the color of mud. Must've been on the streets for at least a week. Probably twice that, by the looks of it. He looks like he's dreaming. His arms are folded tight around his chest, and his eyes are closed.

"Ay!" I step to him. My shadow looms. "You lost?"

This snaps the kid out of his trance, and he starts to shiver. He doesn't even look like he has a home to run away from. Maybe there's a place for him with Auntie Sania and Auntie Nawal at the marayu with the rest of Kos's orphans.

"Hey. What's your name?"

The kid opens his eyes, and that's when I see it. White pupils. His irises are brown, but right in the center of each is a flaming sun. He's an aki. I don't see a sin on him, which means his eyes have changed only recently.

Whenever the preachers in the Forum talk about Balance and the Unnamed and sin and purity, it's all lahala. But we barely finish burying Jai and then this kid suddenly shows up. Maybe this is what they're talking about when they talk about Balance. One leaves. Another one arrives.

"Omar," the kid says. "My name is Omar."

I hold my hand out, palm up. "To you and your people, Omar," I say.

It takes the kid a moment, but then he slides his hand over mine. It's coated in dust, and dirt clings to his fingernails. "To you and yours, sir."

"Taj," I tell him. "The name's Taj." Without thinking, I put my hand to his head and rustle his nappy hair. "You're aki now. Let's go meet your brothers and sisters." I turn back and lead him down the hill.

The pepper soup isn't going anywhere.

Chapter 2

Every single time I return to the Forum, the noise hits me like a wall. In less than a minute, my sandaled feet are covered in dirt and grime. I'm hoping the open air and the sun will help me clear my head and the pepper soup will warm my body. I look at the new lion tattooed into my forearm. It still burns. Prince Haris's sin is staying with me longer than usual, which, I guess, isn't surprising considering how big that inisisa was.

The roar of the crowd settles into a muffled quiet, but if I strain, I can pick out a snatch of conversation about someone's cousins coming to visit or about the rising price of dates. Northern and southern Kosian accents mingle together. Above it all, a crier stands off to the side of the thoroughfare, singing holy verse in a voice that booms out over the crowd.

Farther down, the smells announce the open market. A mix of imported herbs, the syrupy sweetness of deep-fried puff puff, the tingling spiciness of pepper soup with fufu. Stray too far, however, and it all starts to smell like sweet-sour refuse.

Between the jeweler stalls, glinting with crystals and rings too bright and numerous to be real, are the booktraders. They display their forbidden wares over spread cloth, ready to be snatched up at a moment's notice. The books are mostly different versions of the Word, the holy text that governs our lives. The pages are folded into cylinders, and you put the book to one eye to watch the text spiral and form new words as you read. Some cylinders are simple, tough leather fabric with black ink. Others are more colorful and ornate, displaying flamboyant curving script. I've looked through enough of these vessels to know that half of them contain not religious doctrine but secret histories, forbidden alternate tellings of the origins of Kos, of the world, texts proclaiming that sin can't be bought or sold or Eaten.

I spot a kid twirling one of the books in his hands. He's got the thing pressed up against his face, burying his nose in it. I lean back a little bit and can see that the insides don't have words but drawings. I know this book. This booktrader sells adventures: young aki questing to find a magical amulet to purify all their sins or something like that.

Two stalls down, past the herb seller, is a guy who sells stories of princes and princesses who look a lot like the Kayas. They're never named, but everyone in Kos knows who the prince is that got caught in another lady's bedchamber in last week's installment. It was probably Haris. The real people in Kos, the people getting dirty in the Forum, the people trying to make their way through the dozen or so languages being spoken at any time, they know the royal family isn't pure. We all know. Many of us Eat their sins. We just have to pretend they're pure as river water so we don't get strung up by the gates in front of our families, and so I can keep earning ramzi coins to send back to my family.

"Oya, child, buy it or leave. This is not a library." The bookseller snatches the book out of the kid's hand, careful not to crush the cylinder. I glare at him and dig into my pocket to find the marker from Izu. I'll pay for the damn book. Let the kid enjoy his adventures.

But then I pull the marker out and suck my teeth. He shorted me even more than I thought. This is barely enough for me to send back home to my family. For a second, I think about tracking him down and chopping his hand for chopping my coins, but then I'd have no more work because I'd be dead.

Suddenly, the bookseller lets out a low whistle and shoots me a pointed look. Then, he settles into a bored gaze, staring off into the distance, but his hands move fast as a goat-fly trying not to get swatted. I see him sliding some cylinders under others, and then he shoves some of them into his rucksack entirely. I hear more low whistles, and I turn to see another bookseller doing the same furtive shuffling, and farther down another. When I hear the clank of armored boots, I understand.

An Agha glides through the crowd, almost as though she's not even walking in the mud, leading a phalanx of other guards. She wears the ruby-red double-sash of higher officers. The Palace guards behind her are nothing but foot soldiers behind a general. She's staring straight ahead, but everyone knows that they've been seen. The booksellers stare down at their wares, and the guards continue past the intersection before being swallowed up by the crowd.

The little kid is still sniffling over having his book snatched away by the booktrader. He probably has no idea the booktrader just saved his life. Who knows what the Agha would have done if she had found the kid spiraling through illegal stories?

I ruffle the kid's hair and duck down an alleyway to make my way home, ignoring the conmen and hucksters that line the shadowy paths: soothsayers promising to read your future for a few ramzi, scammers offering secret cures for those afflicted by physical or spiritual ailments.

Down a side street I overhear a woman pleading with a trader, clutching her shawl close to her chest. "Please, trader, my son, he is beset by sins." She's on the verge of tears. "For many years, he has not been able to lift himself from his bed. And he weeps. Always, he weeps, and yet there is no wound on his body."

I stiffen when I hear this. I should walk away. It's not my problem. But the more I listen, the angrier I get. I've seen this before.

I was much younger. Up to Baba's knees maybe. I clung to his pant leg as he haggled with a Mage to purchase a cure for Mama. A small flock of children hid in the shadows where Baba spoke with the Mage. I remember the Mage called one of them forward, a tiny girl a little taller than me at the time. Sin-spots ran up and down her arms. And I knew it was for Mama, who had been sick for almost a month, bedridden with a sin that none of us could absolve her of.

Even after all these years, Mama and Baba are still in debt.

I want to help this woman, but I would need a Mage to call forth the sin, and that would mean breaking my contract with Izu.

"It is the guilt that is weighing on his soul," the woman in the market pleads. "Please, save my son. We cannot afford an aki. My son will die for want of cleansing, his inyo haunting my home." The poor woman falls to her knees in the mud.

I listen with gritted teeth as the trader promises a cure that will wash away all her doubts and restore her son, rescue him from the guilt that plagues him. I start at the sharp pain in my hand. There's blood running down my fingers. I've been gripping my daga.

The woman pulls out a small purse and slowly counts the ramzi in her palm, then looks at the trader who nudges her on with a lifting of the chin. She hesitates, then pulls out a few more ramzi, counts them. Her purse is nearly empty.

It's all I can do not to take my daga and carve the greedy look off that trader's face. The trader hands her a small vial, which the woman cradles in both hands before secreting it up her sleeve. Relief washes over her face, and she hurries away, head bowed.

I watch her go, then whip back and start toward the trader. He smirks at me, all traces of false concern gone from his face now that he's made his sale. He glances down at my exposed tattoos, and his grin grows wider. He knows there's nothing I can do, that it would be his word against mine, and who would believe an aki? The trader spits at my feet, sticks a rolled sijara in his mouth, then walks back into the crowd.

I push through the crush of bodies in the thoroughfare and follow him. I make sure to push up my sleeves so that people can see my sin-spots. The crowd parts immediately. Most Forum dwellers avoid touching aki, convinced that the guilt and anguish and weight of the sin could somehow transfer to them. It's a bunch of lahala, but it's useful in times like this.

As I get closer to the trader, I try not to choke on the smoke of his sijara billowing behind him.

Now I'm right behind the trader. Leading with my shoulder, I crash right into him. The trader stumbles and falls to the ground. His sijara tumbles into the dust.

"You!" he growls as he picks himself up, angrily brushing off his sleeves.

"Please, sir. My apologies." I bow, lowering my eyes respectfully as he lets out a string of curses.

I wait till I can hear him walking away before straightening up. The trader's full sack of money fills my entire palm. The ramzi would feed the woman and her son for a very long time. But she might also get tricked out of it by another trader. Mama and Baba need the ramzi too. I slip the trader's bulging purse up my sleeve.

I make my way back through the crowd, ignoring the dirty looks of the Forum dwellers who glare at my sin-spots. Their hisses follow me through the winding streets and back alleys until I reach the outskirts of the Forum. Here, the dahia I call my home stretches out before me: a small hill crushed between the outer walls of two neighboring dahia; rusted, falling-apart buildings stacked on top of one another and too many people living in too little space. Intoxicated stone-sniffers sharing alley-space with pickpockets and cutpurses. I cover my nose and mouth with my shawl, then march through the pathways where thieves and cutpurses crouch or wait or idle. My feet avoid the empty vials and glass bottles by instinct. Same with the rivers of waste that flow down the center of these paths. I've been following this route home since I was a child. I could find my way back blindfolded.

Eventually, the narrow path leads me up a hill where I get a better view of the mud-colored shanties. The tin roofs glint red in the dying sun. Up the hill the dwellings climb, as far as I can see, and I catch myself smiling. Home.

But first I need to see Nazim the money broker. The ramzi is burning a hole in my pocket, and at least some of it needs to get to Mama and Baba.

Chapter 3

Being an Aki does carry certain advantages.

The line to see Nazim trails down several storefronts and around the corner from a butcher's stall, so by the time I reach his stall, the flies buzzing around the meat decide they'd rather make a meal out of *me*. I've spent my entire life in Kos, but I'll never get used to the pests. I could certainly do without the flies constantly feeling the need to dive deep into my ears. One catches me up the nose, and I swat at it. I swear, by the Unnamed, if survival is such a basic animal instinct, why are Forum flies so suicidal?

Somebody jostles me from behind, and I nearly fall into the man in front of me. The line is mostly merchants, a few builders, and some younger Forum dwellers, my age or younger. I can only guess at their jobs. Servants of some Palace royal or their sister or wife. Handmaidens, some of them. Maybe a few newsboys, scurrying throughout the Forum with folded pieces of parchment that carry news from one corner of the city to the other. I've seen them around, darting through the legs of older Forum dwellers, the best ones able to get from one dahia to its opposite in half a day. I know Kos, but I don't know the city as well as the newsboys do. They know every nook, every passageway, even the rumored underground tunnels, and for a second I imagine a whole legion of children crawling through passages underneath the city, bringing people news of loved ones or of new merchants arriving or of a message or sermon from a faraway holy man.

A man stops in front of me to adjust his creaking auto-mail leg, fiddling with the metal gears and knobs in his fake limb. The metal that starts below his knee looks clean and sturdy, but it's gray and not at all like the precious metals or glittering stones the Kayas wear. Looks sturdy, but it creaks. The half-limbed mostly hail from north of Kos, and I have to admit that the sight of their auto-mail arms and shoulders and knees gives me the creeps. I shouldn't talk, given that's the way most people feel about aki, and it's true that a lot of the gearhead girls who solder the auto-mail are cute. But still.

The heat's starting to get that wet, heavy quality about it. I can tell because my puff's starting to droop. That doesn't stop the flies. So now I have them to deal with, and the guy in front of me is starting to stink. I'm sick of this.

I break out of the line and march around the corner till I get to the front. I push past the merchants without a word but murmur some apologies for the old ladies. When I get to the front of the line, I give Nazim's door three sharp raps.

Someone grabs me by the shoulder and spins me around.

"What do you think you're doing?" The merchant's nasty onion breath practically knocks me off my feet. Jewelry gleams around his neck and wrists. He hasn't let go of my shirt. Yanks me close. "Back of the line with you, Forum rat."

"Oga." I grin. "You kiss your wife with that mouth?"

The man's eyes shoot wide open. The crowd stirs, anticipating a fight.

A knife comes out, catches the sunlight. The merchant lunges forward.

I catch the merchant's knife with my own, then yank his arm behind his back. He falls to his knees instantly. The gems on his rings shine in the sunlight. Gaudy and wasteful. This guy has no taste.

"Don't do it to yourself, old man," I mutter into his ear as he struggles against my grip. A fly buzzes insistently by my nose, and I blow it away. It's got more heart than the guy on his knees in front of me, that's for sure.

A gasp ripples through the crowd, and I look up to see everyone inching away, eyes glued to my arms. That's when I realize that in the scuffle, my sleeves were pulled farther back, and now the tattoos on my forearms and fingers are in open view. "Look at that aki. I've never seen one with so many marks," one of them whispers.

I kick at Nazim's door again and hope I don't have to wait like this too much longer. The merchant is starting to struggle harder, and the murmurs from the crowd are growing. A couple more seconds, and their shock will turn to disgust and then eventually anger. I pray to the Unnamed that Nazim will open the door. He won't be pleased that I've exposed myself as an aki. There are plenty of folks who won't patronize the same places as aki, but it's too late for that now.

"Let go of me!" the merchant shouts, kicking at me. I yank his arm even farther up, and he yelps and falls down again. Two more seconds, then more knives'll come out.

Come on, Nazim. Open the door already.

I'm running out of time. The line has dissolved, and now a crowd of men forms around me. They're ready for violence. I press my back against the door, holding the merchant in front of me as a shield.

"Nazim." I kick at the closed door. "Any second now!"

More men push to the front. Someone pulls a dagger out from his sleeve. More follow.

I guess this is how it ends then. Thanks to some Forum flies and my big mouth. I let go of the merchant and kick him toward the crowd. I crouch, pulling my daga free. It'll be like fighting sin-beasts, I tell myself. Only about fifty of them. At once.

Just as they're about to charge, the door opens behind me.

I fall backward onto the poor money broker, who catches me in his arms. Nazim rights me, his shock turning into amusement.

"Taj," he says, raising an eyebrow.

At the sight of the money broker, the crowd of merchants instantly softens. I wait until they put away their blades before I stand up and sheathe my knife.

"It's hot, sir. You know how the weather can sometimes make us behave."

Nazim is shaking his head. *I know.*

With a firm hand on my arm, he ushers me through the doorway and into his office. I don't let go of the breath I've been holding until I hear the door close shut behind us. Another day in the life of an aki.

On his desk are neatly arranged piles of parchment with what I can only guess are accounts written on them. Nazim takes a seat behind his desk and motions to the chair opposite him.

"Please," he says in his clipped, proper southern dialect.

I brush the dust off my cloak, run my fingers through my puff, and try to get it nice and round again. It's cooler in here than it was outside. Much cooler.

"Taj, I would really prefer if you didn't make a business of driving away *my* business."

"Nazim, I try. Really, I do." I sit down and sprawl my legs. The straighter his back is, the more mine wants to curl. The straighter his legs when he sits, the more mine lounge. "But you have some very unseemly customers outside that door. I might have even seen some smugglers. Illegal spices. Forbidden texts. You never know who might come to your door with some dirty ramzi that needs scrubbing."

"Now, Taj," Nazim says, "you know I do not discriminate in my provision of services. I am at the behest of the community."

"Sure." I fish the pouch of coins out from under my shirt and toss it onto his table. It lands with a satisfying thud.

Nazim gives me a long look, and I can tell he wants to ask where I got that much ramzi from. But his business relies on discretion, so he merely sits back in his chair. "Now, will we be sending all of this home?"

He wants to know if I want to keep any of it for myself, but I remember the marker in my pouch and the sin I Ate to get it. "Yes. All of it."

Nazim dips his stylus into the inkpot, pulls a sheet of parchment from a pile, and scribbles on it in silence.

I wonder if he ever thinks about how those figures and names he writes on his sheet will turn into money for families to feed themselves. I wonder if he ever thinks of the lives attached to the money he sends and receives. To be honest, I wonder if any money brokers think about that sort of thing.

As Nazim writes, I close my eyes and think of Mama, and I think of Baba. I try to remember their faces, but other faces swim into view. Smirking princes and preening princesses. It's getting harder and harder to see them, Mama and Baba. Their faces.

I never told Nazim about that time Mama got sick and Baba had to hire an aki to cure her. And I never told him about how much it had cost us. But he has probably heard enough stories like it—he would not be surprised.

Nazim clears his throat. I open my eyes to see that he's divided the ramzi into small, equal piles. I can't tell how long he's been looking at me. I quickly blink away any trace of tears. There's a gentleness to Nazim's smile. Like he wants to nurse me to health or something. I shift my eyes away. I don't need pity. I can't feed Mama and Baba with that.

"So, how does it look?" I mutter.

"It looks fine, Taj." Nazim slides a piece of paper toward me. "The code."

I take his stylus, dip it in too much ink, then scribble a series of numbers. It's the same series of numbers I've been using ever since I started sending money back home to my parents, a code known only to me, Nazim, and my parents. Nazim halves one of the piles and separates it. His commission.

"Is there anything else today?"

"No, I'm good. Thanks for this."

"As always, my son." He nods, his eyes soft. "Be well."

"You know me," I say as I head for the door. I don't know if the crowd is still out there, waiting for me to emerge. Part of me doesn't care. "Have I ever not been able to take care of myself?"

I wave lazily over my shoulder and walk outside, shutting the door behind me.

The line outside is orderly again. There are new people at the front. None of the regulars who were moments away from gutting me. I almost wish they were still there. I'm itching for another fight, and I can't figure out why. Then I remember the marker in my pouch and how badly I was cheated for Eating Prince Haris's sin.

When I get home, a bunch of aki are gathered in a room on the top floor of our dwelling around a massive plate of fufu. Everyone has a small bowl of pepper soup next to them. Dented metal bowls of water for hand-washing ring the table. Bo's there. So's Ifeoma. The bear tattoo running along her arm is fading. Jai's cousin, Emeka, sits next to her, rolling his bit of fufu into a small ball with one hand, then scooping it into his bowl of pepper soup before slipping the whole thing into his mouth. He has a new stud made of coal in his ear, and I remember he was there at Jai's burial. A couple other aki sit or lie around the room. Sade has her legs stretched out, a snake tattooed around each ankle. She fiddles with the blue jewel on her necklace while Tolu stands by the window overlooking the neighboring dahia, etching ever-widening circles into the clay with his daga.

I pause at the doorway, taking in the familiarity of it all. When I make my way into the room, all heads turn.

"Taj!" Sade shouts and pulls something out of the bag next to her. It's an auto-mail arm.

"Ewoooo," Ifeoma pleads. "Put that away-oh. We are eating, na."

Sade jumps up and walks over to me. Everyone shifts out of the way, plates rattling as they do. Bo catches the platter of fufu just in time to move it back to the center. Tolu has stopped carving the clay windowsill and only stares, tense. Sade's holding out the metal limb, practically thrusting it in my face. Everyone waits for my reaction.

Emeka sucks his teeth. "You do not know who that thing has touched, Sade. Put it away."

"I found it in the Forum," Sade says, excitedly. "Just lying there. It's a little rusty, but it moves just fine." She twists it at the elbow. Bits of dust and rust fall away, and Ifeoma lets out a yelp and scurries away from the plate of fufu. "It's not a snake," Sade chides.

"You know how they bang metal up north, Sade," Ifeoma shoots back. "They are heretics up there. Unbelievers. Right, Bo?"

Bo silently picks a small ball from the mountain of fufu and rolls it. He has his back to me, but I can tell he's smirking, so I chuckle too.

"The arashi won't find us and burn down our home because a half-limb left his arm in the street for us," I joke. I'm afraid to touch it, but I do anyway, because I can't let the others see me scared. Besides, like Sade said, it's not a snake. The metal is supposed to be cursed, Unbalanced. Man's attempt to replace what the Unnamed has taken out.

It's cool to the touch. And except for the grooves where dirt has caught, it's as smooth as our water bowls. I run my fingers along its fingers. The joints feel weird to touch, but it doesn't bite or burn like I half expect it to. "See? It's nothing." I toss it to Tolu, who lets out a shriek and covers her head.

"TAJ!"

Everyone bursts out laughing. Emeka falls on his side, clutching his stomach. Fufu stains his shirt because he couldn't wash his hands in time. Bo's shoulders shake as he tries to hold in his chuckling. He calmly washes his hands, then gets up and walks over to where the auto-mail arm lies on the ground. He picks it up, turning it around in his hand.

"It balances just fine," he says, joking. "Back home, most of the men are miners. It is common to lose an arm or a leg in an accident farming metal for the Kayas. Is it wrong for those from the north to make us gifts like these?"

And that's when I notice that little aki in the corner. Omar. That kid I saw after Jai's burial. He hasn't moved this whole time. He's so distraught he can't even be bothered to be scared of a little auto-mail.

Ifeoma glares at the metal limb from across the room. "Eh-heh, when misfortune finds you, we shall see. Keep that thing around and pretty soon we will all be wearing extra coal in our ears."

Bo walks over to me, but then the little aki in the corner climbs to his feet and tugs the back of Bo's shirt.

"What's arashi?"

His voice is so soft, it's almost like he's never used it before. Everyone turns to look at Omar, and I can sense them all softening. Nothing like a homeless little kid who's just discovered he's aki to get all of us to forget our differences.

"Arashi," Bo starts. "They're . . ."

"They're the reason we have work," I butt in, and everyone's all smiles again. "Speaking of which . . ." I fish my marker out of my pocket and hold it up to the light. "It's time for us to get paid. Costa's shop has to be open by now."

Bo throws his hands up in the air. "But we were eating. Let us at least finish our fufu."

"Eat as much as you want," I say, heading for the door, "but you know what they say: Make hay while the sun shines."

Sade follows me. "Time and tide wait for no one," she shouts, grabbing her armband and daga on the way out.

The others get up and gather their things, but Bo sits firm.

"I have not eaten all day. If this spoils, may the Unnamed punish you." He nods in Omar's direction. "I'll see you in the Forum later."

I nod and look over at Omar. His eyes are wide.

"Let's go, little one. Time to get some fresh air."

I look to Bo and grin. He rolls his eyes but smiles back.

I can't pull the same trick I did in the Forum when I go to redeem my marker: show a little sin-spotted skin and scare people out of the way. Because now I'm standing in a line of aki. And, well, sin-spots are nothing they haven't already seen.

Most of the aki in line are closer to my age, which is nice because then they're not staring at how many tattoos I have, or fawning over me. Omar is next to me. I pretend not to notice how he follows me closer than my shadow.

The boy looks up. "Sky-Fist," he whispers.

I wince, but it's better than Lightbringer. "Omar, right?"

"Yeah." He sticks his hand out, palm up. "May the Unnamed protect you, Sky-Fist."

I slide my hand palm-down over his.

When Omar pulls his hand back, eyes glowing, I can see the fresh mark of a snarling rat on the inside of his wrist. I hadn't noticed it before. A small sin, maybe a theft or a vicious bit of gossip. He doesn't have an armband or even a daga yet. I can't imagine how he managed to finally kill the inisisa. It must have exhausted him.

"Congratulations." I nod at the mark. "Your first?"

He nods, suddenly shy.

"How was it?"

"It?"

"Killing it. Eating it, you know." I can barely remember what it was like when I was in his shoes, but I do remember it wasn't fun. "You look like a tough kid. I bet it was easy."

"It was right before I met you." Omar stares at his sandals, shuffles back and forth. "The beast was fast. But once I got past my fear, I knew what to do. The hard part was after, when I had to Eat the sin." Omar looks up at me and fishes a marker from a pouch inside his shirt. "The Mage gave me a chit and told me to come here to collect my money."

I can see from the marker's etches that he's only gonna get a couple ramzi. Hopefully, he doesn't have to worry about sending money to anyone else for food. Hopefully, he just has to worry about himself. He goes back to scratching the life out of that tattoo, and my heart kind of breaks for the kid.

"You can't scratch it like that. You're gonna hurt yourself bad if you keep at it."

"It hurts," Omar whispers through gritted teeth. "How . . . how do you make the feeling stop?"

"Stop scratching." I shrug.

"No." Omar hesitates, then taps his finger against his temple. "In here. I feel bad, like I did something wrong. Only I know I didn't."

I grab his hand, close my fingers over his tattoo so he can't get at it anymore. "That's not your sin to worry about. Those feelings? They're not yours. Just think about yourself. Nobody else."

I flex my free hand so he can see the tattoos that wind around my fingers. "We're supposed to carry the guilt, and the more we think of our sins, what we did, what we thought, the more we are supposed to hurt. But these aren't our sins. We didn't do this. So these aren't ours to think about. Make sense?"

I can tell from the look on Omar's face that it doesn't, but someday it will.

"Don't think about the people who sinned. Don't think about the sin and who it was done to. Just think about killing the sin-beast and getting paid. What's the only thing in the world you should ever think about?"

"I . . . I don't know."

"You." I let go of the kid's wrist. I can tell Omar doesn't quite buy it, which makes me kind of glad in spite of myself. He's skeptical by nature, like me.

The kid looks around at all the aki gathered here. With the coal or the jewels studded in their ears. With the stones in their necklaces or bracelets or anklets to remind them of their pasts. With their sin-spots to remind them of their present.

"We can't ever go back, can we?" His voice is small, but there's a new edge to it. He's learning how to be angry. "We can't ever go back home?"

"Once our eyes change? No." I can't remember the last time I saw Mama's and Baba's faces. This kid is gonna have to get used to that.

"My sister's Jeweling ceremony is soon." He sniffs, then balls his fists at his side. "I can't go now because I'm aki."

I'm not good at this. Usually, Bo handles this part. Whenever aki get homesick or mourn the life they've had to leave behind, he's the one who takes them aside and cheers them up. He's the one who helps them adjust. Me? I'm just the handsome big brother they're all supposed to want to be like.

Someone shouts up ahead, and all of a sudden the line breaks up, everybody pushing one another out of the way. Instinctively, I put my arm out and move Omar behind me, then I shoulder forward. The aki I pass are pretty well marked. I know from experience that not much will set them off, but they'll fight way too hard for what they think is theirs. I get to the front, where a bunch of aki are gathered. Costa, the lizard-faced redeemer, sits behind a protective steel mesh barrier.

"That's not what it says on my marker!" Ifeoma shouts at Costa, who just sits with his arms folded. "I'm supposed to get two ramzi! That's how it's notched."

Costa leans forward and points to a piece of parchment nailed to the outside of his booth. On one column a list of sins, on the other, a series of numbers. "These are the rates, you ruby-lickers. I do not decide them."

"Those weren't the rates yesterday!" Ifeoma slams her fist against the steel fencing.

"How're we supposed to know what all of that means?" growls Sade. "You know most of us can't read that nonsense."

I shove my way to the front and pull my marker out, then smash it against the fencing, right in Costa's face. "How much does this get me? And don't you dare say anything less than six ramzi."

I wait, breathing hard. Everybody waits. He wouldn't dare defy Sky-Fist. The Lightbringer.

Costa bows his head. After a second, I realize he's chuckling.

"Gutter-rat," I shout, hitting the fencing because it's the only thing I can think to do. "Who changed the rates? How do we know you didn't just write these out this morning?"

I keep talking, hoping something will stick. Maybe I'll say something that'll hit, that'll either get him to change his mind or that'll calm the restless aki behind me. Everybody's got their eyes on me now. "Some of us got mouths to feed," I drop my voice low, too low to be heard by anyone but Costa. "We got families."

"An aki? With a family?" Costa sneers. "That seems like the answer to a riddle that doesn't exist."

Something snaps inside me. I pull my daga out of its sheath, slowly so that everyone can see. "Pay me what I'm owed, or I cut through this fence like hot oil. Then we'll see about rate changes. How does that sound?"

Costa's gaze darts to the left, past my shoulder, then to the right, and I turn around, too late, and see that there's half a dozen Palace guards at the back of our crowd, ready to knock our heads in. The fight instantly goes out of me. It's not worth it.

I sheathe my daga and slide my marker through the opening in the fence. "Fine," I growl, shoving my face right up against the fencing. "What does this get me?"

Costa makes a show of examining it, checking its markings. Then, he tosses me three measly ramzi, and I scoop them up.

I wish there were something I could say, some small threat or insult that would hurt him, do real damage, but I can't think of anything. So I walk away, the look from every aki I pass burning into my back fiercer than any sin I've ever Eaten.

I walk and walk to clear my head and lose track of where I am, but a quick look to the left, and I can see, over rooftops, the ridge that surrounds the northern dahia. I realize I'm close to where Auntie Sania and Auntie Nawal live, two older women who practically raised me after I left home to begin Eating. I smile, remembering how their pockets were always full of chin-chin for young aki, meant to wash the taste of sins out of our mouths. It's a poor dahia, but it's far enough away from the Forum and most other parts of Kos that the people here generally get left alone. It's as quiet a place here as you can find in all of Kos.

The sound of scuffling draws my attention. I turn to see Omar climbing over a pile of stones in an alley and heading my way. Uhlah, this kid is never more than three paces behind. I keep going, hands in my pockets, pretending not to see him, but he falls right in step beside me. He puts his hands in his pockets too. Sticks his chin up just like I'm doing. We must make quite the picture strolling through the dahia like this.

I know he's got a million questions for me, but he's gonna have to learn to speak up for himself, so we walk in silence through the winding streets of the dahia. They widen, then narrow suddenly, so that if you don't know your way around, you're likely to run smack into a wall.

Then I hear it. Drumming.

We come to the wide boulevard, and coming around the corner to our right is the first line of dancers. Four of them spread across the width of the street, their brightly colored robes flowing in the wind as they twirl and stomp in unison. Their wrists and ankles and ears glisten with gemstones. The light catches their jewels and makes them look like moving human-shaped stars. Rounding the corner behind them is the first drum line. Their hands move so fast against the massive drums strapped to their waists. Their muscles gleam with sweat.

Local Kosians come out from their homes and join the tail end, arms swinging with their own dance steps, children doing their best to mimic the adults. I can see where some of the aki get their moves.

"What is it?" Omar asks.

I don't bother hiding my grin. "It's an Ijenlemanya. A parade."

"What are they celebrating?"

I can feel my heart getting bigger with each second I watch the Ijenlemanya. This is Kos. "It's a funeral without a body. Odans from south of Kos brought the tradition with them. A celebration of life." Finally, a tradition that has nothing to do with sins and aki and us bearing the guilt of others. A tradition that doesn't make me feel like a piece of parchment for others to write their sins on. Or a rubbish bin where they can dump their worst parts. "Sometimes, they do it to celebrate a birth in the dahia. Sometimes, they do it when a child of the dahia scores well in school. Sometimes, to celebrate a marriage." I shrug and my smile widens. "Sometimes, they do it just because. A celebration of life. That's why they say it's a funeral without a body. It's a celebration. The grave is empty."

The air is clearer around the parade, almost as though they're clearing out the inyo that choke us when we walk through streets they roam.

The revelers head down the street and slowly disappear behind another corner.

"Hey, do you see that?" Omar points at a robed figure standing across the street from us. His robe shimmers silver where the wind rustles against him. The gray is darkening, slowly, starting from the cloth at the bottom near his feet and moving upward.

The call to prayer sounds, and I put my hand on Omar's head. "Time to go." Pretty soon, Kosians in every dahia will come back out of their homes and surround the large black Cubes in the center of their dahia and sit in silence to commemorate the Original Storm that created the dahia. They will pray to the Unnamed to protect them from arashi none of them has ever even seen.

My good mood evaporates. All this fear of monstrous arashi that only appear when there's enough sin in a city to draw them, it's all lahala meant to control us. Anybody with half a mind knows that those Mages send us all over so that there will never be enough sin in the entire city to call down their wrath. If there are arashi, they've done a pretty good job of steering clear of the Kaya Palace.

"There are no arashi." I don't realize I said it out loud until I catch Omar staring at me. I realize I'm thinking of the question he asked Bo when all the others were eating fufu earlier. "There's only the way your wet clothes hang heavy on you during a storm and the way your stomach growls when it's empty. Don't let anyone tell you otherwise."

The robed man across the street hasn't moved, but his robe has gotten darker. It's completely black. Then I listen.

Wait a second.

The afternoon prayer call sounded not too long ago. And the sun's too high in the sky for the next one. Something's not right.

"Come with me." I hurry up a small ladder pressed against the side of a house, then scramble along the roof until I get to where laundry hangs on clotheslines. Omar's right behind me. I squint, and that's when I see them, up on the hills that overlook the dahia. Wreckers. Hurlers. Catapults loaded with brick and stone and burning bundles of wood stand ready.

The man who stood across the street from us is gone. Uhlah, that wasn't a Mage. That was a Palace animist. Sent by the Palace to the dahias. It all makes sense now. The way his robes shimmered—it was metallic thread with the power to detect the amount of sin in the air. The darker the robe, the greater the amount of sin.

That animist's robe was pure black. My stomach twists.

This isn't a call to prayer. It's a Baptism. The Palace is going to "cleanse" the dahia by razing it to the ground.

The first Wrecker launches. A flaming ball of wood and stone hurtles through the air, and I'm frozen in horror as it crashes into a home close enough that the impact knocks me onto my stomach. In an instant, I realize that it must have landed less than a hundred meters from Auntie Sania and Auntie Nawal and the orphanage. Omar and I stumble from the impact.

"We gotta go." And we set off at a run along the rooftops of the dahia while homes fall to pieces behind us.

CHAPTER 4

I KNOW HOW this all goes.

Every once in a while, when some Kaya feels like it, brigades of Palace guards swarm through the Forum and out into the dahia, where families like mine live in shacks and mud-colored homes.

Then up on the hills surrounding the neighborhood, Wreckers and Hurlers are wheeled into place, pulled by servants hoping to work off their sins with manual labor. Meanwhile, the families in the slums cower in fear. Some won't know where to go or what to do; they're the recent arrivals. Maybe they can no longer afford a place in the Forum; maybe they're coming from outside of Kos. Maybe they're just unlucky. Meanwhile, the rest of the dahia will begin packing up their lives and running away. The Hurlers, those massive wooden contraptions, will fling their shots, and stone and brick will arc high into the air then crash into the houses below. Frightened children will scurry, crying for help, and some of them will run straight into the arms of Palace guards and the Agha Sentries lying in wait to round up more potential aki.

I know how this all goes. Because that's how they got me.

A boulder flies over my head and smashes into the building next to me. I dash down an alley and nearly crash into a father racing in the other direction. He stops to pull forward his two sons, their mother following close behind. I look to see what they're running from, and there it is: the telltale red of a sentry's robe. The Agha Sentry moves at the head of half a dozen guardsmen, and they stalk down the path like a river that breaks down everything in its way. They're calm, their eyes sweeping back and forth, looking for new aki recruits. I look back, and I'm relieved to see the family has vanished. But so has Omar.

There's no time to look for him.

I round the corner and run through the market, now abandoned after the warning call sounded. The jeweler's stall is unattended, but people are too busy fleeing for their lives to steal. The cylindrical books are scattered all over, trampled, their pages exposed and torn. The wind scatters some loose sheets over the ground, unraveling them, revealing the illegal stories the booktraders were hawking.

Quiet covers this stretch of street. The only sound is the occasional crash of boulders into homes. Maybe the guards and Mages have already been through here. I'm about to leave when I hear something skitter. I stop, look both ways, then spot something moving in a crevice too thin for a body to fit in. It's not until I'm crouched right in front of the slice in the wall that I see the pair of golden eyes. They shine straight through the shadows. It's a little girl. I can only see flashes of her face, the dark skin of her cheeks, some of the dust and plaster pasted to her forehead.

I reach out my hand and let her get a glimpse of the tattoos on my arm so she knows I'm not one of the guardsmen. "Hey, what's your name?" She doesn't move. I shuffle closer. "It's OK. Where are your parents?"

She's not crying or shaking. She's completely still. Maybe she's in shock. Other than me, she's the only thing still breathing on this street. In my head, I map out the street I'm on and the surrounding quarter. Behind me, the shuffle of boots against dirt. The guards.

"Come on," I hiss. "Come on, we gotta go." She's exactly the type of child they're looking for, the type that gets swept up in these Baptisms. The type the Mages will test to see if she can Eat, if she has aki potential. The footsteps are getting closer. If they find her, I won't be able to stop the Mages from taking her. From separating her from her parents. If they're still alive.

The girl sticks a hand out. I take it, pull her out, and hitch her small body up on my side. She's wearing a green robe, and one of her sandals hangs loose. Now that she's in my arms, I see that she can't be more than five years old. "What's your name, little one?"

She turns away, and I think I see a smile. With my free hand, I thumb some of the dust and plaster off her cheeks, but I only end up smudging it further.

"It's OK. Now hold on tight." I shift her onto my back and make sure she's wrapped her arms tight around my neck. Then we're off.

At first, I want to take her to the Aunties. They'll know what to do, but my gut is telling me to head for the outskirts of the dahia, where the guardsmen are least likely to patrol. The destruction from the Baptism is random. Untouched blocks of houses and shacks one instant, then nothing but rubble the next. Occasionally, we'll hear screams, and the little girl'll bury her head in my neck.

"It's all right, little one."

We're about to hop out from around a corner when I hear a moan. I freeze. It could be anything. Could be something I dreamed up. Could be the moan of an uncleansed inyo wandering Kos. But I wait. That definitely sounds like a person. Still alive. We turn, and, half-buried by a collapsed wall, a man struggles. He grits his teeth and pushes against the bit of stone wall that pins him to the ground. He's covered in dust, and broken tree branches and bits of metal surround him.

I shift to cover the girl's eyes, but it's too late. She's seen him. Before I can stop her, she pries herself out of my grip and lands with a soft puff on the ground.

"Baba," I hear her wail through sobs. She tugs at the arms of her father.

"Sweetheart, let's go," I whisper.

It's not that I don't feel for her, but the man is doomed. Guardsmen are coming through for another sweep. There's no saving that man. But maybe I can save her. As if I summoned them with my thoughts, the good-for-nothing, ruby-licking guardsmen appear and, just off to the side, a Mage. Hunting for someone just like her.

I don't know what to do. Leave and live with this girl's fate on my conscience or sacrifice myself in a fiery burst of heroism—even though after I die, they'll probably snatch her up anyway. I flick my arm, and my daga slides out of its sheath and into my hand. I crouch into my fighting stance and move in front of the girl and her wounded father. Maybe the other aki will tell stories about me. Maybe they'll talk about how the Lightbringer gave his life to save a little girl from the clutches of the Mages. The thought of a statue of me being built in a dahia makes me chuckle.

When the guards see me, they pick up their pace. Now they're practically charging toward me. I'm ready to spring.

May the Unnamed preserve me.

Something heavy rushes right past me, a blur of black and brown, and crashes into the Agha Sentry. The column folds in as several more people rush in to break up the guardsmen. Aki! I shout with surprise when I see Bo leading the charge. He tackles one of the guardsmen, then plows like an ox through the whole troop while the others jump in and cause chaos.

I turn and see with relief that Auntie Sania and Auntie Nawal have followed them. They crouch down by the girl and her wounded father. I can see dirt under their fingernails where the Aunties probably tried to dig people out from underneath the rubble.

In the tussle down the alleyway, the Mage gets tossed to the ground. He yelps. The little girl, distracted, lets go of her father, and Auntie Nawal sweeps the girl into her arms. Down the way is a small gaggle of kids, some the girl's age, some younger, some older. Auntie Sania gives me a familiar look. The kind of look that tells me it's time to do the difficult thing. While my best friend is fighting off guards, I gotta chaperone a bunch of weepy little kids to safety.

There are just over half a dozen of them, some in rags, some in dresses. None of them have a speck of sin on them. I catch Auntie Sania's gaze and nod, then I rush ahead to make sure the path's clear. When I look back to see what happened to the girl's father, he's nowhere to be seen. I pray to the Unnamed that he made it out.

As our little parade makes its way down the empty streets, I scoop up some of the smaller kids, smiling big to make sure they're looking at me and not at the crushed remains of their homes or the arm sticking out from under a piece of rubble. Some of them are old enough that this isn't their first Baptism. Even so, you never get used to this.

I'm still carrying one howling boy in my arms when I start to recognize the streets. There's an untouched balcony that still has potted plants on it, and farther down a blanket hangs from a second-story window. It has a spiral painted on it in many colors. Handprints spot it, small enough I know they belong to a kid. Or kids.

I realize I'm now within an hour's walk from Mama and Baba's house. I could go see them. Right now. Go look for them. Make sure they're OK. I could let them know they don't have to worry about me, that my money will be coming, same as always. With a little extra this time.

But the kid in my arms starts whimpering, and I have to bounce him a little bit to get him to quiet. We don't know if any Mages or guards are around. I can't stop thinking about how unblemished this little boy's arms and legs are, pure where mine are marked. It makes me feel dirty, and I know I can't let Mama and Baba see me like this. Mama would avoid looking at my marks, would whisper, "What have they done to you?" and Baba would just stand there, still as a statue, with that look on his face like he knows I'm suffering and he's suffering because of it, but neither of us knows any other way. No, they don't need to see me like this.

It's not too long before Auntie Sania up ahead motions for us to stop. Auntie Nawal continues down the empty street and looks both ways to make sure it's clear, then leads us down a dark alley to a wall covered by a wet curtain. She raises the curtain to reveal an opening, and we hurry through. As soon as the flap closes, both Aunties look at me sternly, in that way that makes me feel guilty. Like I should be taking better care of myself.

Auntie Nawal steps closer to me. "Bo tells us you've been getting into fights lately."

I look away and run a hand through my hair, puffing out the side because I can't think what else to do. "Bo talks too much."

"I don't think there are very many people in Kos who would agree that talking too much is Bo's problem." Auntie Nawal snorts out a laugh. "You should stop by more often. There is always a warm meal waiting for you here."

I nod to the hidden entrance to the marayu, the orphanage. "You have a lot more mouths to feed now. Besides, I can take care of myself." I shrug. "Whenever I get called to the Palace to Eat, I come back with a full belly anyway." I wink and turn to leave.

"Taj," Auntie Sania calls out. She has chestnut eyes that tug downward at the edges so that even when she smiles, she looks sad. "Your hair's gotten so long. Do the girls like it?"

"Yes, Auntie. The girls like it." The smirk slips off my face. I feel tired all of a sudden. "Auntie, I have to go."

"Be well, Taj." She puts a hand on my exposed forearm, noting the new lion on it.

Both women vanish into the enclosure.

I turn and see Bo leaning against a wall at the mouth of the alley. He's got a small tear on his sleeve, but other than that and a little bit of dust in his hair, he doesn't have a mark on him. When I get next to Bo, I wrap my arm around his neck.

"You've been talking about me behind my back?"

I try to wrestle him to the ground. Before I know it, he's got both of my arms locked behind my back. How he moves so quickly, I have no idea.

"It's for your own good, brother," Bo says. He's not even breathing hard. I slither out of his hold and glare at him.

"I'm hungry. Zoe's?" Bo cracks his neck.

I nod. "Zoe's."

All around us, people are cleaning up from the Baptism. Pulling precious broken things out from under the rubble. Sweeping the entrances to their homes. Restacking stones.

"You think I'll have any luck this time around?" I ask. My back is screaming at me, and my knees tremble with fatigue.

"What if we run into girls from Ithnaan? You think it'll be the same ones as last time?"

Bo chuckles. "You better hope not."

"Well, if they don't like my hair, at least Auntie Sania says it's nice." I start to pluck at it, try to get the curliness to puff out all the way. There's dust and grit and sweat all in it, so I have quite a bit of work to do if I'm gonna be presentable by the time we get to Zoe's.

Chapter 5

The sound outside, in the Forum and in the dahia, is sharp. It crackles in your ears. Different languages, the clink of ramzi in purses. Here, at Zoe's, with the lights low and shadows cast over everything, everything's dulled. It's loud, but it strikes the body differently. Maybe it's just because I'm always more comfortable here than out in the streets. I know the streets, was raised in them. But I'm always on guard, eyeing corners for Agha Sentries, listening for the telltale stomp of heavy boots. Always thinking of where I am in relation to Mama and Baba's house, how far, how close have I wandered? Here, at Zoe's, where I can take a pull from a shisha pipe in peace and blow clouds of smoke into the air, it's like my brain slows down. And the cushions here are soft enough to curl up and fall asleep on.

But as soon as I walk in with Bo, I tense up. The place is packed tight tonight, and there's a different energy in the air. Electric, exciting . . . somebody's gonna fight before the night's over.

Shisha smoke of every flavor hangs thick in the air. Strawberry, lemon, mint, apricot, apple. Gamblers slap dominoes on a table nearby and roar at one another. By the bar, two women with beads in their hair discuss trade routes along seas I've never heard of before, while another who has a warrior's brand running along her left shoulder blade threads her way around tables with a purpose I can only guess at.

The doors whisk open and in walk the Scribes. There used to be only seven of them in this dahia, but now there are more than twice that. Their shirts, made out of dulled stones pulverized into shining threads, shimmer in the candlelight. Their shirtfronts and pants are painted with colorful sin-beasts. Some of them have scarves wound around their mouths and noses. Colorful paint stains their fingers.

The Scribes operate at night, tagging parts of the Wall around Kos with fiery paintings of inisisa. But instead of painting shadows, they give them colors so that the creatures loom blue and red and orange and all sorts of other colors over the dahia. Even carrying their buckets of berry-dye and stone-crushed paint, they're too fast to get caught by the Palace guards or the Agha. But when the Scribes do choose to come out during the day, they do it like no one else. The way they walk, the way they dress, the way they make their own path and don't follow anyone else's. Any kid in Kos who, at some point, doesn't want to be one of the Scribes has something wrong with him.

One Scribe looks over her shoulder and catches sight of me and Bo in our corner. As soon as she pulls down her headscarf to reveal her face, I smile. Marya.

In three long strides, she meets us, then pulls a cushion from another table, and we form a loose circle. Her silky dark strands of hair peek out from under her hood, and paint-stained fingertips poke through her gloves. Her shirt is tight over her leathers.

"To you and your people, aki," Marya says, sliding her hand out, palm up.

"To you and yours, Scribe." I slide my hand over hers.

We slap our hands together, and it makes the most satisfying sound in the entire Kingdom of Odo. It's so good we can't stop laughing.

"Any new ink since I last saw you, Taj?"

I pull back my sleeve and show her the new lion.

"Fresh," she says, tracing it with a paint-smeared finger.

I wink at her, roll the sleeve back down, and put the shisha pipe to my lips. "Stay. I'll order you a pipe."

"Eh-heh!" Marya looks to Bo, who smirks and raises an eyebrow. "So, Taj, you are breathing diamonds now? You sneeze and emeralds just fall from your nose."

"I simply do not work for free, Marya. Enough with this lahala." We're laughing so hard I can barely keep the shisha smoke in. "Really. Stay. It's been too long-oh. Next time I see you we'll both have beards."

"I can't. We have some new Scribes who are gonna do their first tags tonight." She leans in close. "Brought them here to put some oil in their gears. Get rid of that pesky fear." She winks, then slides off the cushion and stands. With her index and middle fingers together, she touches her head and her heart, then turns and leaves. Obi-njide. Holder of my heart. Something they say in the south. Ask a northerner and they'll say it's just dainty, effeminate southern lahala. But there's no other word for it in Kos. Marya, the girl who ran the streets with me after I left home and before the Mages snatched me up, the girl who would use her cloak to shield me from the rain when Kos was flooded and we homeless kids had to sleep on roofs, the girl I stole food to feed. She's not a blood-sister. And she's more than a friend. If I had a family stone, I would give it to her to wear. But then everyone would think she was my heart-mate and we'd be forced to marry, and neither of us wants that. It's not like that at all. I'd rather wear auto-mail than get married.

Bo gives me that look. That "I know you're up to something" look, but I just chuckle and take a pull from the shisha pipe. A massive cloud of apricot-flavored smoke billows before my face.

A medicine man walks by somewhere with his vials, his wares clinking inside his cloak like wind chimes. Halfway across the hall, a young woman with a wrap across her chest and beige trousers heavy with gear pouches sits with another gear-girl. The second one wears her hair in locs, held back by a red head wrap.

I notice the girls, and I can tell that Bo notices me noticing them, because he's got that warning look in his eyes. That "Taj, don't make me have to rescue you again" look.

"Bo." I nudge him. "I have a plan." When he doesn't respond, I nudge him one more time, and I can see the annoyance on his face.

"Please, Taj. Not now. My entire body is sore."

"Whose fault is that?" I shoot him a murderous glance.

"My apologies for saving your life." He puffs and exhales a cloud of shisha smoke so thick it hides his face for a second. "Again."

"This'll be your reward." I shake his knee. "C'mon."

He closes his eyes again. "No."

"Why not?" I know Bo sees the girls. And I'm pretty sure they wouldn't mind the way his muscles fill out his shirt. Bo's quiet, but he does all right for himself. "C'mon, at least give me a reason."

He raises a hand and beckons me close until my ear is right by his mouth. I lean in.

When Bo belches, it's like he's spitting fire up both my nostrils. I topple backward into my cushions, hands over my nose and mouth. "Uhlah! What did you eat?"

"A gum I put together. Made from the resin of an herb I bought from a western trader." He chews as I look at him in horror. "For my stomach."

"By the Unnamed, Bo." My nose still burns.

"Better out than in."

"Always something with you," I mutter. Eventually, the burning in my nose stops, and I can breathe again.

As I grumble and settle back into my cushions, I see her. A girl in a drab black robe. Her hood is pushed back so that her black-brown hair is visible. Spectacles sit unfastened on her head, holders wrapped behind her ears. I watch as she scatters dried dates over her table, then appears to count them.

"Don't worry, Bo," I tell him, not bothering to look his way. "I'll handle this one on my own."

I place the handle of the shisha pipe on the dish that catches the falling coals and straighten my clothes. Run my hands through my hair to puff it out and get it just right. I might smell a little bit, but so does everyone else here. She won't notice.

I head her way, weaving around tables and in and out of clusters of people ready to flash daggers if the wrong person says the wrong thing. When I get to her table, she's still got her head bent over the dates, moving them around and whispering beneath her breath.

I snatch one up, pop it in my mouth, and sit down in the seat next to her, as smooth as anything.

Her head darts up. "Hey! I was using that." She almost reaches for the date I'm chewing, before realizing she doesn't really want it back.

"If you weren't eating it, you weren't using it." I spit the date pit in my hand, then stick my hand out to her. A peace offering.

She scowls, then her eyes widen in shock. I'm about to ask her if she's seen an inyo when she lunges forward and grabs me by my forearm.

"Ow!" I struggle to get free, but if I move the wrong way, my shoulder'll pop out of joint.

"By the Unnamed," I hear her murmur. "You're an aki."

The way I'm pinned down, I can't see what she's doing, but I can feel her fingers running up and down and around my forearm. Tracing my tattoos. Despite what the other aki might think, I'm not used to girls touching me like this, and my cheeks burn.

"Ah, a lion here. Yes. And here, what is this?" She twists my arm to get a better look. I yelp in protest, but it's like she doesn't even hear me. "A lynx?" She gasps. Suddenly, she lets go of me, and I fall back into my chair, massaging my arm.

Meanwhile, she reaches into the satchel at the bottom of her chair and pulls a parchment sheet out on the table. She's scribbling furiously.

"Hey."

Still scribbling.

"Hey. Lady!"

She looks up, then says, "What does it feel like when you Eat?"

"What?"

"Do the marks burn? Is that how they appear on your skin?"

I can't keep track of the questions. She doesn't even give me a chance to tell her she's speaking too quickly. I'm starting to think I should've stayed with Bo and his poisonous breath.

"Lady, I'm happy to answer your questions, but how about some tea first?" I take some ramzi and toss them onto the table. They land among the dried dates.

"No, please, allow me," she says excitedly. "What are you having?" Before I can decline or even tell her my favorite kind of tea, she's already gone.

I sit there, my mouth slightly open, until I feel Bo lumbering up behind me. I wave him off. "Don't worry, Bo. I have this under control. You're gonna ruin it." He ignores me, reaching over my shoulder to snatch up a date.

"Sure, Taj. All right." He pats me on the shoulder, turning to leave.

The girl reappears with a tray of tea, most of it already sloshed out of the cups. When she sees Bo, she gasps, and the tray topples. I reach out and catch it just in time, but scalding tea still splashes onto my hands. I manage to set it all down nicely, arranging the small saucer of milk and the teapot and glasses and the bottle that holds the honey. But when I turn around, the girl doesn't even notice. She's already tracing the marks on Bo's arms just like she did with mine. It's tough not to feel at least a little jealous.

"Another aki," she says. Gleefully.

Meanwhile, I'm trying to get the honey off my hands. My fingers have already gotten sticky.

"Do you know this one?" She gestures to me, and already I've become "this one." I can't even be angry at Bo. He could not have planned to thwart me so expertly.

"Yes," Bo says, trying not to laugh at the expression on my face.

"Here, sit, sit." She puts out a chair for him, then sits back down. She leans forward and stares at both of us intently. I slouch, because what's the point in even pretending I have a chance with this girl now?

"You'll have to pardon me," she says, catching her breath. "I just . . . I don't come across too many aki and—"

I put my hand out and look around. "Please, umm . . ."

"Oh!" She puts a hand to her chest. "Aliya."

"OK. Please, Aliya. Not so loud." She's got a question in her eyes, so I elaborate. "The rules are a little lax at Zoe's, and people feel free to mix more than out in the Forum, but we aren't exactly the most popular types in Kos."

"What he means to say," Bo says, now the suave translator, "is that we aki aren't welcome here. Officially. It is not glorious work, what we do."

"Oh, of course," Aliya says. "Even though I haven't completed my Mage training yet, and I've never met one of you in person, I know all about aki. We know your work—"

"Of course you do," I mutter. "We make you rich."

"Taj!" Bo glares at me and kicks me under the table.

"Sorry," I murmur. "Forgot my manners." I reach over and pop a date in my mouth.

"He gets like this sometimes," Bo tells her. "Moody."

"Is that a side effect of the Eating? All the guilt and torment of others?"

"No, this torment is all his own." He laughs.

If my skin weren't so dark, I'd be bright red by now.

"Well, you aki may be looked down upon, but what you two do is necessary. Important." Aliya hasn't touched her tea. And she hasn't taken her eyes from either of us.

"Thank you for the encouragement." I smile blankly.

Bo gives me a warning look but lets it slide.

Aliya starts to play with the scattered dates on the table. "I'm sorry. I spend so much time down in the archives I forget what it can be like here, that there's a particular kind of order and that some people should be treated one way and some should be treated another. In the archives, I forget that some people are born to be hated. I'm sorry if how I've been speaking has hurt you."

"It's not your fault," I say quickly. If some people can afford to stick their heads in the sand and forget what it's like for the rest of us, good for them. I want to point out her ignorance, but I don't have the heart to anymore.

"I should explain myself." She sits up, straightens her back. "I'm studying to be an algebraist, and I'm still trying to understand how everything is connected. It's wonderful. The ways the tau function can be applied to identify the composition of the minerals that make our gemstones is connected to the charting of star patterns. And if you input values for the theta function and subtract mock-theta values from that, you produce the number of sides of the shrine in each dahia and . . ." She stops. "I'm sorry. . . . I spend so much time in the Ulo Amamihe, the Great House of Ideas. And . . . well, I forget that not everyone speaks this language. It's just that . . ." She gets excited again. "The formulas, they're written everywhere. They're written in the shape of our city, the dahia, the shrines, the sin-beasts covering your bodies—"

"So you know your formulas." I don't know where the edge in my voice comes from, but suddenly, I don't like the way this apprentice is talking about us and where we come from. "Well, scholar, that doesn't mean you know anything about the dahia. Or about what we do."

I grab a glass and pour myself some tea, then, with a spoon, add a dollop of honey . . . and my fingers are still sticky. I take a sip of the tea and grimace. It's cold.

Aliya is quiet for a moment, watching me stubbornly slurp down the tea.

"You're right," she says finally. "I don't know anything about being an aki, but I want to learn. Would it be all right if I spoke with you two further? I've never conducted an Eating. I haven't even seen one in practice. But to be able to reconcile these images with what's spoken of in the texts would greatly advance my studies and—"

"Hey." I don't bother to keep the edge out of my voice this time. "We're not experiments. We're just bodies. Collecting all the horrible things the royal family thinks or does so that their pure spirits can rejoin Infinity. They lie and cheat, and we pay for it. Meanwhile, we're left to gather the city's sins. Is that written in your archives?" I get up without bothering to finish the tea. "Come on, Bo. Let's get out of here."

As soon as I'm outside, I tighten my cloak around my neck. The wind has picked up. Bo appears at my side a moment later. The setting sun bleeds red in the streets. Just as we're getting ready to head off, I hear someone huffing behind us.

"Wait! Please, wait." It's Aliya.

We both turn. She's out of breath. Despite my earlier outburst, I feel a little sorry for her.

"Please, I didn't mean to offend. I'm not used to talking to people, to anyone really, outside of the archives. But this is how I see the world. All of it. Trigonometric functions and equations, that is how the Unnamed speaks to me. It is all connected. It all makes up Infinity, and I know that the aki are a piece of it. A necessary and important piece of it." She steps closer to Bo and lowers her voice. I can tell she's looking my way when she speaks, even though I keep my back turned. "On your bodies, I don't see sins, or anything to be ashamed of. I see functions. Equations. I see poems."

"Mage, what we do is difficult, awful work," Bo says. "We find very little solace in our lives because of it. What peace we do find, we are very likely to keep to ourselves or share only with others like us," Bo says. "It's easier that way."

"But can I see you again?"

Bo smiles at her and slides his hand out to her, palm up. "May the Unnamed protect you, Aliya."

After a second, she slides her palm over his. "And you as well."

Then he turns, and the two of us head toward home. We don't get very far when we hear footsteps behind us.

"Wait!" Aliya shouts, running up to Bo. "One question. Please, before you leave. Why are your sin-spots faded and your friend's are not?" She pants between each word.

Bo looks to me, and all I can do is glare back. It's easy to forget sometimes. We all become white-pupiled. But everyone else's sin-spots fade away with time. Except mine.

Bo turns back to the Mage. "We don't know. We never ask. Maybe someday, you'll find the answer."

"Bo!" I shout.

Without another word, we leave the Mage behind. The lamplights have begun to turn on.

My red drapes flutter in the breeze. The prayer call echoes over the city. A low baritone voice that trills. It's the only sound to be heard for miles.

I'm tired. Too tired to wrap myself in that moth-eaten blanket and stretch my legs out over those threadbare pillows that sport patches of dried drool. Behind me, someone nudges the door open. I lift my head to see it's that little aki I thought I lost in the Baptism. Omar. I'm mad at myself for losing track of him, but a bigger part of me is proud that he made it out alive on his own. He's learning.

"Come in, brother." I make space by the window for him, and he shimmies up to my side.

"It still hurts." The kid hasn't reached for his wrist once since he came in, and I'm proud of him. "It hurts," Omar says again. Quieter. To himself.

"It won't forever," I lie.

I don't say anything else. I just look out and watch the setting sun throw gorgeous colors over the northern dahia. The Hurlers earlier made the place look like broken teeth. But the purple and red cutting through the clouds like a daga still make the slum look beautiful.

In the near-silence of the prayer ceremony, families sit in quiet meditation, forming concentric circles around their shrines. Apparently, it's all supposed to mean something. According to that nosy apprentice, it matters how many sides there are to a shrine or the fact that we sit in circles or the way my sin-spots are arranged on my arms and legs and chest and back, but it's all lahala. I wish I knew why I'm so angry at her.

I can see kids from the neighborhood clambering over the rubble. One of them is carrying a ball, and they start playing.

Another small group crowds around a girl as she arranges shards of colored glass and stones on a wall as the others watch.

The sun angles itself just right, and colors—green and blue and yellow—splash against the rim of the dahia. The children gawk, rapt at the way the lights dance against the wall. Like the dancers in the Ijenlemanya.

I glance at Omar next to me, and for the first time, he's smiling too.

Chapter 6

Omar sleeps under a mountain of blankets. I'm in the doorway of the room in our aki compound where most of us eat, and I've got Bo and Ifeoma and Sade behind me. A couple littler aki crowd behind them in the hall. Ifeoma stifles a snicker. Sade shushes her.

Then I pounce.

"WAKE UP!" I shout, snatching off Omar's blankets and tickling under his armpits. In an instant, he leaps up and swipes at my face. He lands in a fighting stance, but his eyes have barely even opened yet.

Sade doubles over in laughter. Ifeoma can barely hold herself up against the wall.

"What?" Omar mumbles, wiping the sleep from his eyes. "What is going on?"

Bo walks to the boy's side, all stately pride, and grins down at the little aki. "Today's your Daga Day."

Omar looks confused, but we're all beaming.

There is never any graceful transition between the rain season and the summer. There are a few days, maybe a week or two, of relief from the monsoons, the flooding, and the sewage overflow, then all of a sudden the sun returns. The Forum bursts with color; it blinds the eye. And everyone comes out to enjoy it. The streets are crowded with people—children playing and animals brought out after months of being cooped up indoors.

Chickens flap wildly in cages held by their handlers. Some let out their last cries before the meat-man chops off their heads. Goats roam, tethered to their owners by rope. Exotic birds preen for everyone watching. They spread their wings, and their feathers join to resemble multicolored faces looking right at you. Anyone who spends enough time in Kos can tell which birds have dyed feathers and which ones are natural. On really hot days, the dye flakes, and everyone knows who's full of lahala.

We head south toward Gemtown, where all the jewelers peddle their wares. They can't put their shops too close together, because people walk up needing to close their eyes to keep from getting blinded by the jewelry and wind up at the wrong jeweler's stall. So they give enough space for shadows to fall. Here in Gemtown, you pull your cloak low over your eyes. With our white-pupiled eyes shaded and with baggy clothes hiding our sin-spots, we aki can walk around just like everyone else.

Gemtown forms a small semicircle toward the bottom end of the Forum. In some stalls, Kosians can buy fasteners for their ear-stones. In others, families who have been saving up can purchase family stones or gems for a young girl's Jeweling ceremony. But we're here for something darker.

There's one storefront that's barely a storefront at all. From the overhang, a tent flap swishes in the breeze. I hold it open, and the others walk through. Omar hangs back, shifting his weight from foot to foot.

"Eh-eh! Hurry up! Time and tide wait for no one." I give him a soft kick in the backside, and he chuckles as he scurries in. When the tent flap falls behind me, we're shrouded in darkness.

Then a beam of light sneaks through the roof, and the entire room is alight with the rays reflecting off the obsidian knives and gleaming swords and cutlasses hanging from the walls and ceilings. All types of dagas, some with bejeweled handles, some with plain wooden handles, sit neatly arranged on plush cushions behind glass displays.

Bo nudges me, and I notice Omar gawking at the wares.

"Eh-heh. You want your new nickname to be Flycatcher?" I say, laughing. The rest of the room chuckles. Omar smiles, chastened, but still very much in awe.

From behind a curtain in the back, the stonesmith emerges. The jewels he wears around his neck and ankles clink as he walks toward us. His skinny arms poke out from billowing sleeves. He clutches a cane with one gnarled hand and moves with his head down. Everyone clears a path for him. He stops a few steps in front of Omar.

The stonesmith towers over the little aki, then lowers himself, knees cracking as he does, so that they're face-to-face. When he pulls back his hood, the stones embedded in lines along his cheekbones mirror the light in his eyes. He looks like something more than human, and the sight of him always leaves me breathless. I feel the same sense of awe I did when it was my Daga Day and I saw him for the first time.

"Child," he says in his breathy voice. "What do you see here?"

When Omar doesn't respond, the stonesmith tilts his face in closer.

"What do you see?"

"I see . . . I see gemstones. I see jewels and cutlasses and dagas. I see canes with jeweled handspots. I see fasteners for earstones. I see all the colors that ever were."

Bo and I look at each other, our eyes wide. We're both shocked at what the boy says. I don't think either of us have heard him say more than three words at a time.

The stonesmith hums his assent. "That is interesting. I see all of those things too. But I see something else also."

He rises, then looks around at his shop and smiles with all of his teeth. They look like they're made of ivory. "One gray morning, a stonesmith was working in his shop. And a woman came to him. She held in her hands a broken heart and laid it on his table. The man wore a dark apron and had soot and dust covering him from his work, and the ruby jewel on his table was precious and unblemished. But it was broken. The woman asked if the stonesmith could repair her broken heart, and he replied that he would. He mended it and returned it to the woman, and she left him to his work. But she returned the following week to tell him it was still broken. It did not glow. So he worked on the heart for another week, used his best tools, and recalled the wisdom of stonesmiths before him. And he gave it back to the woman. But when she returned again to say it still did not glow, he realized what he needed to do."

The stonesmith turns back to Omar. "So he reached into his chest and took out his heart. He put the woman's broken heart back in his chest and gave her his own. After this, she never returned."

He does this every time. Every single time we bring new aki here for Daga Day, he tells the same story the exact same way, walks the same few paces, stoops at the exact same height, looks at the exact same bits of jewelry. And every single time, it's like I've never heard it before.

"So, little aki," the stonesmith says. "Look around again. Tell me what you see."

Omar stands in silence for a few seconds. Then he says, "Sacrifice. I see love."

"Yes, child. Love."

We all know to remain in reverent silence for this part.

The stonesmith retreats to the back room, then returns a moment later with a daga inside what will be Omar's armband. He holds it out with both hands, and Omar lets it fall into his own. Slowly, he slides the daga out of its sheath and turns it over in his hands, gazing intently at the way it shines. How smooth it is.

Bo steps out of the circle we've formed, and we all unsheathe our dagas. This part is new. Originally my idea, but I let the others think Bo came up with it. I can't have them looking up to me like I'm some responsible older brother bringing them together and building morale.

"This is my daga," Bo says.

"This is my daga," we all repeat, surrounding Omar.

"There are many like it."

"There are many like it." Omar's voice, at first a whisper, grows louder and firmer with each response.

"But this one is mine."

"But this one is mine."

"I must master it."

Our voices are rising so loud all of Gemtown can probably hear us, but I don't care. "I must master it."

"As I master my life."

"As I master my life."

Then all together: "May the Unnamed preserve us."

Silence hangs in the still air. Nothing, not even the jewelry hanging from the ceiling, makes a sound. Until Ifeoma practically tackles Omar and everyone else joins in ruffling his hair, nudging him, and grinning so big that he can't help but grin too.

I hang back a little. Satisfied.

They jostle him until Sade hoists the boy onto her shoulders and dances in a circle while the others dance around them, singing a song about a boy and his new daga.

Omar's still smiling when we leave Gemtown. He doesn't seem to care about anything other than the daga he keeps holding with both hands. He won't stop looking at the thing.

So he doesn't even notice when we get to the ridge of the Sabaa dahia. The cluster of homes and estates in the valley below spreads wider than most of the southern dahia. Small villages dot the outskirts beyond the larger compounds, some of them nothing more than huts, others full clay houses with wells and pens for animals. I realize which village is Omar's when he stops and stands completely still, looking down at what was once his home. We're maybe a couple hundred meters away.

Outside one house, in the backyard, a group of men lounge. Some of them are young, a little older than us. The rest of them are older. And most of them stand by tables, pounding away with hammers.

"Come on," I tell Omar, and wave him along. The others follow as we skid down the hill, one ledge at a time. We get near enough that we can see some of the people inside the house. The sky is darkening, and someone has lit a fire beneath a tree in the home's front yard. The men pound and pound, and the metal clanks, and golden flakes fall to the floor. Then, they slide what remains on the table into calabash bowls filled with just a little bit of water and stir and crush some more.

One of the younger men is given a bowl, and he heads into the home, and I realize with a start that that's probably Omar's older brother. Omar hasn't said a word. Hangs back. He looks on so shocked he's forgotten to put his daga back in its sheath. I bet he never expected he'd get to see home again. Certainly not during his sister's Jeweling ceremony.

The young man heads into the home, and I follow Omar's line of sight to one of the windows. Inside that room sits a crowd of women. I can't hear their words from here, but I know they're praying over the girl at the center of their circle. One of the women takes the bowl from the boy's hands and a few moments later dips her thumb into it. I know she's going to draw a line across the girl's forehead, and so will all the others.

A goat burns over a fire pit somewhere nearby. The neighbors must be cooking for them.

I look around and see that Omar's found a tree to hide behind. I haven't seen him this terrified since that first day, after we'd buried Jai. Bo stands next to Omar, and Sade and Ifeoma stand to the side, in the shadows. Even covered in darkness, their eyes glisten with envy.

The smell of the goat cooking wafts our way. My stomach hasn't been this loud in a long time.

Quietly, I head over to the tree Omar's standing by and rattle the branches. A whole bushel of plums showers us, and when Ifeoma and Sade glare at me, I mouth, *Sorry*, then start picking up the fruit.

Nobody else seems to want any, not even Omar, so I stand and eat by myself.

The women all come out of the house, the oldest at the head and the girl at the rear. The women all wear bloodstained cloth around their right hands. The ritual goes like this: Each family member uses the Family Stone to cut their palm, then they mix the blood with the gold dust and form small lines down the girl's forehead.

Neighbors stream in from nearby, and the smell of good meat almost overpowers me. Maybe if I bite deeper into these plums, I can force myself not to give in to temptation and rush over there and eat that entire goat.

The music starts so suddenly I jump and drop half my plums. Everyone starts dancing. Three of the men have drums between their knees, and the others clap to the beat, forming a ring around Omar's sister. In the center, she twirls and spins. Neighbors reach into their baskets and toss small gemstones onto the ground at her quick feet.

She'll dance until her feet are bloody. Until the minerals from the gemstones and other precious metals are bathed in her essence. And then the women will tend to the girl's feet and smile and tell her now she will bear gilded children.

Marya told me that's how it happens, but this is the first one I've seen in person. I turn to look at Omar, who is peering out from behind the tree,

It was supposed to be a surprise, to give him some peace and closure. But his bottom lip is trembling now, and he's sniffling, holding on to his daga too tightly.

Bo puts a hand to the little aki's shoulder. "Hey, we don't have to stay," he says quietly in Omar's ear. "We can go whenever you want."

"No," Omar says. So quietly I barely hear him. "I want to stay."

So we stay. I chew through all the plums in my haul, but I don't have the heart to rain more down on Omar's head. Seems like too serious an occasion.

I let out a sigh, then watch the village feast. Eventually, the dancing ends and the men clean up and everyone says their goodbyes. I yawn and turn toward the others, ready to gather everyone and head home. But there's no little head poking out from behind the tree.

"Hey, Bo." I look around. "Where's Omar?"

Sade takes a step toward the house. "By the Unnamed . . ."

Ifeoma joins us. "He's aki. If they see him, they'll throw him out. They might even call the Mages. We can't let him—"

"Wait," Bo says. Then he points right to the roof of Omar's family's home.

The little aki climbed up onto the roof of his old home. He's curled up, holding his daga close to his chest. He's going to sleep up there. I know already that there's no way we can talk him out of it.

My room's night-blue by the time I hear footsteps shuffle outside my door. I left the door open for ventilation, but it doesn't make a difference in the summer heat. Even the breeze is stifling this time of year. My pillows are soaked with sweat. Sleeping under the window is no help. So I'm wide awake when Omar tiptoes past my door. He came home after all.

I wait till he's gone, then I get up and follow him down the hall to where he sleeps with a bunch of the other aki. They're all bundled together on pallets on the floor like snoring puzzle pieces. Omar's back is to me as he unstraps his armband and hangs it up on a peg in the wall. The moonlight streaming in through the window catches his wrist and bounces off a new stone on his bracelet.

I'm barely back on my pillows when I see him in my doorway.

"Yeah?" I ask, pretending to be more annoyed than I really am.

"Um. Thank you."

"What? For the daga? Eh, you don't need to thank me. You're one of us now."

"No. For . . ." He looks down at his hands, then at the bracelet on his right wrist. "For bringing me back home. So that I could see my sister's Jeweling." He holds up his wrist to show me the small sapphire hanging from his bracelet. "This was one of the stones she danced on."

I push myself up on one elbow. "Now you two will always be joined."

Omar smiles. "Thank you for letting me see my home one last time."

"It was Bo's idea," I lie. "You should be thanking him."

I turn over, but I can tell he's still watching me. He waits a beat before padding down the hall. It feels like forever before I finally fall asleep.

Chapter 7

The sound of knocking at my door wakes me. I was in the middle of a really good dream.

It wasn't the type of dream you remember completely. It was the kind of dream where the details are blurry, but the feelings remain. As soon as I wake up, I want to go back. There was a pretty girl in it, and sky as blue as the crystals Mama wore around her neck. I'm sure there was other stuff I liked in there too. Whoever's at my door is still knocking, and I shut my eyes even tighter. Maybe if I wait long enough, they'll figure out how to get whatever they need from someone else and they'll go away. But I know I'm not that lucky.

The footsteps draw nearer, and the knocking gets louder.

I give up and peel my head from my pillow. I've drooled all over the thing. Again. I wipe the saliva from the side of my mouth, rub the sleep out of my eyes, and run my fingers through my messy hair.

It's Omar. Looks like we're joined at the hip now.

"There's a Mage downstairs," Omar says quietly. "He's come for Bo."

"What?" Then I remember the night at Zoe's and Aliya, the Mage girl with the glasses. "Is she still there?" She was cute. A little strange with all that talk about equations, but still cute.

I hop up and rush to my window to see if they're in the street. I can see the top of the Mage's hood. Bo is standing next to her, fitting his armband around his bicep and tugging his shirtsleeve down over it. He stretches his neck from side to side, rolls his shoulders back.

On my way out of the room, I snatch my armband and knife from where they hang on the wall. I struggle getting my arm through, fumbling with the straps as I take the stone stairs three steps at a time. I burst out the front entrance just as I slip my knife into its scabbard and run right into the Mage.

The Mage stumbles back. The hood slips a bit, exposing the Mage's face. I'm absolutely certain both the Mage and Bo can hear the disappointment in my sigh.

It's not her.

This Mage I don't recognize. He has skin as thin and pale as parchment. His eyes, narrowed and glinting like silver ramzi, look me up and down. A smirk curls the Mage's lips.

"Ah, the Lightbringer," he says, and I can hear the venom in it.

I catch Bo's eye, and he doesn't seem fazed.

"Got a job," Bo says, adjusting the straps under his sleeve. "At the Palace."

My eyebrows shoot up. "The Palace?"

Bo nods and shrugs, like he's seen it all before and I'm the wide-eyed new kid he's stuck with. Like we get called to the Palace every day. "So you'll be needing backup then?" Even though we both know Bo can take care of himself.

Bo rolls his eyes, and I stifle a chuckle.

"Come on. How much could it hurt to have some backup? In case there's just too much sin for you."

The Mage steps between us. "Enough. Only those with prior approval from the royal family may set foot in the Palace. You were not selected for this job." He twists his mouth. "Aki."

I slide my daga out of its sheath and twirl it between my fingers. "I'm not doubting my fellow aki's abilities. Not in the slightest. Nor am I in this just for the money. I believe you should work for everything you're given." I wink at Bo. "Tell you what, if it turns out you don't need my services, it's free."

My daga whistles with each pass, each twist. Suddenly, I shoot the knife forward, inches from the Mage's chest, then pull it back and run my index finger over the tip, as if testing its sharpness. "But. Say the sin-beast gets out of control or runs loose. Or, and may the Unnamed prevent this from happening, it devours my fellow aki here. Then, you've got a sin-beast on the loose *and* you're out an aki. It can't be too easy to come across guys as good as us, can it?"

The Mage hesitates.

I snap the daga back into my hand. The Mage's face slackens, and I try not to smile. "Just tell the royal family they'll finally get their chance to meet the Sky-Fist. The one they call Lightbringer." I slip my daga back in its sheath. "I guarantee you they'll relish the opportunity."

Even if Bo and I were stacked on top of each other three times over, we still wouldn't be able to reach the vaulted ceiling above us. Ornate crystal chandeliers hang overhead, filling the hallway with light. The guards at the door have their pikes out in front of them, and their backs are like planks of wood. Banners hang along the marble walls emblazoned with the Palace sigil. Portraits of the holy men sit in between. They stare down at us, their eyes following our every move.

I stand a little straighter, push my shoulders back. I don't slouch like I usually do. I have a theory about the people who live in places like this. It's not just about the royal family. I see it wherever the well-to-do scholars and lawyers and religious officers live. They build places like this with ceilings high overhead and walls very far apart to make a person feel small. They build places like this to make it seem like human beings don't live here. People don't live here. Things bigger than people do. Out there, you're angry at the royal family that governs Kos and dictates everyone's lives. In here, you're scared of them.

I wonder if I'll get to meet any of the Kaya family. Bo's the man of the hour, and I'm just supposed to stand around while he takes care of business, but will I still get to stand in the same room as King Kolade? Marble statues of him litter the Forum. Maybe I'll catch a peek at his sister, Princess Karima, who, they say, has the ear of the arashi. The stories say she's carried about in—these are the exact words—a cloud of arashi-breath that makes her glow like the stars.

Bo takes a deep breath. He always pretends to be so serious, like he's setting an example for me. The one time he smiles? When he's about to Eat. I think it's the way he copes with sucking the venom out of sin-heavy people. We all have our ways. I always try to let go of the tension in my bones. To let my body flow on its own. It's like a choreographed dance I've memorized. Sometimes, I catch myself. Sometimes, I'll get too excited to kill the inisisa.

Very early on, when I was just starting to Eat, Auntie Nawal would take me aside and caution me softly about my eagerness to Eat. She called it sin-lust. I think it made her sad. So, instead, I try now to just focus on myself, my movements. I try to remember the powerful things I can get this body of mine to do.

"You OK?"

Bo's voice snaps me out of my daydream.

"Huh? Oh, sorry," I say. "I was just in my own head. Thinking."

"Stay with me, brother."

A door up ahead opens and out sweeps a girl, one I've only seen in portraits and from a distance during royal processions: Princess Karima. She's even more beautiful in person. I have to stop myself from gawking. The light shining through the ceiling windows turns her dark hair gold, like the train of her dress. On anyone else, the precious metals smelted into cloth would look wasteful.

"Hopeless," Bo snorts, seeing my expression.

The girl stands only a few paces from us, with warm brown eyes and full lips that curve into a smile. A loud cough from the Mage makes me remember my place, and I quickly bow.

"May the Unnamed protect you, Princess," Bo and I say together.

"And you as well, aki," she says softly.

I straighten and peek up at her face. I'm surprised to see there's no sign of disgust when she sees my tattoos. Instead, there's a kindness in her eyes that shocks me.

"May I?" she asks.

"Princess?" I ask in confusion.

"Your arm," she says.

Stunned, I roll my sleeve back and offer my right arm. For the first time in a long time, shame rises like bile in my throat. Back in the Forum, I'm used to the hisses and the sneers at my sin-spots, but here, in the beauty of the Palace and before the princess, I'm ashamed. They're telltale signs that I do not belong. That I am someone lesser. I'm the most sin-heavy thing here.

The princess takes my forearm in her hands and turns it over, eyes roving across my cursed ink. I nervously glance at Bo and the Mage. The princess focuses on one mark in particular: a group of small dragons whose flight patterns encircle my wrist and extend up to my bicep. As she examines the fresh lion on my forearm, I rack my brain for some formality, some sense of ritual. Is there something I'm supposed to do? Like kneel or duck my head? Is it blasphemy to continue looking at her shining face? Am I supposed to say something? Before I can come to a decision, she lets go of my arm.

"These are so dark. Your friend's have faded, but yours have not. What you do . . ." Princess Karima doesn't search for words. She waits for them to come to her. "I hate that you must do it."

So do I, I want to tell her, but I feel the Mage's heavy gaze on me, and I stay silent.

"What do you call them?"

"Your Highness?"

"Your markings. What do you call them?"

I look at my arms, turn them over. I call them many things. Brandings. Sin-spots. Markings. Sometimes I call them by the sinners that gave them to me. Liar. Thief. Adulterer. Brawler. "Sins, Your Highness. I call them what they are."

Princess Karima looks at me, like she can see straight through my rib cage directly into that space where my soul is supposed to sit. After a long moment, her brow smooths and she smiles again. It's like a mask has dropped back over her face, reflecting nothing but a kind of amusement with the world. But I know what I saw.

A door opens behind Princess Karima. "Please," she says.

I'm not surprised to see Izu again, waiting for us. Maybe he likes my work. Even though he has his hood up, I can see the glint of his polished eyes. Princess Karima waits at the door, and I realize there's no reason for her to follow us inside.

"May the Unnamed protect you," she says with a small bow of her head, then she's gone.

I watch her go before I remember myself and trail a little behind Bo as we enter the private chambers. I still have no idea whose sin we're here to Eat. Usually, I don't care, I'm just here to do a job, but something about the way the princess looked at me makes me think this is not a regular job. My stomach twists at the thought.

The blood-red curtains inside the private chambers are pulled back, and sunlight floods in. Books are scattered about the floor with torn-off pages floating in the cross breeze. Ornate rugs hang from the wall with tiny, perfectly angled geometric patterns stitched into them with golden thread. One of the rugs has been removed from its peg and lies crumpled up a few feet away from the altar. I have a hard time believing anyone in the royal family is this messy, or that someone isn't immediately here to tidy things up. Then again, we're not exactly the royal family's most important guests.

Someone stands by the large windows toward the back of room. His back is to us, and I crane my neck to try to glimpse his face. When he turns around, I stifle a gasp.

King Kolade has a sharp, narrow jawline, with eyes the color of clean river water. His blond hair, which brushes against his shoulders, is black at the roots. A simple crown sits upon his head. His dark brown skin, blond hair, blue eyes are striking. There's no one else who looks quite like him in all of Kos.

I bow at the waist, making sure I see nothing but marble tiles.

I feel a shadow pass over me. When I lift my head, I see Izu standing over me and Bo.

"You," the Mage hisses.

Bo rises. Izu's hood is still up, but his eyes are as sharp and cold as shards of ice.

"And you," he says to me, "by the wall."

The Mage moves in close to Bo and speaks in a quiet murmur. I strain to hear him. "This will be quick," Izu sniffs. "A small sin-beast, a lizard most likely. Do not expect too handsome a payment, aki."

I stand by the wall, beneath a row of prayer rugs, just a few feet from the guards who stand at the door. Kolade's servants, dressed in white robes that contrast starkly with their pitch-black skin, rush past me and into the hallway. The room settles into a heavy sort of quiet. I can practically wrap my arms around it.

I'm not surprised the servants left so quickly. A Mage had been called. Two aki, covered in sins, stand at the ready. There can only be one terrifying conclusion: King Kolade, supposedly the most pious man in Kos, needs to have a sin removed. Maybe they already know, and all of this is just to keep up appearances, present the illusion of ritual. Just for show, like everything else here.

Izu and King Kolade head to the center of the room and stand on an intricate star pattern made up of small golden tiles. Its points radiate outward to all the room's corners. The Palace guards pull the drapes shut, stamping all the light out of the room. It feels wrong to see King Kolade get down on his knees before the Mage. Izu places his palms on King Kolade's forehead.

Words I can't understand spill out of Izu's mouth. They're in the same language as our holy verse, but there's no music in them. The words are harsh, ugly.

Halfway through, King Kolade seizes. He clutches his chest. His eyes bulge. Convulsions shudder through him. Gritting his teeth, he pitches forward. His moan turns into a growl. I sneak a look at Bo to see if he's nervous.

Feelings rush through me. Vindication at seeing a member of the royal family kneel before someone else. Satisfaction at seeing them in pain. But the ritual is also a reminder that the Kayas sin just like the rest of us. If an aki ever spoke of this, a Mage would discover it, and the sin-eater would vanish. No one would ever know what happened to them. Exposing the royal family would mean preparation for a swift burial. There are days when I want to climb up on a dais in the Forum and shout out to everyone in Kos that the royalty carry sins just like we do. But I'd barely be able to finish a sentence before a guardsman would cut me down. No one is supposed to know about this part. It would be treason of the highest order.

King Kolade falls to his hands and knees, retches, then retches again, then vomits thick black bile onto the marble tiles. The brackish puddle stirs. The sin-beast is coming.

Bo's dancing on his toes a little bit. He's already got his daga in his hand.

King Kolade spits the last of the sin out. Izu helps him to his feet and leads him to a chair. King Kolade sinks into it, exhausted.

I raise my eyebrow. If a small sin takes that much out of the king, then maybe he really is that pious.

Bo walks to the writhing puddle of ink. It begins to take the shape of a tiny lizard. He flips his knife in his hands, flips it again. He's smirking a little bit, and I can tell he's thinking what

I'm thinking. Typical royals, wasting precious ramzi on an aki for a sin like lying.

Just as Bo gets ready to stab the thing dead, the lizard explodes outward, crackling with energy. It grows and grows and grows until its scaled back brushes against the ceiling. Tremors shake through it. Arms burst out of its torso. Scales ridge its back and belly. Its long tail whips back and forth, whistling past my ears. It's no longer a lizard, but a dragon.

The dragon drags its claws against the floor. It crawls toward Bo, then stands to its full height, towering over him.

I'm paralyzed. I wonder if I should rush in to help, but there's the risk of distracting Bo. He needs every bit of his focus right now.

The dragon lets out a roar right into Bo's face so loud I can feel it in my bones.

Bo doesn't flinch, but when I look closely, I can see his hands shaking. It's the first time I've ever seen genuine fear on my best friend's face.

The beast charges, fangs bared and wings beating the air.

Bo leaps to the side and darts to the window. The beast stomps toward him, growls rippling in its inky throat. Bo turns to face it, flips his daga in his hands. The dragon jerks his head to one side to avoid it. With its head bowed, Bo jumps at the dragon and slides his knife between its fangs. He's standing on the dragon's bottom jaw, using his arms to keep the mouth from snapping shut with all his strength. He shakes with the effort, glistening with sweat. Already, he's straining. He can't last much longer like this.

The dragon tries to close its mouth on him. Bo gives one last push, stretching the dragon's jaw open even farther. He has a small window of opportunity. He plunges his knife in the beast's mouth, and the dragon's jaw dips down and crashes to the floor. Bo falls with it, his legs collapsing beneath him. The entire room shudders. Plaster falls from the ceiling. Bo clambers to his feet, and I can see he's limping. He's hurt. The dragon picks itself up and sends an earsplitting shriek that rumbles throughout the room. Bo goes for a foreleg, but the beast raises it, and he misses. Bo loses his balance and slides along the floor. The dragon dives for him, but Bo scrambles out of the way just in time.

I want to leap in. This one is too big for him. But something keeps me frozen where I stand.

The dragon's swishing tail lashes above Bo's head, swatting at him. He ducks, then dodges, dancing left to right as the beast's heavy tail tries to crush him. He's favoring one leg, and the beast notices. In one swoop, the dragon's tail swings toward his injured leg, and Bo cries out. The beast's tail wraps around his ankle, hoisting him into the air. His daga slips out of his hand. Upside down, he grasps for it, but it's just out of reach.

My heart is pounding. Maybe I can run in and knock his daga up to him, but I don't know what the punishment will be if I intervene. And I might just get in Bo's way. Bo might die today.

Bo flicks his wrist. The cord wrapped around his forearm snaps the knife back into his hand. In one movement, he slices through the beast's tail. The beast lets out a roar and arches its back, sending Bo somersaulting through the air. He hits the floor so hard I wince.

He's not moving.

He squirms, tries to pull himself forward. There's a small trail of blood under him.

The sin-dragon turns around slowly. Its steps are deliberate. Certain. It knows it's about to feast.

The room darkens. King Kolade hasn't moved from his seat, watching with weary indifference. He can't be bothered with the death of a lowly aki. Izu shows no concern either. No worries that this sin can't be defeated, or fear of the sin-beast's power. Maybe they believe I'll be able to handle the weakened thing once Bo is gone. Maybe they don't care if I die in the process too. My fists shake at my sides.

The dragon rears. It opens its mouth wide, tenses, then rushes straight for Bo's body.

Before I know what I'm doing, I break away from the guards, daga in hand, and leap over Bo's body.

My hands go up.

"STOP!" I shout.

And the beast does.

Chapter 8

The beast is staring at me.

Its head is tilted to one side. Tendrils of black smoke peel off its body. It considers me, like it's trying to figure me out. Do the inisisa think? I wonder. What, by the Unnamed, could this one be thinking right now?

Bo lies on the floor behind me, completely still. But I think I can hear him breathing. That's what I tell myself. He's still breathing. He's still breathing. He's still alive.

I take a small step to the side, and the dragon turns its head. Looks me straight in the eye. It seems like it can only see me clearly when I move. I remember hearing about animals like this once. They could sniff you maybe, but it wouldn't be till you tried to run away that they would find you. My daga handle is slick in my hand. Slowly, I tighten the strap around my wrist. I have no idea how much time has passed. But I need to move. I can't move, but I need to.

Bo lets out a soft groan.

The sin-dragon tenses. I jump forward and twist, plunging my knife right into the nape of its neck.

Its roar echoes in my ears, rattling my brain. The dragon writhes beneath me, more fiercely than anything I've ever fought. Then, I'm flying.

When I hit the wall, I can hear the snap of bone. I fall to the floor with a thud. Taking a shaky breath in, I come up on one knee. Something wet and warm dribbles down the back of my neck. I put my hand to it, and my fingers come back red. I cough, and pain wracks my ribs.

The dragon looms over Bo's body. My knife is still stuck in its neck. The inisisa convulses, barely holding itself together. Its inky body starts to become thin and patchy. I can see right through it. Tendrils of smoke rise up from its scales; its shape grows blurry and hard to discern.

I try to stand on my feet and can't. My entire body aches. The dragon takes one step toward me. Then another. Then it dissolves.

In waves, its body loses form, and it turns completely to smoke.

Little exploding stars cloud my vision, and my head pounds. I put a hand to my forehead and stagger to my feet, checking for broken bones. But as soon as I stand upright, the sin slams into my throat like a spear pinning me to the wall. It's never hurt this much before. I fight it, I try to swing at it, kick at it, break away, but I can't. Tears stream down my cheeks. This time is different. This time, I can't take it. I'm paralyzed. The sin has taken hold of me. Every bone in my body, every inch of skin, every muscle. I can feel it in my arms and fingers, in my legs and my toes. It fills the space between my ears and behind my eyes. Everything is going black.

Guilt squeezes my heart. I gag on the massive sin forcing itself into my body. I can feel the pain turning into a grief-filled kind of shame. It latches on to every thought running through my brain. Why didn't I jump in to save Bo earlier? Why was I so cruel to Aliya? Why did I lie to Omar about how Eating gets easier with time? Why haven't I sent more money to Mama and Baba? I feel guilty for every single step I took in the Forum, for hiding my skin from others.

Suddenly, it stops. I see Haris, the golden-haired princeling, standing in front of me. This is impossible. The one whose sin was burned into my forearm as a lion. I stumble toward him and reach my arm out for help. Or barring that, for him to cut me down. Any relief from this pain. The princeling is near enough to touch. He's real. My fingers brush against the crest on the princeling's chest, then he disappears.

I open my eyes, then begin hacking. There was no princeling. It was just a hallucination. That's never happened before. Why was there someone else in King Kolade's sin? And why did that sin change shape?

Light returns to the room as servants part the heavy red curtains. Everything is suddenly made of sunlight, and I have to shield my eyes. The sin turns in my stomach. I can barely hold it down. But I can breathe again. Finally.

Bo's on his feet by now. Despite the pain thudding in my body and echoing through my mind, I can feel myself grinning. I knew it. He's alive. He favors one leg over the other, and there's a tiny stream of blood leaking down his face, but other than that, he seems like he came out of it in one piece. We both did.

Izu stands at King Kolade's side. Looking at the king's face, I can't tell what he's thinking, or whether he's even processed what he just witnessed. He's just as expressionless as that sin-dragon was. I stand straight. My back aches. Then, gingerly, I make my way to Bo and the others. It feels like I just got stomped on by a pack of bears . . . or, I guess, attacked by a ferocious dragon made up of evil and sin.

"Aren't you glad I tagged along?" I say, trying to crack a smile. Son of a stone-sniffer. Everything hurts.

When I make it to Bo's side, a servant rushes in holding a small gilt-edged box. The servant, standing before King Kolade, opens the box. Its contents glow so bright both the king's face and the Mage's are bathed in white. A small smile plays across Izu's lips. Izu nods, and the servant closes the box and hands it to him.

I lean over to Bo and whisper, "That's gonna feed us both for two months at least. Maybe three." No matter how they split it for us, it's gonna be a magnificent haul.

Izu, box in hand, heads for the door.

"Let's go," I say, and Bo and I trail behind him. My mouth is already watering at the thought of all the puff puff I'm going to buy at Zoe's.

"Arrest them."

I whip around, and King Kolade is standing there, arms folded across his chest. He glances at the Palace guards. "I said, *arrest* them."

"What?" Bo hisses as the Palace guards each grab an arm. "What's going on?" He winces. His bad leg almost gives out.

They drag my friend to the floor. Even as beat-up as he is, Bo can still fight, but there are too many of them, and they pin him.

Another group of guards bursts through the door. They're coming straight for me.

"What's going on?" Bo shouts, his face pressed to the tiles. The fight drains out of him, and he stops resisting. He has no energy left.

I look to Bo, then at Izu, who now stands in the doorway, his expression saying nothing at all. He turns and continues walking down the hall.

The guards are just a few paces away now.

"Run!" Bo shouts. "Run!" And for the second time in a half-moon's time, he saves my life.

I snap out of my trance. I can hear the guards stomping after me. There's nowhere to go. The guards are blocking the only exit. I look left, right, nothing but wall. The room is still in shambles from our fight with the dragon. No way to climb up to the ceilings.

The window.

I can't think of how much everything hurts. I make a break for the window, running as fast as my lungs will let me. I jump and crash straight into the glass.

It shatters, and I'm flying through the air. It's crisp and fresh in my lungs, cool on my face. My limbs swim through the air. Wind plasters my tattered clothes to my body. I land hard on the stone pathway connecting two palace towers. Guards at both ends turn at the commotion, see me, and begin marching forward.

Come on, Taj. Get up. I don't even bother looking before I vault over the wall. In the air, I pray that the solid ground isn't too far below me.

"Stop him!" guards shout. "Stop the aki!"

I hit the grass and roll down a small hill. When I stop, I hear the rushing of a shallow river. It courses, snakelike, through the gardens. I splash through it, and in the distance I see the main gates. The guards at the entrance have received the call to arms. A series of shouts echoes around me. I veer away from them and see a span of gate overgrown with vines where no guards have been stationed. I squeeze my body through the bars, bruising my ribs and tearing my clothes so that they are practically rags on my body.

Suddenly, I'm at the edge of a cliff formed by a man-made hill carved into the landscape. I chance a look behind me. More Palace guards.

I jump.

Chapter 9

My feet hit the ground. My legs crumple under me as I roll. I scrape my hands and knees on twigs and dry grass and pray I don't smash my head on a rogue rock. Bruised and aching, I finally feel myself slow down. I've reached the bottom of the incline. When I get up, my hands are shaking. There's nothing around me but towering barriers of ivy on either side of winding dirt pathways. It's impossible to tell which way is out. My chest feels tight, and suddenly I realize I'm panicking. I can't remember the last time I felt this scared. I have to snap out of it. Thinking about what will happen if I get caught isn't going to help. When I'm safe, I can ponder things at my leisure, like perhaps why the Kayas want to arrest me for doing my job. And what they're doing to Bo right now.

I run around one corner of hedges, then another, hurrying down a trail, but it's just a dead end. I hear footsteps and double back. I crouch low against one wall and wait. The footsteps draw nearer. Slow, ambling footsteps. Shadows lengthen around the corner, then a young couple comes into view. They wear flowing white gowns. The young prince has a sword at his belt and a Palace crest embroidered on his sash. They walk by, and I thank the Unnamed that they can't be bothered to notice the battered aki crouching just out of sight. I wait until I can't hear them anymore, then hurry away, down another path.

More footsteps. And these are heavier—the distinct thud of work boots on hard earth.

Palace guards.

They whisper to each other just within earshot. They're trying to find me. I strain my ears and can hear them agreeing to split up. I reach for my strap, then realize that I left my daga behind. It's sitting there on the floor of King Kolade's chambers. It takes every broken bone in my body not to mutter a curse.

I turn to try a different path, but my shirt catches on a twig. Just my luck. I pull, and it tears. The sound quiets the guards. I can hear them drawing closer. I tear myself loose, running as fast as I can.

It feels like I'm running in circles. Just when I think I've found my way out, I run into another green wall. All I hear now are the commands of Palace guards. They're closing in on me. Path after path after path, then finally a light. I careen around one last hedge and find an open field. I see the Forum in the distance. There isn't even a gate between us.

My heart leaps into my throat at the sight of the familiar shingled roofs and dilapidated columns. And I run as fast as I can.

As soon as I enter the Forum, bodies swarm around me. That familiar push. I never thought I'd feel this happy to be caught in the crowded, smelly, noisy public square, to find the alleyways I know so well, to be surrounded by all the hawkers, the jewelers, the booksellers. All is just as I left it. I take in a deep breath and smell the warm waft of pepper soup.

Heading toward home, I notice the beggars hiding in the dark and the comatose aki who have either Eaten too many sins or are simply weary of their work. The Crossed.

I think back to the heavy footfalls of the Palace guards and shudder. What would have happened had they caught me?

No. I squeeze my eyes shut, pushing the thought away. When I open them, I stand still and breathe in my freedom.

Just as I inhale, though, I hear it: the clank of armor immediately behind me. Shrieks and shouts erupt from the crowd as the guards barrel past people, cutting an arrow's path straight for me.

"Out of our way!"

"Arrest that aki!"

"Grab him!"

I set off at a run. The crowd parts for me, even as I weave my way around bodies, around stalls, through crowds listening to the holy men.

But as much as they despise aki, the people in the Forum are on my side. I may be nothing, but at least I'm not a Palace guard. Many of the merchants and Forum-dwellers move slowly or shuffle in the way of the oncoming guards to give me a bit more time to escape.

I spot a staircase spiraling up around a house and dart up the stone steps, eventually coming to a roof from which I can see most of the city center. The Forum is laid out before me, the streets shaping quarters that look like honeycombs. From here, I can track the guards and see just which swarms they're struggling through. I can see where they are, where they're coming from, and where it looks like they're going. From up here they look like streams of ants with blood-red sashes wrapped over their chests.

My clothes whipping in the wind, I get a running start and leap onto another roof, where someone's laundry dries on clotheslines. I land hard on my feet and grab for the line, using it as leverage to swing myself over to another shingled rooftop, accidentally taking a damp tunic along with me. As I soar through the air, I can see the hill where the shanties sit in the distance, where I know the Aunties can protect me. I land on a slanted sheet metal roof and clamber over the edge, then slide down the other side. When I hit the gutter pipe, I push off, reaching for another rooftop ledge as I go flying forward.

I scramble up the side, taking a breath at the top. I look down at the streets below and try to gauge my progress. The soldiers are bugs in the distance, heading in the wrong direction. I can barely hear them barking orders. I take a deep breath, let my shoulders roll back, and feel the tension go out of my body for a second.

I turn, take a step forward, then immediately regret it. My foot slips on something slick. I hit the shingles hard and start sliding down. I grasp at the shingles, trying to stop myself, but they fall away beneath my grip. I hit the ledge hard enough to let out a grunt and fall over, hanging on to the roof by one hand. I glance down toward my dangling feet. The alley below is far. Hard as I try, I can't swing my other arm up. I'm gonna have to fall.

My body tenses. I let go.

As soon as I hit the ground, I crumple onto my side. Dust swirls around me as I writhe in the dirt. Pain bites through my ankle. Definitely sprained. I don't recognize the smells and sounds here. Everything feels unfamiliar. I can't tell which dahia this is. I manage to push myself up against the wall of the building I just fell from so that my hurt leg is stretched out in front of me, straight. My clothes have torn open, completely exposing the sin spots on my arms and chest. The laundry, now dirty, falls from my hands. It's better than what I've got on though. I slip the stranger's shirt over my body. My pants are shredded, but there's nothing I can do about that.

I lean against the wall of the house, trying to get my balance back. It takes so much energy to keep pressure off the bad ankle, but I have no idea how much longer I can go on. I don't even know where I am. People are talking, I can hear it coming from the windows above, but the lilts are in the wrong place, and their words get clipped off after the wrong vowel. I can't understand a thing they're saying. The strange language follows me down empty street after empty street. I have to keep walking. I know the guards are still after me, and even the Unnamed would not be able to protect me from what they'd do to an aki. The worst part is that I have no idea how far the shanties are from here. My stomach drops. My heart thuds in my chest. Panic. I feel as though all of a sudden, there's nothing but forever between here and home.

My shoulders dip. My knees buckle. It feels like someone's wrapped a chain around my sprained ankle and is slowly tightening it. I keep going, but the world starts to go gray.

I collapse.

Chapter 10

Someone's shaking me.

I catch the very tail end of a dream: Princess Karima, glowing. And she's reaching out a hand to me. I know she's a hallucination, like the princeling. I know she's not real. But still I try to lift up a hand to get to her, to touch my fingers to hers. She drifts away. Something's holding me back.

"Taj? Taj!"

I blink. The world is fuzzy. Slowly, it hardens, the lines becoming clearer until I can finally see the face in front of me. "Omar."

His name comes out of my mouth thickly, like drool. My lips crack when I smile. "You're not supposed to take care of me. I'm supposed to take care of you."

"Taj, you have to get up." The kid has been trying to pry me loose from the wall, but he stops. "They're looking for you."

I struggle to turn my head and look around. This place is alien to me. Then I remember running. So much running. And a roof. Slipping and falling in an alley.

I try to ruffle Omar's nappy hair, but my hand drops heavy at my side.

"Come on!" Omar pulls and pulls, grunting with each tug.

Things snap into place, and I remember everything else that happened. Eating the dragon. Bo's capture. How long have I been out? The sky is orange and red overhead. Has the sunset call to prayer sounded yet? I try to get to my feet, but my ankle screams in protest.

Bo. Where have they taken him? I need to find him.

Omar slips my arm over his shoulder and helps me along. He's practically carrying me. "They've started raiding homes and snatching up aki."

I frown. Guilt curls in my stomach. Can't think about that now. Once I get to safety, I can settle down and start figuring things out. I'm no help to anybody if I get caught.

In the distance, it sounds like war. Shouts and commands and pleas. People struggling against one another, pushing and shoving and pulling, other people crying out in pain. People weeping. I grit my teeth. All this because they're looking for a runaway aki. All this because they're looking for me.

Omar pulls me down another path and into a small curtained opening we both have to duck to get through. This is the marayu. That's when I realize why I didn't recognize the dahia. It was Baptized not long ago. Homes toppled and temples destroyed and buildings demolished. After a while, it's hard to keep track of whose dahia has been most recently destroyed. The Kayas have made it unrecognizable. But Omar knew the way. I want to thank him for it, but I don't have the energy to form the words.

Darkness hangs low in the room. Someone has put out a pallet against one wall, with a bowl of water beside it.

"Lie down," Omar tells me. He helps me onto the pallet. He's got new tattoos on his wrists and forearms. He doesn't scratch them. It's almost like he's forgotten they're there.

Omar catches me staring and smiles. There's a bit of pride in it. He doesn't bother to hide his sin-spots here. Not anymore.

"I'll be back," says Omar. "One of the Aunties will come by. She'll see to you." Then he's gone. There's more confidence in his voice. It's gotten deeper, more sure of itself. I'm proud of him. He sounds like he can take it now. He's no longer that lost, weepy little boy watching us bury Jai. It's bittersweet, though. Amazing how quickly Eating forces an aki to grow up.

I watch him go, then lean back on the pallet.

What's going to happen to Bo? Is the king rounding up aki because of me? I can feel the guilt creeping back in. Maybe it's the new sin burning its way over my body, but when I look down at my chest and stomach, there's nothing new there. This guilt is mine, not King Kolade's. An image flashes in my head. A prison cell. Cold and gray and damp. Would Bo be alone or surrounded by other aki? Would there be anyone we know, anyone we'd recognize? Maybe the Palace guards captured only the younger aki, Omar's age or younger, who haven't yet learned how to evade the guards and escape.

Suddenly, fire burns through my calf, cuts at my skin like

a knife. The pain grips my left leg like a vise, carving up my thigh to the small of my back, where it branches out. I can't see what's happening, but I can feel it. Every line. Every curve etched deep into my skin. I know that wings are spreading across my shoulders and sharp claws are burning down my arms to curl around my biceps. I squirm on the pallet as the tattoo of the dragon's neck and head form on the back of my own neck. Its open mouth appears just beneath my jaw with a tattoo of black fire spraying needles of hurt into the back of my head. The world turns red, then gray, then black. The pain leaves me breathless. It's never hurt like this before.

I hear a rustling of the curtain, and a lamp is lit in the corner of the room, spreading a small circle of golden light over the familiar sight of Auntie Sania kneeling by my side, like she's done so many times before. Her long white gown pools around her knees. Weathered fingers glide through my hair and lift my head, and warm soup hits my lips.

"Slowly, Taj," Auntie says to me.

I try to swallow, but it goes down too fast, and I gag and sputter it back up.

"Slowly," she says again.

I manage to get some of the broth down, then she lowers my head back onto my pillow. Silver spots float in my vision again, telling me that I'm in pain even though I no longer feel it. Like my body's breaking down, but I can't tell how or where. I blink them away, because I know now not to shake my head. When I open my eyes again, Auntie Sania has her smile turned down on me.

"Good to see you again, Taj."

"Auntie," I say weakly.

"It's all right," she shushes me. "Auntie Nawal sends her best wishes. She is tending to the others." Other aki swept off the streets and out of the hands of Mages and Agha Sentries and Palace guards during one Baptism or another.

I can't help but think about when I first arrived at the marayu to stay with the Aunties. It all comes back. The grief of leaving Mama and Baba when I became an aki. The looks on their faces when they discovered what I could do, when they saw the white pupils of my eyes. I close my eyes, and I can see the sadness in Mama's. And I see Baba's stern gaze, trying to hold things together, trying to hold the family together. I see their room at night after I've snuck into the doorway. I see the fear that wracked them every night as they waited for Mages to arrive and take me from them. Their faces are so clear in my mind right now. As much as it hurts, I want to hold on to this vision of them.

Tears leak down the side of my face.

Auntie Nawal had taken me in. She'd been the one. After I'd run away, it had been her. Marya had told me about the marayu and the Aunties who took in aki who had been thrown out of their homes or who, like me, had run away. I remember refusing, not wanting to be separated from my obi-njide, my sister in everything but blood, the holder of my heart. But she had found the Scribes, and I needed a home. Auntie Sania had given me the first meal I hadn't had to steal in years.

"Omar," I whisper, suddenly remembering the little aki.

"He's safe here." Auntie Sania looks me over, and I can tell she's scanning for new tattoos. "You've been busy." She soaks a cloth in warm water and squeezes. "Sweetheart, you should find a nice girl." She presses the cloth to my forehead. Relief. "Surely there is safer work out there for you to do. Maybe take up a trade. Stonesmithing. You were always good with your hands."

I chuckle and try not to choke. I think I'm catching a fever.

"Taj, what happened? Why are the guardsmen looking for you?"

I stare at the ceiling awhile before I speak again. "They took Bo."

"Bo," Auntie Sania says. It's not a question.

"We were brought to King Kolade."

"The king called you?"

"Yes. And he . . ."

A crash. Loud voices in the other room.

"Keep quiet, child." Auntie Sania's movements are swift and practiced. She has done this many times before. She moves the bookshelves that line the walls, kicks dirt around, then drags some chests across the floor to make the room look like an abandoned storage closet, all of the furniture arranged to hide me.

Before I can say a word or get up from my pallet, Auntie Sania puts a hand to my shoulder. Strong enough to force me back down.

"Shhh," she whispers. "I will deal with them, Lightbringer." She winks.

She blows out the lamp, and the smoke follows her out of the room.

I eye the curtained entrance Omar carried me through. The curtain sways. Shadows cross it. Guards rushing by. Then nothing.

The noise in the other room grows louder. I hear Auntie Nawal's voice, then Auntie Sania's.

"There are only children here. These are too weak to Eat. Do you see? They are nothing but orphans. We are permitted to work by King Kolade himself." Parchment unrolling. "See here our decree." Pushing and stomping.

Then, suddenly, a panicked cry.

"No! You can't!"

The booming footfalls draw closer. I need to get out of here—I can't just lie down and wait for them to find me. I push away the blanket. Just as the first guards kick away the door to the room, I scurry through the curtain and out into the alley.

"There he is!"

Guards fill the street. I look left. I look right. Palace sigils everywhere.

I make a run for it. Something hard smashes into me out of nowhere, hurls me into a wall. Pain wracks my whole body. My ankle gives way under me, and I hear a definite snap. Rough hands bring me to my feet.

"Is this him?" someone barks.

"We are looking for the one named Taj," says another guard. "Are you him, aki?"

As I struggle, I catch sight of Auntie Sania's face. Palace guards flank her, ready to grab her if anything happens. One of the guards sneers when he sees my expression and unsheathes his sword. He slowly holds its point to Auntie's stomach. I struggle harder in the grip of the Palace guards. If they hurt her . . .

"Leave her alone," I hiss through clenched teeth.

The guard holding me kicks my legs out from under me, and I fall to my knees. A cheap trick, and I wish more than anything that I had my daga with me so I could make him pay for it. "Auntie!" I call out to her, because I don't know what else to do.

"Boy, what is your name?"

I can't give them the satisfaction of answering. I won't.

"Bring the servant," their leader hollers.

One of the Palace servants steps through a wall of guards and looks at me. I recognize him as one of King Kolade's servants, the one who brought Izu the box full of ramzi. The disgust is plain on his face. He doesn't even bother to hide it. I sneer right back because he's just as much under someone's foot as I am, only I get paid and he doesn't. He's got no right to look at me like that. I manage to get myself to smirk. At least I'm someone worth chasing down.

"It's him. That is the aki that ran from the Palace," the servant says.

The guard holding me jerks me upright. Two more guards grip me by the arms and drag me away. I try to turn around and see Auntie Sania's face. She stands there between those two Palace guards, her fists trembling at her sides. She fights tears as she mutters a prayer under her breath. I know she's trying to keep calm for the others, the little ones who are surely watching from the windows of the orphanage overhead or from their other hiding places. They watch her, and they watch me. I almost miss it, but one of them, a little girl perched by a window, presses her index and middle finger together against her heart, then raises them in my direction. I squint and see her white pupils. Aki. The same way Marya and I say goodbye. I smile, but before I can return the gesture, the Palace guards drag me around a corner.

I hobble on my ankle, trying to keep balanced—anything I can do to walk on my own or at least pretend that I'm doing this of my own free will. But the pain in my ankle is nothing compared to the burn of the sin that wraps around my body, a burn so strong it feels as though the dragon I killed is breathing fire right onto my skin.

Auntie Sania's whispered words reach me. A prayer growing more and more faint until it's gone, broken off in mid-speech. Unfinished.

My body's on fire. I go limp and let myself fall. I'm not going to make this easy for them. They'll have to carry me to prison.

Chapter 11

In the dream, I'm a little kid. Maybe up to Baba's waist.

Mama's been sick for a whole month. In the last few days, she's been unable even to walk. Her skin has gotten paler, and Baba sits at her side almost all day, patting her forehead with a wet cloth to cool her fever. Sometimes he picks me up, bounces me on his knee, tells me stories. But most of the time, I try to stay out of the way.

I hear knocking at our front door. Baba rushes out past me, and I spend a few seconds in the doorway to Mama's room, watching her breathe slowly, then cough so hard my own chest hurts. She wheezes, trying to catch her breath. Tears spring to my eyes. I've never seen her like this. There must be something I can do. I think I can make a potion, like from the storybooks Baba reads me. A healing potion.

I go into the kitchen and climb up on the counter to find herbs and a bowl to mix them in. The door opens, and Baba walks in with man in a black robe right behind him. The robe has a golden fist threaded on it. They walk by so fast they don't even notice me, but I see a little girl trailing behind the man. Her shoulders are hunched, and I can't see much of her face. She doesn't look much bigger than me. There's a collar around her neck. The robed man leads her through the house by a chain. She doesn't make a sound. Her brown clothes are dirty and torn, and her curly hair is tied up in a poof on her head.

I wobble on the counter, try to grab the handle of a cupboard, and crash to the floor. Calabash bowls shatter around me. Oh no, Baba's going to be so mad if I wake Mama up. Two seconds go by, then three, then four. No stomping footsteps. Slowly, I bring my head up. I hear voices mumbling softly.

The biggest pieces of the broken bowls are easy to gather. I toss those into the rubbish bin out back and sweep the smaller pieces into a corner with my foot.

They've pulled the curtain shut over Mama's room, but I can peek in through a space in the beads.

The girl has tattoos of animals running up and down her exposed arms and legs, like an aki. What is a disgusting aki doing in our house?

The robed man turns to Baba and says a few words I can't hear.

"Yes, Mage," Baba says back. Then he stands against the far wall, and I lose sight of him.

The Mage kneels by Mama's bed and whispers strange words.

Mama sounds like she's choking, and I grip the edge of the doorway. I need to save her. This Mage is hurting her.

I burst through the curtain. Mama is shaking on her bed, and everyone else stares at me, including the girl with the white-pupiled eyes. A puddle of black ink spreads toward me. Tendrils shoot out from it on either side. They turn into legs—eight of them—scratching at the floor. It's the biggest spider I've ever seen. I know what it is from the scary stories my friend's older siblings tell, from whispers in the streets.

It's a sin-beast. Inisisa.

"Taj!" Baba yells. "Taj! Get out of here!"

I scramble backward, and the spider leaps for me.

Something sharp stabs my foot and I yelp, running out of the room. I can feel it chasing after me. So fast. I run through the living room, knocking over chairs and cushions. I leap on our couch, and it follows me, pausing only for a little bit to look at me before chasing right after me again. I'm backed up against the wall. It stands between me and the kitchen.

I can't escape. I squeeze my eyes shut, waiting for it to attack.

"No!" someone screams.

In a flash, the little aki girl bounds into the room and leaps onto the spider's back. Her knife glints in her hands, and she stabs the inisisa in its rear. It swats at her, and she crashes against the far wall. It turns to face her, but she recovers quickly, lunging for it again. This time she plunges her knife right between its beady eyes. The beast tries to jump toward her but wobbles, then collapses completely.

The little girl wipes blood from a gash on her forehead. She steps forward and plucks her knife out of the sin-beast.

The beast turns back into the puddle it had been when I first saw it. In a single stream of dark ink, it rises from the floor and shoots into the aki's open mouth. The girl trembles, then falls to her knees, coughing. She coughs like she'll never stop coughing, but eventually she gets back up. When she glances my way, I see tears streaming down her cheeks.

There's a new tattoo on her face: a spider with four legs running down her left cheek and four legs running down her right.

Chapter 12

I wake up to softness.

I'm lying on cushions. Satin. Definitely expensive. And, of course, I'm drooling all over them.

The visions of Baba and the Mage and the little aki who Ate Mama's sin-spider are fading. I rub my eyes, trying to chase away the rest of the dream.

When I sit up, there's no pain in my body. None. I touch my arms and my chest and feel my legs, trying to sort out how I could have healed so quickly. My bad ankle is bandaged and elevated on one of the pillows. I squeeze my eyes tighter, then slowly open them, trying to figure out where I am.

The entire room is white and gold, bathed in sunlight. Have I died and reached Infinity? Surely not with this many sins.

"I must still be dreaming." My stomach rumbles. There's a platter of fruit on a marble table inlaid with gold. Grapes.

Slices of melon. I rush to it so fast I nearly knock the whole thing over. I'm swallowing before I even finish chewing. Juice dribbles down my chin. It all tastes so good. I can't remember the last time I tasted fruit so perfect—just the occasional bruised apple that makes its way to the Forum market. For a second I forget not to put weight on my ankle and sink down in my left hip. Pain shoots up my calf, and I have to hold on to the table to keep from falling.

Fine. Definitely not dreaming.

That means the Palace guards got me. I know that much. But why would they bring me here? The chase. I remember Auntie Sania and Auntie Nawal and the look on Auntie Sania's face as the guards dragged me away. Then I see flashes of me darting across rooftops. Rolling down hills in the Palace estates.

The sin-dragon.

I drop the fistful of fruit I'd been holding and look around. There's a mirror on the other side of the room. Framed in gold filigree, it's as tall as I am. I lift up my shirt and turn around. There it is. The fresh mark of the dragon on my back. The wings spread across my shoulders, and its claws come down my arms to circle my biceps, its scaled neck burned into mine. The open mouth breathes tattooed fire up the back of my head and into my puff of hair. It's all there. King Kolade's sin.

I tug at the strap of my pants, pull them down a little just to see how far the tattoo continues when I hear a shuffling.

I whirl around and reach for my daga, but my armband is gone.

The door opens, and there stands Izu.

I relax, but only a little.

"What's going on, Mage? Where did they take Bo?"

The Mage's hood is pulled back, and his thinning hair has been combed over a scalp that shines in the lamplight. He glances at the plate of fruit and frowns when he sees the mess I've made.

Instead of answering, Izu pulls a box out of his sleeve, and he places it on the table next to the fruit.

"Why was half the Palace after me?"

Izu motions to the pillows, then pulls a chair from by the door and sits down. He leans forward when he speaks, and even though he appears relaxed, it looks calculated, like he's doing it just to throw me off.

I lean into the pillows, but not so much that I can't leap up and strike if the moment calls for it. "Tell me where Bo is."

"Let me begin by apologizing on behalf of the king for your rough treatment. Really, we wanted to secure you and your services. Your friend, well, call it guilt by association."

"Services? What are you talking about?" I know I should be watching my tone. A Mage like Izu could easily fit my life in the palm of his hand, squeeze it into nothing, and I'd be out of work and scavenging on the street again for however long it took before I wound up in prison. Baba would never pay off his debt. But I need to know where they took my best friend. "Where is he?"

"He's home."

"What?"

Izu picks at a bit of cloth on his robe, flicks away what's probably the remains of an insect—although I have a hard time believing any sort of insect would dare dirty this room, which, I assume, is part of the Palace estates. "Yes, a moneylender purchased his freedom. He might still be in prison were it not for that."

Nazim. It has to be. I can't imagine what kind of danger it must have been for him. To put himself at risk of being noticed by the king. It must be like coming out of the shadows for him. Which, if you're the type of businessman who occasionally deals with less than savory customers, is the worst thing you could possibly do. If they decide they want to look into this moneylender who suddenly has an interest in aki, that could threaten his business . . . or his life. I can see Nazim in my head now, back straight in his chair, scribbling figures onto his parchment with his stylus. I think back to every single time I wondered whether or not he took any interest in the lives of people around him, people whose fates and fortunes he scribbles out on that paper.

I want to ask if Nazim has tried to pay my way, but I don't want to get him in deeper than he already is. "You said something about services. What do you mean?"

Izu looks down at his lap and straightens the folds in his robe. His eggshell-colored eyes glisten. "The king was very impressed with your abilities. And he and I have been in discussion for a very long time as to the proper use of your kind. There is a talent that you possess, most certainly, and we mustn't let it go to waste."

What is this lahala? *Talent?* He sounds like that apprentice Mage at Zoe's. Then it strikes me. It takes me only a second to realize that right now I'm sitting across from her teacher. That girl, Aliya, who talked so dreamily about equations and sin-beasts and shrines and how my body is covered in poems, is studying under this Mage. The same ruby-licker who drags me out to Eat sins, then never pays me all of what I'm owed. The same ruby-licker who bursts into people's homes and steals their children to become aki.

"So far, you have been earning just enough money to get by, and I understand a recent change in rates has made it all the more difficult for aki like you to build a livelihood," Izu continues smoothly. "Those with your talents, well, they make do. But the lesser among you, they are left to fend for themselves. They can't Eat nearly as well as you, and yet they are forced to take on more work than they can handle. To feed themselves. To feed others, maybe?" At that last part, he raises an eyebrow at me. A chill raises gooseflesh on my arms.

"Why are you telling me this?"

"I understand your mother and father live in the Khamsa dahia."

I clench my fists at my sides. I want to punch Izu in the face, half because he can't give a straight answer and half for mentioning Mama and Baba.

"That dahia recently endured a Baptism."

I lurch forward, but Izu raises a hand to calm me.

"They're safe. For now. But who's to say how long that will last?"

"You're threatening my parents now?" I hiss.

"On the contrary, I want to keep them safe." Izu smiles. "How would you like to guarantee their safety, as well as enough money in *your* pockets to keep them taken care of for as long as they live?"

"What?" My spine straightens. "What are you talking about?"

Izu stands and helps himself to the plate of fruit. "You would be in the employ of the Palace," he says, his back to me. "You would be paid out of the official royal coffers. A handsome salary, most definitely above your station. But you would be conferring on the royal family a grand service." He turns, meeting my eyes.

"And what would that be?"

"You will serve as King Kolade's personal aki."

"What?"

Izu doesn't respond, only hands me the box. I open it to find my armband and the knife I left behind. The armband is new. Polished.

"So," he says, "do you think you'll be needing these?"

I say yes.

Chapter 13

It turns out the room I woke up in wasn't even the room where I'm supposed to stay. Just the first place the guards dropped me when they dragged me back to the Palace.

Where I'll be laying my head isn't nearly as big as the rooms in which I've Eaten sins, but it's a palace compared to the shanties on the hill back home. The window faces west and opens out over Palace grounds that I now remember having rolled down and crashed through back when I was trying to get as far away from this place as possible. I kick off my dirty flats at the door because this room is too holy to walk through with those on. The tiles chill my toes. The floor is smooth and unyielding, like the soles of my feet are getting massaged. My bed has a canopy with sheer white sheets tied at each corner. The pillows look like the fluffiest clouds I've ever seen.

I walk up to a closet with heavy, intricately engraved wooden doors. I press my face close and realize the doors are decorated with carvings of what I see now are meant to be arashi. Terrifying and beautiful at once. This is what we're all supposed to be afraid of. Their wings sprout from hunched backs, and the faces are too big for the bodies. Growing up in the dahia, I always heard stories about how the arashi came down from the sky and razed the earth, paving it clean for each dahia to be built anew. I used to sit with Mama and Baba among the other dwellers of the dahia around each shrine, and we would pray to the arashi, whose essences were rumored to be contained within each black cube. It all seems like so long ago. Seeing these carvings in these doors now makes me think of Mama and Baba again, whose faces grow hazier every day.

So many questions run through my head. Who did this? How long did it take? Could they have imagined that an aki like me would be using this thing, just as a place to store clothes?

I open the closet and find that it's completely stocked. Pants made out of leather. I take them from the wire hanger, careful not to tear them, and press them to my waist. They look like a perfect fit. Robes lie folded on a shelf. I slip one on. It's all white, but some of the threads embroidered in gemstones shimmer in the afternoon sunlight. This robe could feed a house full of aki for at least a month. I put my arms through the sleeves, and it hangs from me, loose and light. Next to the folded robes is a row of sashes. I take the dark-red one, cinch it across my waist, and turn toward the mirror on the inside of the wardrobe. It feels so comfortable. I breathe in the smell of the fabric. It all smells of a light, floral sweetness. Lavender.

Now to see if I can actually move in this thing. I don't want to damage it, though. If I stretch too much or if I tear it, it would be like tossing a quarter-year's worth of food out onto the street.

The back of the robe hangs lower than the front, so I flick the robe back, get it out of the way of my legs, then dart toward the bed and slide: an effortless glide against the tiles. I hop up, leap into the air, snatch at where my daga would be, and fling it at the invisible sin-beast lying in my bed.

When I land, I feel like I'm going to sink forever in those blankets and that mattress. It feels like I went from flying to floating, and I'll never have to touch the ground again. I close my eyes. Just for a moment.

The memory comes to me in fragments. I'm a child, hugging the corner of a wall in our house and trying to keep quiet. I can tell it's early afternoon because of how the light shines through our windows and illumines the jewels of the women who sit with Mama in the meeting room. The door is cracked open, and laughter bursts through, loud and clear. I can smell the lavender so thickly. Mama and the others, they're talking politics and saying names I don't recognize. Places, maybe. Rivers. Cities. I have no idea what they're saying, but the women are loud and arguing and happy. They're making dyes in that room, the scent of lavender heavy in the air.

I'm awoken by a knock at the door.

A young woman with green eyes and her blond hair tied

into a bun stands in the doorway holding a white towel with the Palace sigil embroidered on it.

"Sir, your bath is ready." She doesn't bow her head, doesn't move, doesn't even show a hint of an expression on her face. "We hope the water is at a suitable temperature for you."

"We? Who's we?"

She turns in the doorway, looking like she wants me to walk through. "This way, please."

I follow her through the door, down a small hallway, then into another room, this one smaller than the bedroom but only a little. There's a tub in the middle of the room. Steam rises from the water. I turn to the girl. "Is this mine too?"

"Your meaning, sir?"

"This room. I mean, is this the water closet?"

She neither nods nor shakes her head. "Yes, this is the water closet."

"This is *my* water closet?"

I can't believe it. It's impossible. There's no way this is all for me. "And nobody else uses this water closet?"

"This water closet is yours, as I stated earlier." She's starting to get annoyed with me.

I let out a sigh. It still feels like I'm dreaming, but I don't want to test whether or not the water'll stay warm forever. I undo the sash and slip the robe off, then fiddle with the drawstring on my pants when suddenly I turn. She's still there.

"Are you gonna . . ."

She doesn't move. "I am not to leave your side."

"What are you talking about? You can't watch me undress. Er, the Word forbids it." I can't tell her the exact verse where it says a woman is not to observe a man in his natural element, but I know it's in there. Somewhere.

"I am your sicario, sir."

"What? What's a sicario? Like, a servant?"

She hasn't moved an inch. There's a bucket and a sponge by the tub, but I have no idea who put it there. She holds the towel by her waist and makes no move to shield her eyes. "I am tasked with guaranteeing your safety, your well-being, and with solving any and all problems that may arise with regard to your condition." She waits for me to move, but I'm frozen, confused. Finally, she rolls her eyes.

"You are not attractive to me," she says bluntly.

Eh-eh. The rudeness with this one!

Still, it's enough to eventually get me out of my clothes. I climb in, half expecting the water to burn me, but it's actually at the perfect temperature.

Before I can protest, she's at my side, taking the sponge out of the bucket and squeezing the excess water out.

She takes my tattooed arm. Her fingers are rough.

"Now, tell me. What is your name?" I ask. I'm met with cool silence. I sink deeper into the water. "Look, it sounds like you'll be something of a bodyguard. Which means we'll be spending a lot of time around each other, no? It'd probably make things easier if I knew what to call you."

"Arzu."

No matter how hard I try, I can't completely let my guard down. Izu has threatened to Baptize a dahia if I don't do what he says. He seems willing to keep me here in the Palace, even to feed me and treat me like a royal. But I don't trust him. I need to figure out what he really wants with me. I could spend the rest of my life in this bath and not wash off all the grime I feel on my skin right now.

I lean my head back against the tub's edge. A part of me still can't believe all of this is happening, like I'm outside of my body and watching these events unfold from above. I can see the top of Arzu's head and the little dip in the center of her bun. I can see the slope of her shoulders. I can see where my knees poke out of the water, already gray and clouded around my body. I can see the wings of the sin-dragon emblazoned across my shoulders.

And I can see my body curl on itself in pain when Arzu starts scrubbing my arm as though it had grown a mouth and insulted her.

It felt rough when she did it, but now when I look in the mirror in my chambers and rub my palms against my cheeks, they feel as smooth as a fish's. She gave me bands too, rubber that stretched but was still tough to pull at, said they were for my hair. I don't know what she means; it doesn't get in the way of anything, and I can fight just fine with my puffy hair the way it is, but I try it out anyway.

I pull the band down over my neck, then stretch it and push it back up my face and to my forehead. Now it looks like I have a massive bun at the back of my head, but it shouldn't be too hard to comb out. And it's nice to have my hair out of my face. It feels a bit strange, but I'll give it some time. Now that I've got new clothes and real money in my pockets, I can't go looking like any regular aki on the street. I move with a new lightness. My arms, my legs, they feel unburdened. I don't have to worry about Mama and Baba anymore. If Izu has guaranteed their safety, then that means King Kolade has guaranteed it. It's such a new thought that it makes me smile. For the first time, I know they're safe.

A breeze pushes against the curtains, and I step out onto the balcony. *My* balcony. I don't really know what people use spaces like this for, except it reminds me of when some of us would climb onto the roofs of our shacks or take the highest dwelling on the hill and spend the early part of the night counting the stars until they got too numerous. And some of the others would lie on their stomachs and watch Kos quiet down in the distance and try to count the number of people still out. We would try to see if there were more people on the ground or stars in the sky.

The view of the sky isn't panoramic here the way it is on the Hill, but I can see Kos. Nearly all of it. It's all so far away that you almost can't see the Forum from here. Like it's buried at the bottom of the bowl. It's nearly a speck against the Wall.

And that's when I notice it. For the first time, really. The Wall.

On the ground, it's just a fact of life. It's invisible. When the sun shifts to tell you it's a certain part of the day, you don't think of the shadows the Wall casts. You think, *Oh, it's nearly time for evening prayer*, or, *Oh, I'll be eating soon*. But from here, you notice it. I finally see just how high it stands over all of us.

Arzu shows up next to me. She follows my gaze, stares straight ahead. "Your meal is ready, sir."

I smell it. A massive plate of fufu and, next to it, a bowl of pepper soup with chunks of goat meat swimming among the greens. On another plate, freshly baked puff puff, the fried balls of dough coated with crystals of sugar. A dish of rice baked in a sauce made from blended peppers. I smell all of it. Out there, I never dared to even dream of food like this. It only makes you hungrier, especially when the last thing you ate was a day and a half ago and stale by the time you got it anyway. After I sit down, I take small bites, savoring each mouthful. Each one reminds me of the aki back home. They will never taste food like this. I swallow thickly, then push the food away without finishing.

I stand and walk toward the window. Kos looks so small from up here. I could fit it all in my hand. The stonesmiths, the seamstresses, the miners, the farmers, the aki, all of them seen from this high up are ants. From where I stand, you can't make out any people in Kos. Just things. Only things.

"I'm going for a walk." When I turn, my robe billows, and it's so dramatic. I hate it. I make it to the door, and Arzu's right behind me. "What are you doing?"

"You're not permitted to leave the Palace grounds unaccompanied."

I really can't get rid of this girl. "Well, what if people think you're my"—I lean in and try my sultriest gaze—"my heart-mate."

She keeps her eyes steely, but I swear I see a faint smirk. "Trust me. They won't."

Defeated again.

I open the door, and right in front of me, close enough to smell my breath, is Princess Karima.

I freeze. My mind goes blank.

Arzu steps next to me and bows at the waist.

I notice and do the same.

When I look up, a small smile plays on the princess's lips. She wears a dress emblazoned with emerald gemstones. Her obsidian-colored skin, the same color as my daga, shines. She seems to glow from within.

I stand there and don't even realize for how long before I notice her hand, stretched out to me, palm up.

"To you and yours, Taj."

Slowly, I slide my hand over hers. "To you and yours, Princess."

Her smile broadens as she withdraws her hand. "It is impossible for me to express how delighted I was to learn that you've joined us." She peeks into my room and looks over the chambers: the walls, the ceiling, the furniture. "If the room is not to your liking, please let me know, and I will personally look into filling your needs."

"Thank you, Princess."

When she chuckles, she shows her teeth, perfect pearl-colored teeth. But then she quiets, still smiling. And staring. Like she's waiting for me to say something.

Arzu tightens the leather straps on her wrist gauntlets. "He was just preparing to leave."

"Oh?"

"An outing." Arzu nudges me with her elbow.

"Oh, yes," I say, finally snapping out of it. "The Palace food is wonderful, but it's not like home."

The princess smiles and steps aside. "Do let us know and we will have our people prepare exactly what you need, how you need it. Spare no expense. We are at your service, Taj."

Isn't it supposed to be the other way around?

"Enjoy your outing." Before she turns to go, the princess leans in and places her hand on my forearm. "I very much look forward to seeing more of you," she whispers into my ear.

I watch her go. My skin tingles where she touched me.

Chapter 14

People in the Forum clear a way for me now.

Not because they can see my sin-spots or my white pupils. Not because I'm aki. This time, it's not because of anything I do or anything I say. No one calls me Sky-Fist anymore, or Lightbringer. People see the fine metal threads and cower. They see my clothes, and they fear me. Even the booktraders pretend not to see me.

The books look just as I left them. Some cylinders carry more elaborate golden script than others, some covers are bound tighter than others, some have gilt lining their edges. But I haven't been away long enough to forget how to tell which ones contain forbidden gossip about the royal family. Long-lost twins, revenge plots, bumbling relatives, and scheming children. There's one toward the right in a pile in the middle, buried under a couple of other books. I can almost hear it calling my name.

As I reach for it, the booktrader tugs his robe at the shoulder, and, behind me, other traders shuffle their wares. With a hand I can barely see under the table, the booktrader in front of me slips a book out from the bottom of the pile and the whole tower collapses. He stoops to fix his book display, but the one I'm looking for doesn't reappear. It's gone.

I look around and don't see any guards. Any Agha Sentries or Palace guards around are too far away to notice anything over here between the jewelers' stalls. What did they see that I didn't?

Arzu.

She's standing too close to me and has that griffin-going-hunting look on her face. She may not be dressed like a Palace guard, and, in her leathers, she's not wearing the Palace colors, but her back is straight enough, and her hand rests on the pommel of the knife at her waist to signal that she's not a Forum-dweller. Judgment is written all over her face. Guess she has enough disdain in her reserves for all of us and not just me.

I back away from the reassembled pile of books. I nod an apology to the booktrader, but he doesn't react. Probably doesn't even notice it.

No one bothers me now that I'm completely covered. The scarf around my neck bunches to hide the dragon's head that rises up my spine and into my hair. Nobody can tell I'm an aki, and the Palace colors demand respect. I can walk through the Forum without getting sneered at or spat on or kicked by some errant foot. Nobody's going to try to push me to the ground, pretending they have to rush somewhere.

It makes me uneasy, but I force myself to relax, to enjoy it. Don't I deserve a little respect? I catch sight of some Palace guards and want to test just how good this protection is. Arzu breathes right down my neck. I strut, and the crowd splits before me. When I get closer, I realize that I know this one. This guardsman in particular. He's one of Costa's guys. A local, hired out to work the Forum. Whenever we try to redeem our markers, he's one of the first to start cracking heads. Sometimes, he doesn't even wait for us to speak up or get mad about getting shorted again. His club hangs at his waist. The leather wrapped around that wooden bludgeon is dark from all the blood that's stained it. I make to walk past him and bump my shoulder into his stomach. Hard.

He grunts and stumbles a few steps back, then straightens again. The Palace guard goes for his club, but I don't flinch. I stare him straight in the eyes, and he freezes. The only people milling around us are regular Forum-dwellers. No Agha, and all the other guardsmen are elsewhere, lounging around or looking for other aki to beat up on.

"Who am I?" I ask through gritted teeth. I know this guy remembers me. He has definitely seen me before, when I've complained to Costa or made a scene in front of him and the other guardsmen and the aki collecting their pay, promising to burn this whole thing down if he and the Mages didn't start doing right by us. I'd occasionally overhear Costa conferring with some hired-out guardsmen, the Bulls, discussing what to do about me like I was some kind of leader or like I would head any sort of rebellion. Felt good to live in the lie, for them not to know any better. Now this guardsman in front of me is holding himself so tight he's starting to tremble.

"Who am I?" I ask him again.

"Respectfully, sir, I've never seen you before in my life."

He might be telling the truth. How many people as brown as me wear Palace colors in the Forum? He might not recognize me in this new outfit. So, smirking, I pull up my right sleeve, just far enough to reveal the lion tattoo I'd gotten from Eating Prince Haris's sin. I know he's seen this before.

"Who am I?" It feels so good to do this. Every single time a Bull like him has sneered at me or chased one of us down or beaten us within an inch of our lives and shown no remorse, all of it is right now getting balanced in the ledger. This feels like Nazim righting accounts in his book. It's all starting to even out. "Who. Am. I."

"Your name is Taj, sir." Then, more softly, he repeats it. "Taj."

My head is still foggy with power. I let the sleeve fall and step back. The smile won't leave my face, even as I turn to go.

Without looking, I can tell that Arzu is frowning again. Maybe she doesn't approve of me getting whatever small piece of revenge an aki can get in this city. Or maybe this is just how she is all the time.

Once I get away from the Bull, my mood turns. This walk has turned out to be not nearly as pleasant as I'd wanted. I need to get rid of Arzu. She's getting in the way of my fun. Auntie Sania and Auntie Nawal might see us together and get the wrong idea. And I can't walk through Kos all dressed up like this and have girls thinking my heart-stone is no longer on the market.

The alleys we pass only lead to dead ends or are too narrow to squeeze through. I've never seen Arzu run, but from the way she's always tensed up, I can tell she's ready. She's probably fast too. I don't want to take any chances. Nothing will probably happen to me, but she doesn't care about Forum-dwellers, and I don't want anyone accidentally getting in her way and getting cut down just because I wanted to get some real fresh air.

Toward the end of the main thoroughfare is a food stall, and on hooks hanging from wooden beams that cover the eating area dangle red and yellow and green peppers. Perfect.

"I want to get something to eat," I tell Arzu. "Let's go."

We find an open table, and she sits across from me. As soon as we settle, two merchants sitting at a table behind Arzu see us, get up, slap money on the table, and leave, vanishing into the crowd. Another small group does the same, then a small huddle of men whose auto-mail legs creak and groan as they get up from their seats, until we're the only ones left. I nearly duck my head in embarrassment. For the first time since I can remember, I don't have to walk around with my sin-spots out there for everyone to see, and Arzu has to ruin it by following me like a Forum-fly that won't quit.

The foodseller brushes his hands on his dirty apron and comes to our table. The thing about being associated with the Palace is that now everybody trembles when they realize they have to talk to us. Already, I hate it. "To you and yours, oga."

He doesn't wait for my reply. "How may I be of service today, sir? Madame?"

Arzu looks to me. She's never been here before. I was counting on that.

"Two plates of chicken-sticks. Ten for each of us." I look to Arzu. "Trust me, you're going to love these. You may not think you're hungry now, but chai . . ." I snap my fingers, grinning, then look back to the foodseller. "Different peppers." And I count them off on my fingers. "Wahed sauce for the first, then ithnaan, thalatha, arbaa, khamsa, sitta, sabaa, thamanya, tisa, and ashara." I beam up at him. "Thanks."

Arzu watches him leave, then focuses on me. "Those are the names of the dahia."

I wink at her. "You learn quick. Yes, I just asked for different sauces on each of our sticks, so you can see which ones you like. Have you been out to the dahia? No? None of them?" When she's silent, I shake my head with disappointment. "Well, each dahia does theirs differently. I personally think they're all good, but I'm a peacemaker, and I only fight when I have to."

It doesn't seem like she registers sarcasm either.

Neither of us talk until the wings are brought on two wooden boards, one for each of us. I act like I've only got eyes for my wings; meanwhile, I'm scanning sight lines and gauging the width of alleyways, memorizing paths and noting the direction of traffic up and down each side street.

I take the first wing and point to the corresponding breaded chicken wing on her board. "May the Unnamed preserve us," I say, blessing the food. I tap my wing against hers. "To health." It tastes so good. It has rough texture, and the sauce is sweet on my tongue. "The wahed sauce," I say through a mouth full of white chicken meat, "is flavored with various fruits. That's why . . . when you're in that dahia . . . you see orchards."

I swallow in one gulp, catch my breath. "They put fruit in everything. They've got orange-flavored this and lemon-peppered that." I clean mine to the bone, then toss it into the thoroughfare. The chicken wing remains vanish in a parade of sandals and boots.

It's fascinating to watch Arzu chew mechanically through these. She chews a line horizontally, rotates the skewer like it's a spit, then chews another line. She eats like a gear-head put her together. And when she finishes, she arranges the sticks in a perfect line.

I'm halfway through the fourth wing when I look up. She's stopped eating and is staring at a half-eaten wing like it has slapped her in the face. I quickly stop smiling. "Oh, that's the arbaa. It kicks a little bit. It's still sweet like the wahed, but if you eat it too quickly, it's like someone stabbed nettles into your tongue. Sorry, I should've warned you. The others are much less deceitful."

Arzu nods and doesn't finish the fourth wing, places it half-finished alongside the others. That stick doesn't line up.

We both start on the one with khamsa sauce, and I chew a little more slowly than she does. She does her line thing once, rotates, then does it again, then mid-rotation, she stops. It takes almost all of my energy to keep from laughing.

"My . . . my stomach."

"Oh, it'll pass. You must not be used to these. Don't worry."

She reaches for one that's farther along, skipping several.

"No, don't do that! You can only really appreciate them if you go in order." I reach for her half-eaten khamsa wing. "Here, I'll take that off your hands." I blaze through both hers and mine.

We each take our sitta wings, and I tap hers with mine. "To health!" I didn't believe it was possible, but her face has gotten even paler.

She starts licking her lips. Mechanically. "I can't feel . . . I can't feel my lips. What has happened to my lips?" Tears bloom in her eyes. She swipes at her nose. "My face." And now she's turning red. Red as the sauce on these wings. Red as peppers.

I have my hand over my mouth, but I can't hide my laughter this time. "By the Unnamed, you're crying real tears."

"I have been poisoned." She sucks in air, but that only makes her mouth burn hotter. "Water." Sweat pours down from her forehead. Her sleeves darken with each pass she makes to wipe it all away.

"It's not poison. It's just the sauce. You're not used to it. Don't touch your eyes!"

But it's too late. With sauce-covered fingers, she tries to rub away her tears. She howls and flails about, knocking into the table and falling over. This is the point where I'm supposed to make a run for it, but I have to at least help her get inside.

"Here," I say as I pull her up. She walks with arms outstretched, blinded. I lightly push her toward the restaurant. "He'll get you some help. I'll be right behind you."

Hopefully, the foodseller will find her some milk and help her flush out her eyes. I wait a few seconds, till she vanishes around a corner, then I'm off.

I sprint around a few corners and down some darkened side streets, jumping puddles I don't even have to look for because I still remember them. Then I slow down and dare to look behind me.

I can finally let go of that breath I've been holding. She's gone.

Chapter 15

When I look up, I see where the sun is and catch the angle of shadow the Wall casts, and then the call to prayer sounds. The city becomes so quiet that my footsteps are the loudest things I hear. Slowly, however, I wind my way through the edge of the Forum toward the Arbaa dahia, the darkness growing thicker until I make it to a thicket of shrubbery near the base of the Wall. I know there's an opening in the hedging somewhere, and when I find it, I get low and crawl through. Free at last.

When I come out on the other side, there's dirt all over my white robe. My red sash is wrinkled, and the thick blue stripes coming down from my shoulders to my waist are all twisted and askew. At least I feel more like myself this way. I've never kept clothes clean for very long.

I hear voices ahead of me.

The wall that circles Kos, that keeps us safe, is a massive expanse of gray before me, going on infinitely in both directions, but after my eyes adjust, colors bloom to life against the stone. Some of it looks like letters, but the pink and red and orange and blue have been splashed on to create beasts. Inisisa that tattoo the Wall like they tattoo my skin, some taller than me, some battling one another, some making their way in flight over the Wall. It's the work of the Scribes.

I follow the trail, and, sure enough, there's a group of them huddled together and talking from behind their scarves. The shimmering cloth is tied loosely around their heads, and when they paint, they pull the cloth up over their mouth and nose to keep from inhaling the pungent fumes. The Scribes claim it's worse than walking through inyo-infested dahia where the uncleansed souls of the dead wander. I think they're right. I've gotten used to walking among the inyo, breathing them in. If your dahia has ever been Baptized, you've done it before, been surrounded by inyo. You've had to live with them.

My scarf, when I pull it up, won't stay over my mouth and nose, so eventually I give up. When I get close enough, everyone stops. The conversation cuts dead like it fell off a cliff.

I realize in the dark they can't recognize me, so I pull my scarf all the way down and slip my hairband down to my neck so that my hair breathes freely.

"Taj?" It's Marya. She's got her hood up, and strands of dark hair peek out and frame her face. Her gloved fingers, with the tips poking out, are covered in blue and orange paint. Her still-wet brush dangles at her waist. "Taj, is that you?" I can hear joy in her voice, and for the first time since before I fought that dragon, it feels like I'm home again, like the city of Kos recognizes me.

She's wearing a gray shirt with an eagle painted on the front, cinched at the waist. Another Scribe behind her wears a robe covered in painted lizards. A smaller aki nearby shows off his new shirt to a couple of the others. A gift from the Scribes. He flaps the shirt so that it looks like the tiny birds on it, the inisisa representing thievery, are flying up his chest.

More aki cluster by the Wall, checking out the latest painted sin.

Scanning the paintings, I remember how the holy men would talk of a time when beasts roamed the earth. Before there were aki and Mages. The beasts roamed the world freely and spoke directly to us lowly humans. The Scribes tag the wall to memorialize this time. They do so in vivid color, as opposed to the black ink of actual sin-spots, so that everyone can see the images, even against the drab backdrop. Looking at the Scribes now, I feel the inevitable pinch of envy. They weren't cursed with the ability to Eat, they weren't born with the Hunger, they just felt out of place. The way they dress, the way they talk, the way they refuse to bow and kneel and scrape before all the people they're supposed to bow and kneel and scrape before. Being able to run away is always better than being taken. I wonder if any other aki watch them, admiration glowing in their eyes, and think the same and feel just a little bit jealous.

Marya picks at my robe with her dirty fingers, and I don't mind. I've missed her.

"Chai! Where did you find these? Oga, tell me the name of your dressmaker, I will make sure he is caned in the Forum for wasting these gemstones on you." She eyes me up and down, turns me around to see how it all fits together. "This is all metallic," she murmurs in awe. "The time it must have taken." Then she straightens, fists on hips. "You obviously haven't learned how to take care of clothes. You could be draped in gold, and it would all be soiled within the hour. That is a month's worth of puff puff you're wearing right now, and it is already soiled."

"Doesn't seem to suit you, brother." Someone steps forward. Bo. Relief rushes over me. Izu had promised me that he was safe, but it's a totally different thing to see him standing before me. I want to ask him about Nazim, the moneychanger, and how he bargained for Bo's freedom.

But when Bo speaks, there's a new air of confrontation in my friend that I've never seen before. He refuses to meet my eyes, instead looking me up and down. "In fact, it looks like you are preparing to pound yams. Is that what they have you doing over there, Taj? Pounding yams?" He sounds like he wants to fight me.

"Well, you're welcome for saving your life." I smile, hoping to ease the tension. Bo's sporting a new scar that slides around his left eye and down his cheek from his fight with King Kolade's sin-dragon. And his limp hasn't gone away.

"Yeah, the Palace guards let me go. Didn't give a reason. I see you've made it out all right." He snorts. "You practically glitter now." The way he says it makes me want to break his nose. "This is what they dress their servants in, eh?"

He plucks at my sash, and I step back, gritting my teeth. Marya looks at both of us, worried. What's his problem?

Bo crosses his arms over his chest. "Can't see a single sin on your skin the way you're covered up. Wouldn't want your new overseers to let the Forum know they've hired a common aki to Eat for them, would they?"

"Bo, what are you talking about? It's not like I'm stealing your work. By the Unnamed, there's still more than enough sin to go around."

"I bet they feed you pretty nice too. Goat meat on your plate every night, eh?"

"Bo."

He takes a step forward, but Marya stands between us, a hand to Bo's chest.

"Brothers, stop this lahala. Now."

She speaks with steel in her voice, but Bo and I are still spoiling for a fight.

"Leave it!" one of the younger Scribes suddenly cries out. "The guards!"

All at once, everyone scatters. The Scribes snatch up their tools and trays and pour their paint out into the dirt. They vanish in the shrubbery. Bo gives me one last glare before he does the same. I get ready to head in after them when I see Arzu leading a small army of guards. Sweaty, breathing hard, barely able to hold herself up, and fuming with rage.

"Sir," is all she has to say. Her eyes are still rimmed in red.

I follow her back to the Palace.

Chapter 16

My bed in the Palace is still softer than anything I could ever imagine touching. But I'm so angry I spend the night shaking, fists balled up at my sides, wishing Bo would walk in so I could smash a shovel over his northerner face. I'd bet a thousand fric he thinks I've betrayed him somehow, but that's absolute lahala because he gets to walk free throughout the Forum while I'm trapped here doing nothing. Trapped.

I can't tell how much time has passed, but the sky is as dark as my daga outside my window. Arzu is nowhere to be found. If I even breathed of leaving the Palace again, she would probably leap out of the shadows and tackle me to the ground.

Before I know it, I'm out of my room and wandering the halls. Maybe if I stomp around for long enough, I can let go of some of this anger. At the very least it'll help me stop thinking about Bo and how he got the other aki to look at me like I was some sort of traitor, even though I did nothing to them. I saved his life. A smirk crosses my face. He's probably just upset I was able to defeat that inisisa and he wasn't.

Up ahead, noise leaks out from one of the rooms to the right. The door is partially opened, and I can see the glow of candlelight.

Something to do, I guess.

I get to the door, and through the sliver I see vibrantly colored cushions and lounge chairs. The walls look like buckets of glittering paint were splashed on them. A few kids my age sit on pillows in a circle around a small lamp. They laugh and shout like the rest of the Palace isn't trying to sleep.

"On your mother's opal, eh, I will find that girl, and I will crush her ruby. Do you think her brother can stop me? That stone-sniffing ditchdigger? All of those northerners. Lay a hand on me and CHOP!"

The room erupts with laughter.

I remember how I used to feel about the Kayas and about the royal family before I got here, how they weren't worth a fraction of the gemstones they wear, and still aren't. How they look down on the rest of the city and all the dahia and how we are all supposed to believe that they are the purest among us, wholly and completely without sin.

I turn to leave, then I hear. "Eh-eh! Where are you going?"

They can't possibly be talking to me.

"Come here, come here!" A pause. "What are you, deaf? I said come here!"

I push the door a little bit open, and now I'm angry again. Thankfully, it's no longer Bo whose nose I want to break.

I open the door all the way so I have an easy escape.

When the candlelight shines on my face and my clothes, they look me up and down. One of them grins, showing his teeth.

"So you are the new servant, eh?" says one of them, wearing a full robe with red and green stripes, rubies and emeralds alternating all the way down from his shoulders to his knees. They all wear pristine white pants. There are four of them. The other three wear single-color robes: blue, brown, and silver. The one in stripes seems like their leader.

"Eh-eh! Come join us!" The one in the stripes shifts over to another cushion and pats the one he just left. He has his hood pulled close to his face. I can barely see his eyes. "If you refuse us, I will have you caned for your rudeness. What is your name, boy?"

Every single word out of his mouth makes me angrier. The way they look at me or talk at me like I'm some sort of exotic servant. I can hear the arrogance in their voices. Nothing bad has ever happened to them. No misfortune. When has this one's stomach ever been empty? But I walk in and stand over them. They watch me in silence.

"Rest," says their leader, chuckling. "You are not working. You are with us now, so you will never work again."

On the table in the middle of their circle is a metal dish with powders in varying colors on it. Next to the one in brown is a bowl that holds a smaller version of what women in the dahia use to pound yams. Its wide bottom is covered in blue and red and purple dust. I look at the dish again with the lines of powder, and my stomach turns.

Stone-sniffers.

The leader slaps me on the back while the one in blue takes one of the small, thin pieces of metal, whose edge looks sharper than my daga's, and chops a piece of the ruby powder off the line. In a single deft movement, he slides it onto the back of his free hand, puts his hand to his nose, and inhales.

The others are giggling even more than before. I can tell from the backs of their hands that they just sniffed too.

On that table: rubies and opals and emeralds, while beggars and those in Kos with nothing put crushed coal up their noses and kill their minds. Miners in the north would work an entire year to supply the gemstones these royals have crushed into powder to put up their noses.

When I flick my arm to get my daga into my hand, it catches on my sleeve, exposing the sin-spots that run up and down my right arm.

Everyone freezes. Their eyes bulge with wonder. Then the one in stripes grabs my arm and slams it on the table.

"So this is how they look?" he says. "When you Eat sins, this is where they go?"

I glare, my lips pursed. I flex my arm, but his grip is surprisingly strong. Even though he's joking around and laughing and doesn't seem to pay attention, he can guess what I want to do to him.

"Eh! He is wearing our sins. Look at this." Then, with a finger, he traces the griffin by my elbow. "Whose is this?" He points to the boy in brown. "Is this your sin? What does a griffin mean? What sin is that?"

Before I answer, he sees the lion tattooed on my forearm. He stares for a long time, entranced.

"Haris," I say beneath my breath. I don't even realize I've said it until he looks me in the eye and grins. He pulls his hood off his head. "You're Haris."

I didn't recognize him in the soft glow of the candlelight. I'd only seen his face at a distance, then recognized it in a vision, both times in broad daylight.

"This one is mine?" he asks quietly. "I don't even remember what this one was for."

"When you smashed that jeweler's stall!" shouts the one in brown.

"Or maybe when you tried to take that coal-woman's ruby, eh?"

"If the lion is from a visit to the coal-woman, this aki would be covered in the prince's lions. You see?" the one in silver leans over and pulls my sleeve up even farther. My stomach turns so much I'm ready to vomit. "Here is a bear, and here a snake." Then the one in silver considers me. "Unless you can get different beasts for the same sin?"

I can feel heat rising to my cheeks. I pull my arm free and grab my daga from my armband. The entire world is covered in a sheet of red. Tears spring to my eyes. I want to fight, but harming royals is the most heinous sin of all—it would mean certain death.

We all turn at the sound of footsteps in the hallway.

"Cousin," Haris sputters.

I whirl around and stop dead. Princess Karima stands in the doorway, her face a porcelain mask, betraying nothing.

"Cousin," she says softly. She sees everything but says nothing else.

Slowly, I calm my breathing, but my chest is still so tight. I fumble my daga back into my armband and brush past the princess without saying a word.

I spend the rest of the night on the balcony, staring at Kos in the distance.

The sun is high over the wall when I feel Arzu's hand on my shoulder.

I get up, and when I wipe my face, my cheeks are still wet with tears.

"Sir, is everything all right?" Arzu asks, and for a second it sounds like there's genuine concern in her voice.

"I'm fine." My loose sleeve slips, and I see there's still powder residue on it. Revulsion and anger twist in my stomach.

"Well, sir, you have a visitor."

"Tell them to come later." I walk back into my room. "I need sleep." But just as I turn to my bed, I see who's standing in the door.

She wears a Mage's robes, and her spectacles are tangled in her hair. The Mage from Zoe's.

"Aliya," she says, as though I could have forgotten.

"Good morning," I say groggily.

"Princess Karima wanted me to tell you that she is hosting a poetry competition right now, and she requests your presence. It's a bunch of kids from the dahia, the absolute smartest, and it's always a special occasion. I've been told to expect a wonderful afternoon of equations and proofs today. There will be plenty of Palace advisers, kanselo, and other algebraists, some of the best in all of Kos. They will all be judging. It really is a lot of fun, and I—" She stops, then smiles. "I'm babbling. Well, Princess Karima wanted me to tell you that you're more than welcome to come."

She leaves, then, a few seconds later, pokes her head back through the doorway. "And welcome to the Palace estates. I was very happy to hear that you'd be around." Then she leaves, and it's just me and Arzu left.

I can't even begin to figure out how to feel about this place.

"Sir," Arzu says from behind me, "my advice would be to bathe first."

Oh yeah. That.

I bathe quickly, Arzu still at my side, and dress for the competition. I only end up finding the auditorium by following the sound of occasional, faint applause. Even then, it takes me a few tries to find the right entrance. I open one door, and it looks like I've arrived backstage. From here, however, I can see a few familiar faces sprinkled throughout. Aliya sits in the front row, leaned over, with her chin in her hands. She's got parchment on her lap, but it's like she's forgotten all about it. She stares at whatever's happening on a large chalkboard on the stage. Other

Mages, wearing the kanselo stripes of Palace advisors, fill out the front row along with several algebraists.

Bo worked the wedding of an algebraist one time, and he told me about it. He had been called in to Eat before the proper wedding ceremonies to ensure that both parties were pure when they exchanged vows. He told me about their clean white robes and dresses, and the brightly colored gemstones adorning them. He told me how they made sure he was always out of sight of the guests. He'd been forced to wait by a water closet outside, then brought to a small bedroom in a separate house behind the main estate to Eat the bride's and groom's sins. Afterward, he was kicked out through the back while the Mage collected his payment.

They're mostly men here in the front row that I can see, with a few women algebraists. They're all in simple robes—work attire—and everyone forms a semicircle around the room. In the center is Princess Karima. A few Kayas, probably some of her cousins, sit around her.

She doesn't see me, and I hurriedly look for another way in.

There's another door that opens out onto the far back of the room, so that I can see the board and what's being scribbled on it. The ceiling of the room looms so high overhead that everything echoes—including the sound of the door closing behind me as I try to shuffle as noiselessly as possible inside.

A few heads turn at my entrance, but if I look the part, I better be the part, so I strut in like I personally own this room. I am the Lightbringer, after all. No one is going to respect me if I cower in the back.

But when I get close, I notice that most of the seats are full.

Either Mages or kanselo or algebraists or Kayas in their brightly colored robes. There is one seat, though. And I gulp when I see it's right next to Princess Karima.

OK, Taj. Breathe easy.

It takes me a moment, but I muster the courage and make my way through the back of the semicircle. I take the small steps up to the dais two at a time and plop down in the unoccupied chair, nearly knocking it over in the process. When I get settled and try to breathe steadily again, I see she's looking at me. Her eyes are clear and calm like river water.

I keep my hands in my lap and remain still, even as she reaches over and puts a gloved hand over mine.

She squeezes once, then lets go.

My hands warm at her touch, and they stay that way for the rest of this dahia kid's presentation.

A little boy, dressed in a blue-and-gold-striped robe fills the chalkboard with lines and numbers and symbols: with *e* and pi and something about a golden ratio, but it all goes over my head. I try to follow Aliya's reactions. But her rapture is beyond me. I glance to my right and am chilled to see Izu staring straight ahead, his lips pursed in a frown. Then I notice Haris, slouched in his chair two down from Karima, with that permanent smirk on his face.

My gaze returns to Karima. By the Unnamed, if she could hear the way my heart is beating in my chest right now . . .

A smile graces her face. She's not looking at me, but there is no doubt in my mind that I am on hers.

After several more dahia kids present their equations and

explain their poetry, everyone disperses. A few of the algebraists huddle together and talk about the children. The Mages eye them hungrily, searching for potential talent. Either future kanselo, court lawmakers, or aki. I can already tell that look in their eyes. They don't see dahia children. They see money.

Before the kids are ushered away by Palace guards, Karima has them all assemble at the front of the room before the board. Several long equations fill the board, and the children fumble, some swaying nervously left to right. Others keep their chins held high and their backs straight, and I smile at them. They're trying to show that they're not cowed by this place. That the bigness of this room and the richness of the clothing of the royals and the patches on their own robes mean nothing. That they're just as worthy as the people they're performing for.

I've spent my whole life trying to do just that.

Karima stands before each of them and bows to meet their level, then slips something shiny in each of their hands. Ramzi. Probably enough to feed their families for quite some time. Some of the children remain stone-faced and respectful. A few others smile widely. One of the little boys tries to keep his lips from trembling, but two tears run down his face. As much as I'm sure his parents tried to scrub him before he was presented here, there are still smudges of dirt on his cheeks.

I duck out before anyone can notice me.

The shuffle of my footsteps echoes along the cavernous hallway. Arzu falls into step beside me. I can never hear when she enters or when she leaves a room. If she wanted, she could sneak up on me, cut my throat, and I wouldn't be able to tell until I had joined Infinity.

Just as we're about to turn a corner, I see her stop short in my periphery.

I half turn. Her face is hardened, lips pressed into a thin line. I follow her gaze and see Princess Karima down the hall, talking with someone neither of us can see. She smiles at the person, nods her head, then comes my way. She puts out her hand, palm up. She's not wearing her gloves anymore.

"To you and your people, Taj."

I slide my hand over hers. "To you and yours, Princess."

"Would you like to walk with me?" she says, not quite asking.

"Yes." I look to Arzu, wondering if she'll be coming with us.

"Has your sicario been a good companion?"

"Arzu? Oh, yeah. Doesn't talk much though."

Princess Karima smiles. "Well, I'm sure we can do something about that."

I can feel my face redden as the princess threads her arm through mine. "Please, sicario, will you excuse us?" she says to Arzu, who turns abruptly and heads back the way we'd come.

Princess Karima gently tugs my arm, and I shake myself out of my trance and join her.

We walk for almost a minute in silence, up and around corridors with chandeliers glinting overhead and tossing colors along the walls. Kanselo amble in either direction along the walls. The Palace here bustles with quiet activity. People work here, I realize with astonishment.

"Some of those children are so terribly gifted," Karima says at last. "Some of them will make wonderful algebraists." She leans in like we're in on a conspiracy together. "If we can keep them away from some of these grubby Mages," she says, smiling.

I smile back. "To be honest, Princess, it was all a bit beyond me."

She presses her free hand against my arm. "Give it time, Taj."

I want to ask her about last night with Haris and the other cousins sniffing stones. Surely such sinful behavior would be forbidden here. But when she'd walked in, she'd said nothing.

"I find that Mage very interesting. You know her, I think. The one with the glasses."

I smirk, because I know she's trying to be funny. "Many of the Mages wear glasses, Princess."

"Aliya. Yes, that's her name. She has such fascinating ideas for the children and for scholarship more generally. I think she would make a fantastic student in the Ulo Amamihe. Izu believes that she should become kanselo. He thinks her place is as a lawmaker, deciding what actions constitute sins. I disagree. I think her talents indicate that she belongs elsewhere."

"You have a say in that? Who joins the Great House of Ideas?"

She looks my way. "Well, if a student can teach us how to use our mathematical arts to unlock space and time, as well as find medical applications for them, then we'd be smart to keep her here."

"She can do all that?"

"She's quite gifted."

She stops walking, and I have to stop with her.

"How are you feeling, Taj?"

"I'm well."

"You walk very stiffly. Are you sore?"

I didn't even realize how straight my back had gotten. "No, Princess. Just . . ."

And that's when I realize that the hall we've just turned down is empty. No one's around. Karima lets go of my arm, then pushes open a door to her left. Before it opens all the way, I know that this is my room. I was so distracted by the princess that I didn't even notice. I look around, then she pulls me in, and the door clicks shut behind me.

It's a mess, clothes everywhere, some outfits I've only tried on once.

My face is on fire with embarrassment.

She walks to the center of the room and stands on the eight-pointed star patterned in the tiles. And as she moves, she looks around and considers the place, taking it all in.

Then she turns back to face me.

"You needn't be nervous around me, Taj." She waves her hand at the empty room. "It's just us." She glances at me, then looks ahead. "Everyone here frowns on curiosity. The very *notion* of curiosity is severely devalued. No one seems to care about the world outside the Palace grounds, which is why we are so fortunate to have you in our midst."

"We, Princess?"

She puts a hand to her chest, blushing. "Well, I can only speak for myself. I'm the fortunate one. But I speak of this apathy in my family for the world outside, which even seems to extend to theology."

As she speaks, she moves closer to me until we're standing face-to-face. I can feel her breath on me.

I clear my throat. I've never wanted to be so close to someone as I am to her right now.

"In today's devotional, I was reading about penance and absolution. And what we are called upon to do in service of the Most High, the Unnamed." Her eyes are wide and earnest. She really does care about this. "And the familiar line is that we are but soldiers in a larger battle with our dark portions, but why? Why do we sin?"

I can't imagine the princess sinning, pure and pristine as she is right now, practically glowing.

She puts a hand on my forearm and gently pulls me closer. I think she's about to whisper a secret in my ear, but her eyes are trained straight ahead.

"I've spent much time praying on this and thinking. I believe sin is a necessary part of our existence. The world is richer for the darkness existing in it." Her face breaks into a smile. "Do you see, Taj? The truth is Balance. Light and dark. We are all necessary parts of the tapestry."

My head is swimming. One thought pierces the cloud and clears the fog, and before I can call them back, the words fly out of my mouth. "Even the Mages?"

She stops, looking stricken. I've spoken out of turn. I've probably just signed my own death warrant.

She looks directly into my eyes, unwavering. I've never seen a more beautiful face in my life. Her words make me feel like I'm the only other person in all of Kos.

"Show me," she whispers.

"Princess?"

She takes my hand and guides me to my bed. The sheets are twisted, and the pillows all fell off at some point in the night. We stand right at the bed's corner, my back up against one of the wooden columns of the bedframe. Carvings of arashi press into my back.

"Show me," she murmurs again. She slides my sleeves up my arms.

Her eyes don't widen at the sight of my sin-spots. Instead, she moves closer, hand pressed against my bicep, and traces with one finger the arch of a jungle cat's back as it runs along my shoulder.

Her fingers wrap around my arms, and my hands move to her waist.

I lean back so that the arashi carvings dig into the skin of my back. Karima presses her body against mine and runs her fingers over the curling snakes by my throat. "What sins are these?" she whispers into my neck.

I can't remember them. I force myself not to.

Her fingers spiral down toward my back.

"They're mine now."

Hands firm on my shoulders, she turns me around, so that I rest against the bedpost. "And these?" she asks, sliding a finger down the dragon whose spine runs along mine. "Whose is this?"

Memories return. Of the sin-dragon I fought, the one that nearly killed Bo. "Your brother's."

Her hands stop. And she looks up at me. Over the top of her head I see Arzu standing silently in the doorway.

Karima notes my hesitation and turns. "Well. It seems that someone else demands your attention." She nods at Arzu, who has her fists balled at her sides. The princess lets go of my arms, then takes my hands in hers. "Be well, Taj. To you and your people."

"To you and yours, Princess."

I watch her slip out the door and down the dark corridor.

Arzu clears her throat. "Izu wishes to speak with you," she says, standing in front of me.

Dazed and still on fire with the memory of Karima's touch, I shrug my robe back onto my shoulders and pick my sash up from the floor.

"OK," I murmur.

Chapter 17

Izu's quarters look completely different from the rest of the Palace grounds. Just four stone walls and a wooden desk with a wooden chair that scrapes loudly against the hard floor. Everything here looks like punishment. I can't believe that a guy like Izu is forced to live in a place like this. I can't even see a bed anywhere. No pallet on the floor either. Nazim's office looks like the inside of a castle in comparison.

The warmth I felt with Karima suddenly feels very far away. A part of me still can't believe I was actually that close to the princess—that she actually touched me. The softness of her fingers as they traced my sin-spots, and the sound of her voice as she whispered into my ears.

Izu coughs. I can't tell if it's because he saw my mind wandering or if it was because of the draft, but it's enough to make me remember where I am.

There's only one chair, and Izu places it behind his desk and sits in it. Guess I'm supposed to just stand here, then.

"So. Lightbringer." No matter how much lightness he puts into his voice, he can't get rid of the hiss. "How are you enjoying your new post?"

I shrug and cross my arms, trying to find an interesting crevice in the wall to stare at. "Everyone here is so pure that I don't really have much work," I say, hoping he catches my sarcasm.

Izu smiles, but there's no mirth in it.

I look around and take the place in, trying to seem as nonplussed as possible. Hopefully, that'll convince Izu to hurry up and finish whatever he has me here for.

"Ah, yes. My chambers. Maybe you are thinking to yourself that I am not nearly as important as others may think if my chambers are so diminutive. In our quest to join Infinity, however, modesty is a principal virtue. Sometimes, the most elegant formulas are the simple ones. A lack of material possessions is chief among our duties. So that, lacking in outward comforts, we may rely on the Unnamed for spiritual sustenance. To balance us."

"Guess that makes us aki pretty holy then."

A smirk crosses Izu's face. "Perhaps it does." He reclines in his chair and, surprisingly enough, manages to look comfortable. "And your companion? Is she . . . suitable?"

"Suitable for what?"

"As your guardian."

I snort. "Is that what a sicario is supposed to be doing? Well, yeah, she's pretty good at it. Not sure how she'd protect me from a sin-dragon, though."

Light glints in Izu's snake-shell eyes. They say lizards adjust their body temperature to their surroundings, so they can survive in cold as well as hot weather. Put them in a suffocating room with no windows or in a dungeon at the bottom of a castle during the cold months, and they would survive all the same. Unbothered. Maybe that's why he's so at ease here. "It seems, then, that we've alighted on your main concern."

"Concern?"

"You appear . . . bored . . . with your current employment."

"It gives me a bed to sleep in, so I can't really complain. But King Kolade is not much of a sinner," I lie. "Other than the one time."

Izu pulls a string of prayer beads out of his sleeve and thumbs through them, probably thinking his way into a reply. "I have a proposition for you, then. A job." He shrugs. "The position is much less glamorous than your current posting. And you would be far from the Palace, but there will likely be more danger, more excitement. It seems the domestic tranquility of the Palace does not suit you."

It's tough to get loose in this room when I'm just standing. Like the room itself is telling me that I can't be comfortable. Can't slouch. Can't hunch over. Can't favor one leg over the other. So, I stand straight up, like a fool, and say, "I've never liked feeling closed in. What's this proposition?"

"You would train other aki."

"Train how?"

Izu spreads his hands. "Why, help them master their talents. You are the most skilled aki in Kos."

"I see no lies."

"We can use more like you. These would be younger aki. Some still developing their ability. They have little to no control over it, and many of them have never Eaten before. They would very much value your wisdom and expertise."

I'm trying to find the angle here and figure out why Izu wants me out of the Palace. I'm sure he's nervous having me around, which is probably why he's had Arzu tailing me. The more I think about it, the more I search for a reason, the more I realize it probably has something to do with the princess. That time in my bedroom and the little time I got to spend by the Wall with the Seven Scribes were the only moments when Arzu wasn't breathing down my neck. Which means that even though Izu is making this sound like I have a choice, I probably don't. Arzu's been spying for this Mage.

"These children are young," he says again. "You can pass along the princess's wisdom and knowledge of the Word. If, of course, you haven't been too busy to converse with her."

He does know. The ruby-licker knows about me and the princess. "Are these the same aki you people snatch up during your Baptisms? When you're busy destroying their homes?"

Izu shakes his head slowly. "These children we gather have nowhere else to go. You can help them. We are all working to build a pure Kos. We all play our roles. Mages guide the herd. Aki keep us from succumbing to the weight of our sins." A smile twitches at the edge of his lips. "You can also get a glimpse of what lies beyond the Wall."

"I'll think about it." The only way out is past Izu's desk, and I brush by it, knocking my hip against it. When I get to the door, I hear him turn in his chair.

"Regarding your decision, your haste would be much appreciated. If the king does not find a suitable candidate soon, he may be forced to Baptize another dahia in Kos, hoping, of course, that there will be nuggets of gold in the cleansing waters that pour through those streets. Aki powerful enough to suit his purposes, perhaps."

And there it is. The threat that I've been waiting for. Take this new job or an entire dahia gets destroyed in another Baptism.

"I'll have your answer by tomorrow," I say, fists clenched at my sides. I don't wait for him to dismiss me.

Just outside his door, I pause.

I could go back and tell Izu no. I could hope and pray to the Unnamed that Karima would save whatever dahia Izu would choose. Maybe she would stand between Izu and her brother. Maybe she would do it for me, for the people of Kos.

I double back but stop when I see another Mage sweep into Izu's chambers. Before the person vanishes into the room completely, her hood falls back to reveal the face of a bespectacled girl. Aliya.

She latches the door behind her, but the wood does a poor job of obscuring their voices.

"We want to train our aki. They are so important to this society. You of all people know that. And at the Festival of Reunification, we will celebrate them and all they have accomplished. They are the last line of defense between Kos and the arashi. Were it not for them, this city would have long ago been destroyed by the uncleansed sin that fills it. Finally, the aki will no longer have to live in hiding, shunned by the very people they protect."

For a long time, there's silence. Then beads clicking against one another.

"But, Mage. All those sins . . ."

"That is why I am sending you to the camps to help them, to train them. You have a gift. You can decipher texts at a remarkable speed. You can make connections that illuminate new meaning in the Word. You understand Balance and what one must do to proceed to Infinity sinless. Those aki will need you."

I can't make out every word, but I know the type of person Izu is. He must be threatening her with something. Baptize the dahia where she comes from? Demote her? Forever bar her from the Ulo Amamihe, so she has no hope whatsoever of joining the algebraists in the Great House of Ideas? Whatever it is, Izu has her in his grasp. I press my ear to the door. There's movement. A hushed exchange I can't make out, then footsteps moving closer. Fast. I hear one last whisper before I go.

"I won't let our aki down," Aliya says.

I make a run for it and round the corner just as I hear the door creak open.

Izu's got an angle here. He always does. Now, whatever his plan is, Aliya's part of it. Maybe she'll have the answers I need.

CHAPTER 18

THE NEXT MORNING, at my request, they bring my breakfast tray out to a table on the balcony. I look out at Kos as I eat. It's so small and unremarkable in the distance. It must be horrible to spend one's entire life here and see that whole city as little more than a speck against a massive gray wall. To never see the Scribes' handiwork. To never hear the poets standing on raised daises in the thoroughfare and shouting those stanzas they spent way too much time trying to put together. To never watch the older women and some of their families crowd around the itinerant holy men reciting from the Word or giving their own sermons. To never smell the sweet tang of halal meat spinning on the butchers' skewers or the beautiful sting of pepper soup boiling.

Is this why it's so easy to order Baptisms? If a city where people live is small enough to fit on the edge of your nail, that must make it easier to send Hurlers to destroy those dahia and chase people from their homes. From this far away, you can't possibly see how alive the city is.

Arzu stands at her post near the entrance to the balcony. The way Arzu looks out at Kos right now makes me wonder if she has people from there. Maybe she comes from there.

"What dahia?" I ask, popping a grape in my mouth.

"Excuse me, sir?" she says, and it's gone. Whatever memory she was walking through or whatever song she was recalling, it's gone. And she's all business again.

"I was asking what dahia your family is from." I wave my finger out at Kos in the distance. "Can you see it from here?"

"I'm not from the dahia, sir."

"Where are you from, then?"

She turns to face me. "I was born in the Palace, sir. I am from here."

"But you're not like them." I can't keep the surprise from my voice.

She doesn't move from where she stands, but I can tell that her thoughts are somewhere else right now. "My mother was a servant to Princess Karima."

"Was she a sicario too?"

A hint of a smile from Arzu. "No. Just a servant."

I take a seat by the table and gesture to the open one across from me, but Arzu shakes her head no.

"My mother was not from Kos either. We came from elsewhere."

"From beyond the Wall?" My eyes widen.

"She was a migrant, and she came here looking for work." Arzu nods. "When she began her work in the Palace, she was already heavy with me. I'm sure some of the other Kayas would have wanted me sent away, or disappeared. Princess Karima kept my mother in her employ and allowed her to raise me within the Palace grounds."

Now I take a long look at Arzu, a real one. I notice the veins that thread the backs of her hands. The tightness in her calves where they come up out of her boots. She has the same skin as the princess, only tougher. In her leathers, she looks like the princess's sister or cousin, maybe, kidnapped at birth and trained by sand kings like in a storyscroll I once read as a kid.

"The Kayas wanted to take you from your mother. You don't resent them for that? You're still walking around as their servant?"

"I am not their servant, sir. I am yours."

Just like that, she stops my anger. I can't figure her out. Most people, I can tell what they want pretty easily. And usually what they want in the moment says something about what they want in life, but Arzu . . . how can she walk around and stand in the same rooms as the people who had wanted her mother to abandon her?

"Where's your mother now?"

"Gone."

"And why aren't you with her?" I'm angry again. My chest is tight, and I can't figure out why. "Why are you still here?"

"Why are you?" Arzu snaps, then quickly composes herself. "I apologize, sir."

She lets out a small breath, and it seems like whatever had bound her so tightly has loosened. "I must remain here in order to repay a debt. I serve at Princess Karima's behest, because we are bound. My mother . . ." She stops, clenches her fists at her sides.

When she speaks again, she speaks through gritted teeth. "My mother committed a sin in this house. They wouldn't hire an aki to Eat her sin, so she was to be executed. I offered myself in her place."

"What does that mean?" A chill raises gooseflesh along my spine.

"I was to take my mother's place as Princess Karima's servant." The resolve has returned to Arzu's voice, but her cheeks are shining. "To ensure that I never leave and that my life be forever bound to the princess, I was unsexed so that I may never bear children."

I try to imagine Princess Karima in that scene. I'm putting it all together in my head, but it's a blur. Jumbled images of a fair-skinned woman in a servant's clothes, maybe on her knees humbly begging for her life, forehead to the cold tiles wet with her tears. Does her daughter stand by her side? Does she glare at Princess Karima for what she is about to order? I can't imagine that the same Princess Karima who would do this is the one who condemned the system that has aki ragged and poor and hungry in the streets of Kos. The same one who touched me so gently.

"Princess—"

"No, it was not Princess Karima who ordered this," Arzu says. "Her cousin Haris decreed the punishment. Originally, I was to be murdered." She stands taller, raises her chin so that she's looking down on me. The sunlight, when it hits, makes her seem more than human. "Karima saved my life."

For a long time, neither of us says a word.

I wonder if I should tell her to go after her mother. I'll distract the Palace guards while she makes a run for it. I'll sacrifice myself so that her family can be reunited; I'll Eat her mother's sin. Maybe I should tell her it's OK, while I feel guilty that I still know where Mama and Baba live, that they are healthy for now. And safe. I don't know what I can tell her that she hasn't already told herself.

"I want to show you something," I tell her.

"Where is it?"

I nod in the direction of Kos. My city. "It's OK. No peppered chicken-sticks this time."

This time of year, the days get shorter and shorter. I take her through Kos slowly, because I know I may not get another chance to wander like this. I wish I had more time to show her places like Gemtown. But the sun has started to set. And pretty soon, we'll have to return to the Palace.

We make our way in the dark, first through the backstreets, then up through the villages of the southern dahia. I know Khamsa is near. I can feel it, like a humming in my bones. Any time I'm near Mama and Baba, whether I've wandered there by accident or snuck there on purpose, I know where I am. Arzu falls behind me, and as agile as she is, she doesn't know where the puddles are that she needs to step over or the thorny vines that wrap around the walls of some homes and shacks. By the time we make it to the rim of the Arbaa dahia, she has one slipper off and is shaking small pebbles out of it.

The handholds and footholds are all waiting for me. I haven't been here in a while, I realize, but my body knows this place. It moves all on its own. When I seat myself on a small boulder, I pull Arzu up, then I point to the roof of an abandoned shack just in front of us.

"I cannot see it," she tells me.

"It's right there."

"But I can't see it."

I rise to my feet and check my pockets to make sure that everything is there. "OK, just follow me." And I leap off into the darkness and land softly on the roof I know is there.

"Taj?" Silence. "Taj!" She shouts in a hushed whisper. "Taj, where did you go?"

Most of the dahia is asleep, so I lower my voice too. "I'm right here. Just jump. There's a roof right in front of you. Metal. Just jump. If you slip, I'll catch you."

"Taj," she warns. She's annoyed with me, but she's also scared. She's never called me by my name before.

"Don't worry," I say, more softly. "I'm here."

"OK." I hear her shift, hear her slippers scuff against the ground, hear her running, then I hear the soft whoosh of her feet leaving the ground.

She lands with a tumble and nearly topples me over. It's enough to make me start laughing, and even as she comes to her feet and stands over me, straightening her leathers and brushing the dust off, I roll on the roof, clutching my stomach in pain from the laughter. She's completely silent, but I can tell she's glaring, so I eventually settle down.

"Here." I pat the spot next to me. "Sit down. Turn around so that we're both facing where we jumped from."

She does as instructed, and I pull out of the pouch by my waist a fistful of marbles. Mostly blues and greens, but there are a few reds in there. And one yellow, if I remember correctly. I can't quite see them in the dark.

"You have a match?"

She pulls a small matchbook out of her chest pocket, and I take one and light the candle I've brought with us. I smear some of its base on the roof so that it sticks at the angle I need it to be at, then I arrange the marbles in front of it. When I'm finished, rays of color splash against the rim of the dahia wall.

Arzu's eyes go wide in the light cast by the candle.

The colors dance against one another. When a gust rushes by us, the dance turns into a fight. But they flow all the same. And for a long time, we watch the show without saying a word.

The candle goes down to half its original length before Arzu says, "We came from the west. Well, my mother did."

I glance at her, but she's only got eyes for the light show.

"I never saw our land, but my mother would tell me stories. It was harsh terrain, very dry. My people didn't cut the earth for metals like they do here." She brings her knees up to her chest and hugs herself. "We farmed. We raised cattle. We fled the arashi."

"You've seen arashi?"

"In my mother's time, the arashi visited the west frequently. There was no order to their visitations. But each time, they would tear at the land and turn it so that we would have to flee. It would take a year before anything good could grow from it, so we migrated. What you call nomads." She looks at me, and it's different from any other look she's given me. "Your kind exist where my mother comes from."

"What? The aki?"

"Yes, there are people in my homeland like you, but they are honored. They serve as arbiters of justice. And they are healers. We call them tastahlik. When a person's sins render them ill, the tastahlik will cure them by taking on their sins. They are heroes, and they wear their markings proudly." Her face softens. Or maybe that's just a trick of the light. "When my mother told me of this, I thought it was strange that you aki walk in such shame all the time. That you hide your markings." She turns back to the light show. "You sacrifice your body for the sake of others." A breeze threatens to extinguish our candle, but the light persists. "Back in my mother's land, your kind are buried in reverent fashion."

Feelings roil inside of me. So many feelings that I can't figure out what to say. As the candlelight dies down, we head back to the Palace in silence.

I wonder, had I said no to Izu, whether or not this dahia would have been the one he would have chosen for Baptism.

Chapter 19

I wake with a start. It's dark. Still the middle of the night.

No matter how hard I press my palms to my eyes, I can't squeeze out the last traces of the dream. All darkness. But against the black, there were outlines of sin-beasts: a lion and a snake, silhouetted against inky night. Light shone in from somewhere, and I realized they were circling the source. A girl. Karima. They stalked her, the lion and the snake, in increasingly tight circles, and she had nowhere to go. I was frozen in place. I couldn't do a thing to stop them. Then, just as they both lunged at her, I woke up.

Other aki complain about it, night terrors that attack them when they close their eyes. The sins they swallow enter their dreams and torment them. When Bo and I had to share a room, he broke at least three bowls thrashing around in his sleep. It didn't take us long to figure out we had to put the ceramics we ate from in a whole other room when it was time to sleep. But that only happens if you're soft enough to think about the sinners. I get by because I don't do that. The only way to Eat as much as I have, to maintain the Hunger, is to think only of yourself. Which doesn't explain this dream with Karima.

Then I realize that, no, that's not what this is.

I feel my heart drop. This isn't a night terror. It's not a side effect from Eating too many sins. It's me being upset about a girl I'll never make my heart-mate.

I search my brain to try to figure out when it happened. How did she do it? Was it that first time she ran her fingers along my forearms? Touched my sin-spots and didn't back away? Was it when she took my arm in hers and walked with me? When she held me and traced the lines of her brother's sins on my body?

And now I haven't seen her since.

I have to leave. I have to join the Mages in the forest and train the aki. Aliya is right. I can't let them down, and whatever Izu has planned for them, they'll need me.

I feel stupid for thinking things could have turned out differently. It's nonsense to think that I would ever be accepted here, or that someone like me could be treated with respect here. An aki's duty is to Eat until they can't Eat anymore. That's what we're here for. Sins are written on our bodies until the pain becomes too much and we go mad. We Cross over. Then, even dead, after our throats have been cut, our inyo hang around and wander the streets of Kos, leftovers.

I'm just going to be training those young aki to be paraded through Kos for the Festival of Reunification. Only the

Unnamed knows what sort of ridiculous spectacle Izu and the others will make of them, but at least aki are being given proper training now. Omar's tear stained face flashes in my mind. His tattered clothes and wide eyes. I hope to go my whole life without ever seeing one of my own so frightened again. If joining the Mages prevents that, then so be it.

I think about what that apprentice Aliya said about sin-spots being poems, but here at night it's too dark to read whatever might be written on me.

Kos at night is invisible from the balcony. You can hardly tell it's there. I see the Wall and almost nothing else. But if I close my eyes, I can see the Seven Scribes painting sins and writing their messages, tagging the Wall. I can see some of the aki, unable to sleep, like me, lying on the rooftops of their shanties, counting the stars.

I miss them.

Arzu's standing over me when the morning prayer wakes me up.

The rest of the Palace is praying right now.

I wonder if Arzu's mother ever prayed, or if they did that sort of thing where her mother came from. I can't stop thinking about what it would've been like had Arzu been born anywhere else. Always an outsider, maybe she would've joined the Seven Scribes. Maybe she'd be tagging the Wall right now. She wouldn't have been born with our Hunger, but maybe, as a child, she would've been swept up by prelates during a Baptism of her dahia and tossed back out into the streets when the Mages realized she couldn't do what they needed her to do. Maybe she would've stayed with us anyway. Maybe she would've spent enough time in the dahia to get used to our dahia sauces.

"Izu is ready to meet with you," she says.

"Sit with me for a little bit," I tell her. "Please."

She sits next to me, both our backs against the marble. I slip my daga out of its band and flick it from my wrist to my hands, where it dances over my fingers, spins, twirls. It feels good to do this again. All the while, I keep the strap out of the way so it doesn't get cut. It feels comfortable. I can't believe it's been so long since I've played like this.

Arzu turns to look at me. "Have you made your decision?"

"Yeah, this place is awful." I remember Izu and his reason for wanting me out, to separate me from Princess Karima. Then I remember that Arzu is his spy. But a part of me doesn't care about that anymore. Not a big enough part to keep from lying to her, though. "All I'm doing is getting out of shape here. Plus, I don't need to be surrounded by all these people, all pure and sinless and boring."

"Sin excites you?"

"No, but it's just the world's realer out there, you know? People living their lives. Trying to make it work. Telling the occasional lie or being jealous of someone or stealing a loaf of bread to feed their little sister. Fighting a cutpurse to protect yourself. It's not just that it's exciting, it's . . . it's life." I wave the knife in my hand at the Palace, at everything inside it. "This isn't life."

"The Unbalance is out there."

I tap my heart. "The Unbalance is in here too." It's not until the words come out of my mouth that I realize they're Princess Karima's. If I could, I'd bring Princess Karima with me. Show her what it's really like out there. Surviving on scraps, wearing rags, and having to bathe using a bucket. Sleeping crowded, close to others during the cold season. Maybe I was only ever just a toy or something exotic for her. If Forum mud ever did really touch her dress, she'd change her mind about me.

The image from my dream flashes in my mind again. The lion and the snake circling Karima. Just as they're tensing to leap at her, they burst into clouds of smoke, then evaporate. "OK," I say, sliding my daga back into my armband. I push myself up. "Let's go see Izu."

When we get to Izu's office, Arzu waits in the doorway. I walk in and know that I can't give him the satisfaction of seeing me angry. With every nerve in my body, I school my face into an expression as cold as the stone floor beneath our feet. He's got his hands folded in front of him and is already smiling like he knows my decision.

Karima is waiting for me when I get back to my room.

"Taj," she says, excited and worried at the same time. She walks over to me, placing her hand on my forearm, exactly where the lion from her cousin's sin is tattooed. "You're going to the camps. Surely, there is something special planned for you."

"You know of the camps?"

She smirks. "You think there is anything that happens in this place that I don't know about?" She's so close I can smell her lavender perfume. "Taj. I know it is Izu who is trying to separate us, but I can have you stay. He is not the only one here who commands my brother's attention."

"I know. This isn't my place," I say. "I belong with the aki."

I believe that. I do. But still, when she moves her hand up my arm and to my shoulder, I feel a chill run through me and have half a mind to tell Izu no, just so I can stay here with Karima a little while longer.

But then I remember Izu's ultimatum. And the dahia he threatened to destroy. Karima could keep me here, with her, but could she save that dahia? As much power as she has here, she can't truly keep Kos safe from Izu.

"I'll be here when you return," she says, placing a soft kiss on my cheek. I watch her leave, stunned, placing my hand to the spot where she kissed me. She's asking me to choose between her and my home. Sadness fills me. She could never understand my choice. She has spent her entire life sheltered here. The people of Kos are probably nothing to her. I was a fool to think I could be her heart-mate.

It takes me a second to realize Arzu is waiting on me.

"Well," I say, sticking my chest out, "are you just going to stand there or are you going to help me figure out how to dress for training camps? You're the only one I know who's been beyond the Wall."

Arzu smiles. "I do believe that I can help you with that, sir."

Chapter 20

Arzu gives good advice.

One of the first things I do in preparation for leaving the Palace grounds is get rid of that stupid outfit. In my room, I practically tear it off, and then stuff it at the bottom of the closet, almost like I never want anyone else to ever see it again. Maybe if I shove it deep enough into the shadows, I can erase any memory that I ever wore it.

The rags I came in here with are long gone. But there are some undershirts here, loose-fitting cloth with tougher fabric than what is normal, and I take one of those off the rack. The sleeves hug my arms tightly, so I tear them a little to let my limbs breathe. Same with the leather breeches. With my knife, I cut the cuff by my ankle into strips that I can tie together. The clothes are all brown, like Arzu's leathers, and now that I see the resemblance, I smile at my reflection. I've seen how she moves and how even the way she wears her clothes tenses her muscles and works her limbs loose. This'll do nicely.

A retinue waits for me outside my room. Palace guards lead me down several corridors until we get to the main hall, and I stand at the balcony flanked by two staircases that wind their way to the main floor. At the bottom stand two Agha Sentries and ten servants carrying what look like bags of supplies for me. I want to tell them to drop it all, but I don't have the energy. It feels like the Palace is forcing this on me. This is how they're going to parade me to the Wall and beyond.

The massive doors to this part of the Palace open out onto a wide staircase that begins the path leading to the Forum. I step out onto the raised space right before the stairs, and up above hangs a ringed balcony from which public proclamations are delivered. Is this the closest King Kolade ever gets to the city?

Servants stand in rows on either side of me, and the sentries have moved up to the front, forming a V shape, like the tip of a dagger.

I wish Arzu could come with me. As we start moving, I turn back to the stairs, but she's not there anymore. She has already left.

The road here is paved. My flats whisper when I shuffle along. The homes here are made out of the same material as the Palace, only they are smaller. Many of them belong to the algebraists and lawyers and the Palace functionaries. The dwellings sit high up on smaller rolling hills with a single trail branching off from the main road to their complexes. Grass coats the hills. They're so green. Gardens line some of the trails, flowers I can't name making all kinds of colors on the pathways leading to those homes. I hear bubbling, the same bubbling that signaled the rivers threading the Palace grounds, and I realize that the same things also irrigate these homes. The little tributaries I see scattered throughout the hill sparkle in the sun. I can't believe that this too is part of Kos.

We get to the hill, and the Forum spreads before us. Before I can take in the view, the sentries proceed down the trail that will bring us to the Forum's front gates. I almost wish the servants would crowd in around me and hide me from the judgmental gazes of the Forum-dwellers.

The last time I made this part of the trip, it was just me. And a sin-lion had just been burned into the skin of my forearm.

I'd practically tripped down the main stairs outside, then I'd made my way to the front gates of the Palace, where Bo had been waiting for me. And together, we'd walked down the hill. I'd never paid attention to the homes before. I was always so eager to get to the Forum. But we'd spent a moment at the crest of the hill looking out over our home before racing each other down.

This time, the whole retinue makes too much noise. It's enough to silence the music of the market, the melody of Forum-dwellers talking and arguing and singing. Some Forum-dwellers pretend not to notice the troop stomping down the main thoroughfare, but most watch. Or it feels like most of them are watching.

No matter how much I try, I can't keep facing straight ahead. I'm constantly glancing to one side or another, looking for familiar faces, hoping I don't see them.

I frighten them.

Gear-heads sit on stacked barrels, their pockets full of metal parts, legs dangling over the edges of their perches. Maybe some of them recognize me from Zoe's. Maybe they don't.

The people from the Palace parade me around a corner.

I recognize the street, even though it's crowded on each side with Forum-dwellers and men and women wearing auto-mail. I turn, and suddenly, I'm staring straight at Auntie Sania. Auntie Nawal stands next to her. Their hands are folded before their robes. I stop dead in the middle of the street and can't turn away. Servants pass me by. I want so badly to break off and explain everything to them, but what would I say?

The troop stops around me. The sentries have turned to see what is holding up the caravan. I can't stop staring at the women who took me off the street when I was young and still learning about my Hunger and had nowhere to go. I want them to smile at me the way they always did. I want them to pluck at my puffy hair and wonder yet again when I'll find a nice girl to braid it for me.

Something or someone bumps into me. I'm jolted out of my trance, and a sentry stands in front of me.

"Sir," she says. And it sounds in my ears like she's shouting it loud enough for the whole Forum to hear.

"Right," I say quietly. The prelate returns to the head of the caravan. We keep walking.

Aki stare out from the crevices and holes and alleyways they hide in. Half the time, I don't even have to look to see them. I know the feel of their gazes on my back.

Bo is somewhere in the crowd. Hidden. Anonymous. But I can probably find exactly where he's standing. I can't bear to look at him. I can't think through the fact that he's seeing me like this. Ifeoma and Sade and Tolu and Emeka are probably with him. I'm ashamed to think about what expressions they're wearing on their faces right now. They probably think I've spent all this time simply getting fat off sugared puff puff and thinking I was better than them, that I belonged in that Palace rather than out here in the Forum and the dahia. Sade would joke about it, and maybe Ifeoma would find some funny way to mock me, but they would do it as friends. Tolu and Emeka and Bo would see me as a changed person. Not aki. Not Kaya. And they would probably refuse me.

If only I had the chance, I would try to tell them what it was really like in there. I'd tell them just how sinful the Kayas really are, that the food is nothing like in the dahia, that there are Mages everywhere. That there is nothing there worth wanting. But if I told them that, it would be a lie. Like the snake tattoo running along my left shoulder, where Karima once touched me.

We near the main entrance to Kos, the gate that traders and itinerant preachers march through on official business. This is the entrance that no one I know ever uses. It's the biggest patch of Wall the Seven Scribes haven't touched yet.

The gate is impossibly high, and I hurt my neck trying to see the top of it.

I'm leaving Kos.

The thought sits with me for a moment, and I turn back to take one last look at the city I've spent my entire life in. My eyes scan it, the mud-colored homes, the people, the market, the stillness of it, and then I see Omar.

For some reason, that one hurts more than the others. The look on his face is somewhere at the center of sadness, disgust, and anger. He looks like I've betrayed him.

If I could, I'd tell him that I was wrong. That, sure, thinking only of yourself will make it easier to Eat, less painful, but I'd also tell him that sometimes you can't avoid caring about what happens to others. Sometimes you get tricked into it. I want to tell him that I'm saving someone's dahia by doing this. But every time I try to put the sentence together in my head, it comes out like I'm trying to justify myself. Like I'm trying to make myself blameless.

He'll never understand.

When I nod to the Agha Sentry that we can keep going, there's movement to my right, and a Mage shuffles through the row of servants, then stops at my side.

She pushes her hood back and nearly knocks her spectacles off her head. The frames get tangled in her hair, and after some fumbling, she leaves them be.

Aliya.

A full-toothed grin bursts open on her face. "Oh, this is wonderful. I didn't expect to see you! I'll finally get to witness you at work. An actual sin-eating ritual. And you are the best, aren't you? Everyone calls you the Sky-Fist. The Lightbringer."

For a moment, her joy and energy stun me into silence. Then, I feel my face soften. "Just Lightbringer. You don't have to say *the*."

"Oh, right." She shrugs, hugs her bound cylinders of parchment to her chest. "There can only be one."

And that's what gets me to smile. "Right. There can only be one."

Aliya walks next to me all the way into the forest. All the way to the tents and tables laid out in straight rows. All the way to the future waiting for me in that clearing.

"Thank you," I say, but she is already conversing with other Mages outside one of their tents. She hasn't heard me.

It has to still mean something, though. Just saying it.

"Thank you," I say again. This time, it's even easier.

Chapter 21

During breaks from their fight sessions, the smaller aki lug gourds and push barrels of water for the drinking pool and the bathing area. The little ones struggle to keep the water from sloshing over the edges. They know how precious that water is, so they take extra care. Their shoulders are stiff, arms straight as iron rods. Some of them look to me for guidance. Sitting on a small boulder that looks out over the grounds, I nod in the general direction of the drinking pool.

It's free time right now. I watch as one young aki with a long braided ponytail throws combinations against the leather padding of an older aki's mittens. Another group of aki comes by, rolling a barrel along, and I silently direct them to the bathing area.

The aki, at one point or another, marked the trees, some with lettering and others with symbols, showing what dahia they come from. Cliques are forming. Already, I've had to break up a few fights between some of the rowdier ones, and the little aki sometimes don't know where to go or who to turn to, so they move with the older aki from their dahia. Mages occasionally wander through here, like where we aki live and train is some sort of shortcut, but they mostly leave the order-keeping to me. A lot of the time, it's boring. Just me telling some of the kids what to do and acting tough when they decide not to do it.

Another young aki pushes a broom around a clearing, sweeping away the discards from a previous meal: chicken bones and uneaten pieces of moi-moi, and the bugs that cling to it all. In a sandpit in the distance, an older aki helps a younger one wrap his hands with cloth to protect his knuckles while he trains.

Some days, I'm the big brother; other days, I'm the joking friend; others still, I'm the strict overseer. On those days, all I need is a whip.

Truth is, there's too many of them for just me. I think about naming some of the older aki as my lieutenants, dispatching them to oversee the smaller groups, but power corrupts. And I like being the guy in charge.

Besides, they all have to be here. They have no choice. And if I don't train them properly, then they'll have to fight a sin that will beat them, a sin they won't be able to Eat. It'll stand there in front of that paralyzed aki, jaws wide open, saliva dripping fat raindrops from its bared fangs, tongue lolling in anticipation. Young aki are pretty easy for an inisisa to digest.

I leap down from my perch.

"All right. Break's over," I shout. Time to work. "Now, who's ready to take me on?"

A dozen training fights later, I let the kids catch their breath, and I take a rest myself beneath a large tree, part of a circle that rings a small clearing. Some of the training happens here, but for now, it's all peace and quiet. I think nobody rests here because the pine needles prick their backsides and the skin behind their knees. Some of those kids really wore me out, so I don't have the energy to move my legs, just adjust them slightly so the needles sting less. It's a battle, really, between me and the pine needles, to see which one of us moves first. But I'm too tired to lose.

The Wall is a circle, with watchtowers connecting the swaths of stone at certain points. The towers are topped with observation booths. Some days, I catch older aki climbing the forest trees while the younger ones trail behind and watch the sentries and sometimes even the Palace guards amble back and forth. Patrolling. Sometimes, when they're all sleeping and I can't, I climb up to where they sat or hunched or hung, and I watch the guards and listen to them talk and argue. Complain about their children, complain about how little they're paid. I watch them get tired. I watch them worry about how their sons are doing in school, which daughter is hoping to train as a scholar with the Ulo Amamihe. Sometimes, I track when they come and when they go. I don't know why, really. It's not like I'm plotting my way back into Kos. If I leave, then someone's dahia gets Baptized, but I don't know. . . . Seems like a small-enough act of rebellion.

Right now, however, I'm just trying to get feeling back in my arms and legs.

Something moves in the tree in front of me—a rustling on the branches right below my line of sight. The breeze whistles through the leaves, and I swear I hear something or someone whisper. I try to sit up and focus. Nothing. Just a breeze.

Then again. A shadow leaps from one branch to another. One branch bows beneath new weight, then the shadow doubles back. Passes over me, then continues off into the distance. It moves way too fast to be an aki, even another human being. But it's bigger than any forest animal I've seen out here so far. My stomach drops with fear. Could be an escaped inisisa. If it is, I need to get after it fast.

The branches have grown still.

It was a blur of brown and black, the thing. Leaves rustle again. Closer. I push myself to my feet, aches and pains and all, and flick my daga from its strap into the palm of my hand. The beast leaps down, then lands in a small copse of brush right at the base of the Wall, beneath a mural of a horned mammoth crashing through a painting of a wall. Movement stops. I step closer. Closer.

I gasp.

Out slinks a small form. Slowly, it uncurls itself, standing up straight. What? It's a person. She wears gray rags, and every inch of her skin is covered in sins. I can't even tell if, beneath her sin-spots, she had been born with the light skin of the wealthy hill people or the dark skin of Forum-dwellers. A tattoo of a spider marks her forehead, a single black dot with long jointed legs that arc around her eyes and down her cheeks all the way to her jaw. Her hair falls down to the small of her back. She stoops to pick up a twig and, in a few deft movements, twists her hair into a loose bun atop her head. More sins wash down her neck, along her collarbone, and deep into her shirt.

She has even more sin-spots than me.

"You're their new Catcher," the other aki says to me. Her gray rags sway in the breeze, and neither of us has moved. I don't know her name or anything about her, but she feels so familiar. She wears a blue stone on a bracelet around her left wrist.

"You're here to help out?" I ask her, because I can't think of anything else to say. I don't realize how stupid the question sounds until it leaves my mouth. Questions trip over one another in my head, and suddenly I want to know how long she's been out here, what dahia she originally comes from, what the Mages have her here for, what else lies beyond the Wall. Like most aki, there's very little of her past written on her other than the sins she's Eaten. She wears no gemstones in her ear. She doesn't have any coal either, to commemorate the dead. She's the only aki I've ever seen who's older than me.

She flexes her fingers into a fist, right hand, then left hand, then right again, twisting her wrists. She looks restless all of a sudden, like even though she's not going anywhere, she needs to be moving. Her arms settle at her sides, but she still looks poised to strike. She reminds me of Arzu. She flexes her right ankle, cracks her knuckles, then starts to limp past me.

"It is sad what they plan to do with you," she tells me as she walks past. She drags one leg in a semicircle with each step, and I wonder if she hurt herself coming down from one of the trees. She looked fine a moment ago.

"Hey!" I start after her, but suddenly she's able to bend her legs, and she sets off at a run, then leaps into the trees, higher than I've ever seen anyone jump.

By the Unnamed, what was that lahala? And why am I so sure I've seen her before?

Chapter 22

"Snap your hips into it," I tell Remi, the aki with the gray streak in his hair. "Snap your hips into that right. Connect the dots." Sometimes, others will trickle in, aki brought in by a Mage, and this guy was one of them. He'd come in a quarter-Moon ago, and I'd taken him into an empty clearing to help refine his one-two. His jab-straight. "Snap your hips!" I shout to him. "Back of the foot leaves the ground." He does it, a left jab followed by a straight right. "Yeah, just like that."

I jump down from the boulder and scoop up the mittens at my feet. Walking toward him, I fit them tight over my hands and wrap the loose straps around my wrist. Then I plant my feet, shoulder-width apart. I try not to think about that aki I saw by the Wall, the one who called me the new Catcher, whatever that means. Training the new aki helps. A little. "Now do it again, and duck like I taught you." He does it again, jab, straight, then I swing for him with my right hand. And the kid ducks! He sees my eyebrows lift and smiles shyly before schooling the expression from his face. Can't let me see that he's begging for my approval. I shoo him out of the clearing. "Now go work on your leaps. Do that for a few rounds; have a partner count your rounds. And keep practicing this." I mimic the one-two-duck. The aki hurries off, and I'm left with a space that smells like animal dung.

Wild animals sometimes roam. The stink probably comes from them. A lot of forest squirrels, but sometimes mangy dogs stalk through and paw at discarded handwraps. All we need is someone cooking goat off in the distance and a few poets and itinerant holy men, and we'd be back in the Forum. Some of the tree trunks wrapped with padding and cloth have stuffing sticking out of their blankets. The thinner trees slouch from the younger, wilder aki hanging and bouncing on their branches. The trees that haven't been transformed for striking drills have messages scrawled into them. Some are tiny love letters. Some are dahia markings that signal territory. Somebody's missing a slipper—I see it all covered in dust by a patch of weeds.

There's space to move here. To run around. It's not like Kos, where the streets and alleys are so narrow you practically have to squeeze through. We don't have to memorize the trails and tracks here, the way we do the side streets of the Forum. We can run around and wave our arms here. Or, at least, they can. I still have to act like the oga around here.

I wander into a small clearing hoping to see that older aki. Maybe if I wait long enough, I'll see that face with the spider tattoo poke out from the bushes.

Early on, I'd set up a horizontal striking post here. It hangs by two chains from a thick tree branch and swings at chest level. I have to hit it differently than I would an upright striking post because it pivots and catches me in the head if I'm not paying attention. I can either block and swing or pivot and riddle it with punches. Some days, when I look at how we're made to live, when I see the near-endless rows of shacks we're crowded into and the line that develops every morning for the bathing patch, the way the little aki shiver when they upend the bucket over their skinny bodies, when I look at how exhausted everyone is at the end of the day and I remember what I'm training them for, I come here to this striking post. And sometimes, I don't even bother to block. In the back of my mind, I count the seconds to a round, and when I finish, I lean on it, heavily. I can be angry here, in this wide expanse, and I don't have to worry about who's watching.

A part of me is happy she's not here to see me like this.

The Aunties used to worry about how I was angry all the time as a little boy. At least, as an aki, I have something to fight. Here, I have something to hit. And I imagine the Mages would prefer I do it to this bag rather than to their noses. I hate having to train children for this work. If I could, I'd rid Kos of every single sin, just so they wouldn't have to Eat. They could remain with their families, grow up to become jewelers or algebraists or miners. Live normal, healthy lives. But I'm training them to Eat. To eventually Eat so much that they Cross over, then die.

They won't be like me, though. Their sin-spots will fade. Maybe, after time, they'll forget what sins they Ate. They won't be marked forever.

By the time I finish, I'm exhausted. It feels good being this tired. I'm too tired even to hate what I have to do.

After another training session, I wander off to be alone again.

On one stretch of Wall, rain has turned a painted portrait of an ancient rebel warrior into a curved, sliding mess of white and gray against the light brown of the stone. Elsewhere, more recently painted, a runner in sleek, patterned pants vaults over what has been stylized as a piece of the Wall, to make it look like that man whose head is uncovered and whose face can be clearly seen is escaping. Kosian script flows along other stretches of the Wall. Beautiful scribbling.

Scribes were here.

Farther down is where the menagerie begins.

Some of the beasts are beautifully rendered. The painted snake, rearing up to face the boar, painted in profile, with multicolored spikes running along its spine. The inisisa here are splashed with color in some places. The monkey's limbs, eight of them stretched out to make a sort of wheel with bent spokes, create a rainbow, and the griffin caught in mid-flight has wings the color of the morning sun. There's more black here too. Sunset doesn't cast it all in shadow like it does on the other side of the Wall.

The girl with the long hair is here. The one who called me the strange name—Catcher. She has her back turned to me, and she sits in a crouch, wiping paint-smeared hands along the Wall in practiced movements. Her whole body sways, like she's dancing. She's fast, and all of a sudden, a large tail curls along the ridges of stone and fluffs at its end. Then another and another, until seven have formed, like the skeleton of a hand-fan, but caught in mid-swirl. It's a painting, but like the best of the work from the Scribes, it shimmers in the light so that it looks like the sin-beast is emerging from the Wall.

A twig snaps under my foot. I half expect her to dart up and away, but she stands slowly and turns to face me. The spider-dot sits right on her forehead, and its legs run down her face. In daylight, the sin-spots that cover her from the crown of her head to the toes of her sandaled feet are even more striking. She's as dark as me beneath her markings. Paint—orange, yellow, red—covers her palms. She doesn't bother wiping her hands clean. Just stares at me. Silent.

"That was you the other day." Suddenly, I'm right in front of her, and I can't tell which one of us moved. But I can see the wrinkles at the edges of her eyes, and the way the handle of her daga dances against the insides of her fingers. She's so fast I never even saw it slip out of her armband.

"You used to be a Scribe?" I gesture to the Wall.

She says nothing, but tenses, then drops into a fighting stance. I step back and throw my hands up instinctively, in defense, and she lunges at me. She hits me hard enough to knock the wind out of me. We crash to the ground. I can't breathe. Suddenly, she's up again, standing over me while a bear made of churning shadows turns around and faces us.

"Stay down," she hisses. Her voice is deeper than I expected, and something sounds strange about it, almost like two people speaking at once.

The bear rears and roars, then comes down on all fours and dashes toward us. I scramble away, but the girl runs straight for the sin-bear. The spikes running along the ridge of its back flex. She flips her daga in her hands, and just as she and the bear are about to crash into each other, she leaps over it, as smooth as anything I've ever seen. She hurls her daga at it, but it misses. I flick my own daga out and prepare to run in and rescue her. But the girl's strap runs against the sin-bear's neck, wraps around, and the girl lands, pulling with all her strength and yanking the bear onto its back. Her muscles flex and ripple where they show, and she pivots on one foot, slips another daga from a small scabbard at her hip, and drives it straight into the sin-bear's throat. Once the knifepoint pierces the nape of the inisisa's neck, it bursts into a cloud of smoke.

The smoke solidifies into a puddle of ink on the forest floor, then morphs into a column and shoots straight into the girl's open mouth. She doesn't move. She doesn't even tremble. She chokes a bit as the sin races down her throat and into her stomach. It ends as quickly as it started. She swallows, wipes her mouth with the back of her hand. Staggers one step, two, then rights herself and is normal again, except for a new distant look in her eyes.

Her body tenses, and that's when I see it. New ink.

Right at the base of her neck, above her collarbone, a bear in profile, rearing on its hind legs. She takes it without noise, not even a grunt against the pain I know is ripping through her skin. I've seen plenty of other aki react to Eating and the burn that comes with their branding. I've seen them doubled over, completely at the mercy of the process. Some of them fall on the ground, writhing, crying out for their mothers, for the Unnamed, for someone, anyone to make it stop. I've even seen them fall unconscious.

Bo admitted to me once that, very early on, he used to weep.

But this is the first time I've seen an aki not cry out in pain after having Eaten. The first time I've seen someone other than me unaffected by what she has just done. By what has just been done to her. She killed that inisisa almost without thinking, and she Ate that sin with that exact same attitude. Complete instinct.

Footsteps behind us announce the Mages. They arrive in a group of three, and the Mage at the forefront, named Ishaq, wears no hood over his bald head. I've seen him around a half dozen times. I recognize the pastiness of the skin on his face. It's strange, and it never gets easier to look at.

Two aki trail behind the Mages, both of them a little younger than me. One of them, Ras, carries someone in his arms. The other, walking next to Ras, has two shovels over his shoulder.

The Mages say nothing as Ras and the other aki walk past me and the girl, and Ras lays the body down on the ground, and the other aki begins digging.

"Zainab," one of the Mages calls out.

So, that's her name.

The girl turns from watching Ras and his companion dig the grave and walks obediently to the Mage who has called her and who now turns and walks away, Zainab skulking behind them. The paint on her palms has dried.

I've seen this before. Where have I seen this before? My mind flashes to a Mage in an alleyway with a flock of aki behind him. I'm watching as Baba speaks with the Mage and hands him more ramzi than I've seen in my life. Almost as soon as the memory comes to me it's gone.

I head over to Ras. The other boy doesn't introduce himself.

"A Mage called forth a sin for him to Eat," Ras tells me, digging. "He couldn't beat it. The inisisa ate him, then went wild and escaped."

No doubt searching for other aki to consume.

Suddenly, the one with no name begins to shake. His shoulders tremble, and he lets out a sob, then he can't stop, and he shuffles to a row of bushes by the Wall where he can cry in peace. I pick up the boy's shovel and see the comatose aki's face. The eyes of the boy we are burying are blank. No irises. No color in them at all. His skin has turned blue. His lips are dried. He's gone. Eaten. He has Crossed.

I don't recognize the boy, and that hurts. I'm responsible for him, for his training. This is the first one I've lost like this.

I catch Ras's eye. He's older. One of the dahia leaders. Others flock to him. Ras takes the stone the boy wears around his neck, that jewel the boy kept near to remember his past before the forest, and adds it to his own necklace. So that the boy may never be forgotten. The stone, a dull blue, flares when it touches Ras's chest. Someone will soon walk through the camp with coal for those who knew the aki to stud into their ears. To remember that he died. To remember how.

Ras hoists the boy up over his shoulder and carries him away. He doesn't want us to have to see him end his suffering.

When he brings him back, the boy's eyes are closed—peaceful. And there's a streak of blood on Ras's pants where he'd cleaned his daga.

Neither of us says a word as we bury the boy.

CHAPTER 23

IT TAKES A while to get to the Mages' quarters. I think they did that on purpose to discourage wandering. Maybe they really see themselves as apart from the rest of us. I've been put in charge of the dirty, lowly aki, and they can wash their hands of us. But we can't keep going like this.

I have to ask them if they can build a better bathing area and increase the water supply so that the morning wash line isn't so long. I'll tell them that if more aki can wash at the same time, it'll pass more quickly and we can spend more time training. I won't tell them that even aki have dignity to maintain, as much as it may surprise a Mage to hear it. I don't think that argument will play very well with that crowd.

When large tents and a few wooden outposts come into view, I know I've arrived. Mages mill about in their cloaks, many of them with their hoods pulled back. They haven't seen me yet, so I imagine this is what they look like when no one is watching. I even see a few Mages smile. Some of them dare to chuckle. I guess Mages were regular people once. Seems impossible to think about someone like Izu, or like Ishaq, as someone's son. Which is why it's strange to watch a Mage tell a joke. It's like watching a yam sprout legs and start dancing.

I wonder if Zainab lives here too. She's obviously special to the Mages; I haven't seen her much recently, so maybe they keep her in hiding. There are too many questions here. For now, all I need, really, is better bathing conditions for my charges.

When I get closer, a few Mages brush past me like they don't even see me. One woman with silver braids nearly knocks me over, and I turn, daga in hand. I'm about to let her know what I think of her and her kind when I spot Aliya, hurrying toward me with her parchment clutched to her chest.

"Hey!" I shout.

Aliya stops and looks around like she can't see me, then when she does, she heads straight for me, grinning. "Isn't it amazing here? I can't take notes fast enough. I've already witnessed three sin-eating rituals. At this rate, my research will be complete in no time, and I—"

"Aliya," I cut her off. "My kids stink. Like no other. Like week-old moi-moi left out in the sun. Like a wild boar ate another wild boar's leavings, then left them for another wild boar to eat." I can't stand her gushing right now, not when we don't even have proper bathing conditions. "The way the bathing area is set up now, there's no privacy for the little ones.

Or the older ones, for that matter. Tell your ogas they need to build us stalls, or I quit training the aki."

She looks like I just hit her in the chest. "Taj . . ."

"I'm serious. It is not you who has to stand next to them all day."

The call to prayer sounds. Even this far out, we can hear it.

The caller's voice is faint, and I hadn't even heard it while I was arguing. But now that I can focus, the voice makes me feel like suddenly I'm back home watching everyone in their dahia gather around their shrines and sit in silent meditation.

Aliya spares me a glance before heading off to where a group of Mages have gathered. They have their prayer rugs laid out beneath them, and already a line of them, facing toward Kos, have begun the ritual. Kneeling, bowing, then back up—moving in that way that reminds me of Mama and how, whenever she prayed, it seemed as though she were having a conversation with a very dear, very quiet, very kind friend.

Suddenly, I don't have the heart to talk to anyone anymore.

The young aki dance by the light of the campfire. The ones that aren't finishing their meal form a loose circle and stomp a rhythm onto the forest floor with their feet, singing a song I remember having heard in the Merchants' Quarter when Baba used to walk me through the market. I recognize only phrases, but the youth who've come from around there or who'd been rounded up from that area sing loudly, bouncing on their feet, clapping in unison. A song about a trader and a noblewoman and a lost pearl making its way through the Forum.

The dance is contagious, and I find myself tapping along. During the chorus of the song, one sin-eater, sometimes two, breaks away from the periphery of the circle and leaps into the middle, stepping along to the beat faster and faster, arms and legs swinging joyfully through the air. Then they jump out again, rejoin the fringe, and someone else takes a turn to shine.

A couple of the younger aki play-fight by a set of trees, rolling and leaping in and out of the shadows, practicing the moves I've been teaching them.

I bring my soup bowl to my lips, drain it dry, then wipe my mouth with my sleeve.

Ras breaks away from the group of aki who've been sitting by the dancers. He has a soup bowl in one hand and tips it back, slurping it up as he walks. It's empty by the time he reaches me. He slides down the side of the tree with a thump and rests at its base next to me.

He reminds me of Bo, the way others are drawn to him. Automatically, they look to him as a kind of big brother. He's kind that way. Kinder than me. Even if he were the only child in his family, he looks like someone's older brother. He's certainly skinnier than Bo, but they both have the same look of silent strength on them.

"You don't dance?" he asks.

I shake my head. When Ras doesn't look away, I meet his gaze. "You?"

Ras snorts. "They're not ready-oh. If they let me in the center of that circle, forget it. It would be the end of everything, and they would have to go to sleep." He shakes his head. "No, I'll let them have their fun, because I'm a generous man." He looks inside of his bowl, turns the thing over so that different angles catch the firelight.

"Ugh," Ras says. "Not like the pepper soup my mother makes. Ewoooo. Don't let anyone ever tell you that Arbaa pepper soup isn't the best pepper soup the Unnamed ever made us capable of putting together." He shakes his head. "This one aki, you see him over there? He's trying to keep the rhythm, but he's always off. He tried to tell me that the best pepper soup comes from Ithnaan, and praise be to the Unnamed who stopped my hand from just slapping this boy."

He turns to me. "Which do you think is better? And if you say Ithnaan pepper soup . . ."

A smile breaks across my face. It's not that I can't tell the difference. It's that I want to play with him for a little bit. Get him riled up. Mama never really cooked her soup with peppers. Instead, her special dish included spreading sweetened herbs over yogurt and stirring that together with a special tomato sauce. Ithnaan pepper soup has its own merits, that's what I want to tell him, but I just shrug. "My family comes from Khamsa, so I'm agnostic."

Ras raises an eyebrow. A challenge.

"We choose no sides."

Ras nods to himself. "Eh-heh. This is smart. You are smart. Stay above the fray."

I look off into the dark forest and see Zainab standing alone, her arms folded across her chest. She looks on at the dancing by the fire. Without a word, I push myself up and walk to her. When

I get close enough, I can smell something strong and pungent. She doesn't notice me. Or she pretends not to notice me, as she slips a small flagon from its hook by her thigh and tips it onto the back of her free hand. A small line of black and gray dust falls out. She sways back and forth when she puts the flagon back, but not to the rhythm of the music. It's like she's dancing to a song only she can hear. Her free hand remains absolutely still until she puts it to her nose and inhales sharply.

"Zainab," I call out.

She looks up and smiles, but her eyes are sad.

The smell thickens, and I flinch. "What is that?" I ask her. My hand comes up to cover my nose.

"Do you want some?" she slurs. She holds the thing out to me. A stone sways on the bracelet around her outstretched wrist. It glows softly in the night.

I look at it for a moment, then take it and look it over again. Slowly, I unscrew the cap and sniff lightly. It burns my entire face. I hold the flagon out to her, begging her to take it. Meanwhile, I'm trying to spit out the mucus in my throat from inhaling the fumes. Laughter explodes from Zainab. She clutches her stomach, bends over, slaps her thighs. She can't stop laughing. I'm still trying to figure out how to breathe again. It's poison. It has to be.

She takes it, ready to pour again.

"Why do you do that?" I cough before every word. I try to wipe the rest of the burn from under my nose, but the heat lingers. I wince. This must be how Arzu felt with the pepper sauce.

"It helps," Zainab tells me, still smiling.

"But it hurts." I cough again. "It's like sniffing fire."

She examines the flagon in her hand. "It is bad to do. But I do it."

"Why?"

With her free hand, she taps her temple. "It quiets me here." She points to her chest. "And here." And that's when I see it. Tears. Leaking down her face, running along the spider legs that trace her cheeks. "Too many sins." She turns the flagon over in her hands and turns the other way.

Stone-sniffers aren't supposed to look like her. They're supposed to be emaciated, worn-down old men or women unable to find work and make families of their own. Stone-sniffers in Kos, they're supposed to be the ones the city gave up on. They're not supposed to look like Zainab. My first instinct is to feel disdain and disgust for her. How can she do this to herself? But I look at how covered she is, and I understand.

Zainab starts to limp away.

"Wait!" I shout and chase after her. We stand at the very edge of the forest. In front of us is pure darkness. "You don't have to do that." I want to tell her what I learned about keeping the sins out of my head. I want to tell her that all she needs to do is not think about people, not care for them. To just focus on herself and staying alive. She doesn't have to sniff that coal. "What are they making you do?"

"I'm their Catcher."

That word again. "Catcher?"

"When Mages call forth sins for the aki to face and the young ones cannot defeat them, I am sent to catch them."

"You Eat escaped sins?"

"That is what they have me here for."

So, this is how they're using her and how she believes they will use me. As just a bucket for sins. How long has she been here? How many training seasons has she been doing this for?

The sins drawn on this side of the Wall . . . the Scribes didn't paint those. She did. They're her sins.

How much longer does she have? There's almost no bare skin on her left. She shifts from foot to foot, as though trying to get feeling back in one leg. I've seen her do that before. When we first met in the forest and she called me the Catcher.

She puts both hands to her chest. "You are like me. Your sin-spots do not fade. That is why they chose you: This is your future. This . . ." She gestures all around her. "It's not what you think. They'll never want to celebrate us. They will use us to destroy Kos." Then she steps back, and the forest swallows her. I take a step after her, but a hand grips my shoulder. I turn, and it's Ras. He merely shakes his head. Destroy Kos? How?

We head back to the fire. I watch the others dance. I can see their skin. When I finish teaching them to fight, they will go with Mages who will call forth sins for them to fight. If they win, they come back with new tattoos. If they don't, they don't come back at all. Some of them have only begun to gain their sin-spots. For most of them, so much of their flesh remains untouched, unblemished.

And they are still so happy.

This is your future, Zainab told me. I think about the young aki I've been training. I think about the festival, and that conversation I overheard between Aliya and Izu makes less sense than it did before. He wants to bring the aki out of hiding, but I can't for the life of me figure out why.

CHAPTER 24

IN THE SHADOWED enclosure where the stone has been moved from the mouth of the cave and where moisture drips somewhere in the black depths farther on, I sit with a sharp stone in my hands. Like the clearing with the bag I spend hours hitting, this is a place where I know the others can't find me. Where I can let go.

It's been getting worse. My fingers lose their feeling for a few seconds, then it all comes back. And every time I go to sleep now, I get night terrors.

I know the guilt isn't my guilt. I know it's the guilt of other sinners. I know that there's no reason for me to feel this way about myself, that I haven't told that lie or committed that act of adultery or broken that person's arm. But at the bottom of my stomach and in the space that fills my lungs, I feel like I've done those things, that I deserve the pain and torment, that I'm guilty. I know this is merely the sins breaking through the walls I've spent

Patron number: 1110390
Item barcode: 39078083080607

Have a nice day.

04/26/2018
WOOL
SAR
L

my life building. I can't pretend I don't care anymore, and that's how it happens. I think of others—the aki, Bo, Karima—then suddenly the others become the people whose sins you've Eaten.

Whenever I get tired, whenever I'm about to fall asleep, the visions attack. All the sins I've ever Eaten, so many of them, it feels like I'm the one committing them, like my lips are telling every single lie, like my hands are causing the violence. And always, at the end, that vision of Princess Karima, the sin-lion, and the sin-snake.

It has gotten to the point where I just wind up sleeping alone in the forest, away from the tents. Sometimes, I wake up with bruised knuckles from the stone and trees I thrash against in my sleep.

This is probably what Zainab's going through. Maybe, while she sleeps alone on the forest floor, she thrashes in her sleep. Maybe she scatters leaves all around her. Maybe, while walking, she collapses as a foot or a whole leg falls asleep. Maybe her hands tremble when she brings a bowl of stew to her lips. Maybe some of the stew drips onto her rags. Maybe she has to close her eyes against the shaking, trying to will it away. Maybe when she Crosses, every movement is a struggle, and every morning waking up from the night terrors sees her riddled with fear. It's starting to happen to me.

She's going crazy. Paranoid. The festival is just that—a festival. What else could it be? My heart sinks. Maybe that's why she said what she said about using the aki to destroy Kos. She is losing her mind.

This is why Zainab sniffs coal. This is why other aki give up in the middle of a fight with an inisisa.

I squeeze my eyes tight and let out a sigh.

By the time I get enough energy to push myself to my feet, the sun has begun to show over this empty patch of forest, and I can start walking back to the campsite.

Somebody runs past the entrance to the cave, then doubles back.

Aliya.

"Hey, I was looking for you."

"You found me. What do you need?"

Her face softens. "I just wanted to see how you're doing."

"Why?"

She comes into the cave and sits too close to me. "I'm starting to see. The Eating ritual. What it does to the body. It is all so different from what is written in the notes. It is mentioned only in passing in the Paroles, and even when the Seventh Prophet speaks of Balance and the prophecy, there is no mention of what happens to you." She looks up from her hands folded in her lap. "Taj, what happens to you?"

I meet her eyes and straighten my spine. "Whenever you Eat, whenever you consume a sin, you take the sinner's guilt. And it becomes a mark on you." I pull my sleeves up to reveal the sin-spots that wind trails up and down my forearms. Some of them have been burned into the back of one hand and the fingers of the other. "Eventually, it becomes too much. The guilt consumes you, drives you mad." The glass-eyed beggars on the side of the road in the Forum who can't even move to collect the ramzi in their bowls. They're Crossed, cowering in alleyways. The ones who can still move, roaming the streets like ghosts. "It's kind of your destiny. There are no adult aki. By the end, you can't stand.

Can't speak. Can't even see. You just stop moving, and that's when you know it's the end." I shrug. "You can't Eat any more sins." I remember the first time I saw Zainab, when she limped away from me into the forest. Even then, it was happening.

Aliya looks out the entrance to the cave. She's probably thinking of all the aki out there and the fates awaiting them. "How do you know?"

I look at my hands. "You run out of skin." That's when you know.

We're sitting there for a little bit when she says, "I want to spend more time with you." I look up, startled. "In the camps, I mean. With the aki you are training. In my own tent, of course. And apart from the aki quarters, but . . ."

I smile. "I know what you mean, Aliya."

I move a little closer to her, so that we're looking out the cave's entrance together. The leaves shiver, and drops of rain plop their music into puddles that are already forming at the mouth of the cave. I come here to be alone, but it feels good to be with Aliya. Like a different way of being.

I lean back against the cave wall. "I remember the first Eating I saw. I was a child. Maybe up to Baba's hip. Mama was sick. Very sick. Coughing and wheezing. She could barely breathe. She couldn't even get up out of bed. Baba took me with him into the Forum to see a Mage, and the Mage had a whole group of aki with him in the alley. They didn't have many sin-spots on them yet. Some of them were my age. And the Mage had one aki, a girl, on a chain. She had this collar around her neck like an animal. She was the one the Mage brought to our home to Eat Mama's sin."

Aliya is still and silent.

I feel myself drifting into the memory as I tell it. "I wasn't supposed to see it, but I could peek through the beaded curtains. I watched the Mage speak over Mama, and I saw the inisisa escape her. I'd rushed in because it sounded like Mama was in so much pain, and the inisisa chased after me. It cornered me against a wall, but the little aki was able to sneak up behind it and kill it with her daga. Then she Ate it."

Aliya looks into her lap.

"What was it?" she asks, her voice small.

Suddenly, my heart jumps into my throat, and I can't breathe. A spider. "The inisisa was a spider," I murmur. "The sin-spot appeared on her forehead—"

I leap up from where I was sitting, my mind racing. "It was Zainab," I say, stunned. "By the Unnamed, it was her. She was the one who cured my mother."

A couple aki walk by in the rain, then more, and I see a bunch of them holding a blanket heavy with a body. Ras carries one end. I don't even have to see the sin-spots covering the leg that dangles over to know what has happened.

"Zainab." My limbs go numb. I fall to the ground. I feel Aliya's hand on my shoulder, but I shrug her away.

"Taj, I'm so sorry. I—"

I don't hear the rest. I'm already walking away.

The patch of forest they eventually bring her to is otherwise unremarkable. Looks like any other patch of forest. We shiver in the rain that has made the soil moist enough for easy digging. My body trembles, but I barely feel the rain. I barely feel anything. There aren't enough shovels for everyone, so most of the aki stand to the side while Ras and I and two others dig. I don't think anyone else knew who Zainab was or what she did. Some of the girls look at her body and cry, not because this is the first burial they've seen, but because Zainab was something special to them. She would occasionally cross their path, and all they needed to do was glance in her direction and know that they could survive. They could wear all the sins in Kos and survive. Tears burn my eyes, but I keep digging anyway. Digging like it's the only thing I'm meant to do right now, like I wasn't built for anything else but this moment.

The world fades away, and the only sound I can hear is my shovel scraping into the ground and scooping up dirt. I can't even hear the rain pattering on the leaves overhead. I can no longer feel my clothes growing heavy on me.

My arms are on fire, and I stop just long enough to wipe the rainwater from my eyes. When I look up, I see a blur of black. I blink, then that blur turns into robes, and I realize there's a Mage in front of me, back bowed as they dig. Aliya looks up, returns my gaze, then goes back to digging.

The others begin to peel away to escape the rain. It's clear training has been called off for the rest of the day.

The cut on my forearm stings.

By the end, the only ones left are me and Aliya.

When I walk back to camp, my daga is wet with blood from the throat I had to cut, and I have Zainab's stone in a bracelet around my wrist.

CHAPTER 25

I'VE FOUND A fallen tree trunk to crouch on, and I'm squinting as hard as I can at the writing on the Wall.

All that time I spent around Mama and Baba and the books they would bring, and I only ever scrolled through them for fun. They were all pretty to look at—my eye pressed to the cylinder as the words and pictures danced before me.

Beneath the inisisa painted here are words splashed out in the paint Zainab used. She's buried far from her work, her art, but the stone I now wear on my wrist glows from being so close to where she scribbled. Auntie Sania tried to teach me how to read, but I didn't need it. When you're trying to scavenge for your one meal of the day, you can tell how valuable something is by how people treat it, not by what's written down as its price.

I wish I'd been able to tell Zainab thank you. She probably

never recognized me. By the time she'd helped Mama, she'd probably Eaten so many sins and killed so many inisisa that the families all blended together. But if her sin-spots never faded, then she never forgot. As much as I try, I can't ever truly forget the ones I've Eaten either.

The right side of my face goes numb. I shut my eyes tight and try to let it pass, all the while working my jaw. Eventually, feeling returns. It's getting worse.

This is my destiny, Zainab told me.

I wish I'd been able to tell her that it didn't have to be. It didn't have to be hers either.

"They're beautifully done."

I jump and nearly fall off the branch. Scrambling, I get back on and see that Aliya's standing there next to me. She pulls down her glasses and connects the bridge, then she squints like I was doing. "Some of the spelling is a bit off." She glances at me. "I don't mean misquoted verses. But you can see, right?" She points at a bit of script beneath a red falcon's talons.

"Yeah, I see it. The . . . yeah."

She takes a few steps forward, still squinting, then comes back next to me. She sits heavily on the tree trunk. "Do you come here often?"

I shrug. In my head, I'm stumbling over half-formed excuses, things to tell her that probably won't make sense once the words come out of my mouth anyway, but then, all of a sudden, I say, "Zainab was here a lot."

"Oh."

"Yeah, she . . . she did a bunch of these." I point to a couple of the inisisa. "I think she was a Scribe before . . . well, before she got brought here."

"In the Paroles of the Seventh Prophet, we're told that it was like this in the Before."

"What do you mean? Like what?"

She's looking at the inisisa. It feels like she sees something different from what I see. "Inisisa weren't made of sin, because during the Before, there was no sin. They were these magnificent creatures made of light. They were like glass, so that all colors passed through them whenever they walked. Beasts composed of perfectly angled geometric patterns. They were walking equations, explaining the wonders of the Unnamed."

"Not this lahala again. Tell me why this is supposed to matter to me." I know I'm not angry at her. Not really. I'm angry because Zainab's dead, and Izu forced her into this work.

She frowns. "I'm serious. Nobody takes the Paroles of the Seventh Prophet seriously! It's so frustrating." She leaps off the trunk and gestures at the script under the falcon's talons. "All of it is important. And that's why people should get the spelling right! This message doesn't even make sense!" She throws the papers she'd been carrying up into the air, and the parchment flutters to the ground all around her while she huffs.

After a moment watching her tantrum, I hop off the tree branch and start collecting her sheaves.

"I'm sorry," she mutters, stooping to help. "Thanks, Taj, and could you also place them in order? I've numbered each page. But there are also chapter headings in the upper right corner."

She assembles her collected sheets in a stack. "Thanks." Then she comes and collects mine. She gives them a look. "Uhlah, you could've at least pretended to arrange them like I asked."

She's halfway to the forest barrier separating this space by the Wall from the camps when she stops. She hands me a bundle of parchment from the bottom of her stack. "Arrange these for me, please."

"Why? Do it yourself."

She thrusts the papers out at me. "Arrange them." Her voice is no different from before, no louder, no softer, but I take the parchment.

I throw occasional glances her way as I shuffle them, trying to follow the numbers at the bottom of the page and looking for similarities in the script in the upper right corner. She sees me getting rougher with the parchment until I'm ready to tear it up. That's when she puts her hand on mine.

"You can't read."

For a moment, I'm so angry I want to throw all the papers on the ground again and have her stoop to pick them up. It never bothered me before, maybe because most aki don't know how to read anyway. But for some reason, when she says it, it makes me feel like less than nothing.

She sits down next to me, and, by the Unnamed, if I had two million ramzi, I would pay her all of it to leave me alone.

"Taj, I'm sorry." She looks at the papers in her lap. "I forget sometimes. You know me. I understand most books better than people. But I'm learning." She pauses. "I'm sorry about Zainab."

"Is it true that we poison the ground we're buried in?"

"What?" She looks like I've just stabbed her in the chest with my daga.

"You're practically a kanselo. You know things. You're a scholar. Is it true?"

For a long time, she says nothing. Then she cranes her neck and looks at the morning sky.

"Centuries ago, the algebraist Ka Chike would spend entire days at the temple in his village in the south, writing down mathematical equations and rolling them into books he would put to his eyes and manually twist and untwist. He recited the Word, he interpreted dreams of those in the village. Even as a child, he was gifted. But when he began to speak of the Unnamed, he frightened people away. He spoke of the Unnamed not as a single deity overseeing Infinity but as Infinity itself, embodying everything and its opposite. Every atom in all the world. And the spaces in between as well."

I'm watching her eyes glass over, and suddenly, my anger's gone. I feel at peace watching her like this, talking about a thing she so clearly loves.

"An immaterial being who resided in the boar and the bear and the griffin and the cantaloupe and the living grass beneath us and the air we breathe." Her gaze returns to her parchment. It's a jumble of numbers and letters. "Ka Chike wrote that if you divided by zero, you yielded a number as infinite as the Unnamed. And here's what I think." She turns to me, and her eyes are all lit up like stars. "I think that when you multiply by zero, you yield all numbers simultaneously." Her eyes widen.

"You reach Infinity, the Unnamed in its totality. The Unnamed takes infinite forms. The Unnamed fills our lungs with air when we are born. And it pushes that final breath from our lungs when we die. The Unnamed is written in the world all around us." She smiles, and the warmth in my chest grows. "It's written on you, Taj. All of you. Wherever aki are buried, there the Unnamed is also."

I let out a soft snort, but I'm only pretending to brush this off. "Whatever happened to Ka Chike?"

"He became the Seventh Prophet."

"Oh?"

"Then he became mad and died alone and was branded a heretic for the next five hundred years."

"Oh."

The more time I spend in the camps, the more time I need by myself. I'm constantly wandering away after training sessions, skipping meals with the younger aki. Half the time I can't stand being around them, because all I can think about is the future that awaits them as aki. But I've found a familiar spot by some fallen trees. No one will disturb me here.

Sparks pop up from the stone I have in my hands every time I flick my daga blade against a shelf of smooth surface. Late-season leaves crunch under someone's feet. I don't bother looking up. I'm too comfortable at the base of this tree, its near-naked branches hovering overhead. It's late enough in the day that the sun's heat no longer feels like punishment. A small breeze has come to the rescue. And I don't feel guilty about Aliya coming here and finding me like this, because I have wooden blocks on the ground in front of me with letters she made me carve into them earlier. She can tell that even though I'm sharpening my daga, I'm studying my alphabet.

She lands hard next to me, leans against the tree trunk, puts her hand to her belly. A look of actual distress washes over her face. Sweat on her forehead, strands of hair clinging to her cheeks. Her mouth is a single straight line. Lips all pursed.

"You OK?"

She waves me away. "I'm fine, I'm fine." With a sigh, she rests her head against the tree trunk. "Just fasting." Her chest heaves with another breath, then she lets it out, like someone has squeezed all the air out of her. "For the first few days, it's nothing. But by the end?" She shakes her head. "You're not fasting, are you? It must be very difficult for you aki who are training all the time."

"No." I pause in my daga-sharpening, then get back to it. "Mama and Baba did. But I was too young to fast." Suddenly, I'm back home. In this memory, there are tables with bowls full of dates. From the kitchen, the smell of beautiful, juicy meat. Saliva's practically dripping down my chin, I'm so hungry. Smoke hisses from the stove outside, where so much of the cooking happens. Over a fire pit, a roasting goat, its skin nearly black by the time night falls. Bread is baking somewhere close—by the smell of it, almost done. Someone has cleared away the flowers; I can't smell them anymore. My nose only has enough room for the food. Everyone is moving, busy, caught in a secret rhythm, bringing dishes out of the kitchen, bringing bowls into the kitchen, sweeping the stairs, calling out orders to the people in the yard cooking the goat. So much activity, and my stomach grumbles in anticipation.

"You're thinking of food, aren't you?"

Aliya's voice snaps me out of it. I realize I'm still holding my daga and the stone. "No. Just family."

"All the time, whenever the Festival of Reunification approaches and the period of fasting begins, everybody has the exact same questions. Every time!" She turns to face me fully. "And especially as a woman! 'Oh, so you don't eat the whole time? Oh, wow, you must lose a lot of weight!' Every time I tell someone how long I have to go on with fasting, they look at me with their mouth wide open like they're trying to catch flies and they just stare! And then the very next question, 'Oh, but what about water?' 'No,' I tell them. Every. Time. 'Not even water.' Can't chew gum, have to be careful of what music I listen to. Then those last few minutes before evening breakfast . . ." She moans, hand to stomach, and looks to the sky like it has the answer to a question she's too hungry to ask.

"And then you eat so much during breakfast that you can't anymore, but you're looking at that one last piece of puff puff and you know if you don't eat it, you'll regret it."

"Exactly!" She grabs my sleeve. "And it's always the best food. Jollof, and cassava, fufu, chin-chin, egusi soup, moi-moi!" She writhes in pain.

I chuckle, then return to my blocks. "You're making it worse for yourself. I hope you understand that."

She slumps. "I know," she says, pouting.

"Baba always used to lose his sandals in the pile outside the prayer room at the masjid when he and the other men would do their extra prayers."

When we laugh like this, it feels natural. It's easy for me to forget she's a Mage. Especially because of the way she's sitting, I can't see the Fist of Malek embroidered on her robe. Instead, she's a girl who likes to study the Word, who wants to be a scholar, who teaches children the verses when they're not learning how to Eat, who complains about being asked the same questions over and over and over again during the fasting season.

She looks over at the blocks by my feet, squints. "I see what letters you have. Let's see how far along you've gotten."

"It hasn't even been a quarter-Moon yet!"

Out of the seven blocks, she takes two and places them next to each other. "Well?"

I feel embarrassed about how long it takes me to see it, but when I do, it's like light flashing behind my eyes. "Apple!"

She grins, then adds a third to the row, right on the very end.

"Ap . . . ricot. Apricot!"

She switches the first two around, takes one of them out, and switches it for two more from the original pile. It's a mess in front of me now. She sees my confusion and says, "Sound it out. Take each one at a time."

"U . . . u . . . uni . . . university." I'm practically out of breath with the effort that took. I can't imagine all the little aki doing this for however long in the morning, then coming to me to learn how to Eat sins.

But she's at it again, exchanging some blocks for others and rearranging them in patterns I can barely follow.

But I know this one. "Sparrow!"

Another rearrangement.

"Butterfly."

Another.

"S . . . save!"

More switching.

"The?"

Again.

"Princess."

Her expression has changed. There's none of the mirth in it that was there just a few minutes ago. She's frowning at me. Staring in silence. She arranges another message:

You.

Are.

Not.

Safe.

"Aliya, what are you—"

She puts a finger to her lips, staring down at the blocks. When she looks back up her eyes are bright again.

"Better go, Taj. Imagine if the children were all gathered for their lessons," she says breathlessly, "and their teacher was late!"

CHAPTER 26

THE LITTLE AKI and the older aki are starting to see less and less of me. I trust Ras enough to leave him in charge of training, but I wonder what they're starting to think of me. Maybe they just think I'm getting bored and I'm wandering the forests looking for adventure, or whatever it is the Sky-Fist is supposed to be doing. Maybe they think I'm being responsible and discussing changes to their schedule with the Mages. Of course, by now, they've seen the new bathing quarters that I had set up, so maybe they think I'm out there fighting on their behalf. Maybe they've seen me with Aliya. Maybe they think I've made her my heart-mate. I bet they look to see if we've swapped heart-stones. I smile at the thought until I can't feel my left hand anymore. Zainab's stone slips down my wrist as my whole arm falls to my side, dead, and I leap off the fallen tree branch trying to shake it alive again. I squeeze my eyes shut. Panic shudders through me. Please don't let this spread. Not this time.

By the time Aliya shows up at our spot by the Wall, I can flex my fingers into a fist again. And that's how she finds me: staring at my hand like a madman and curling my wrist over and over. I can tell feeling has returned because Zainab's stone chills the dimple in my wrist.

"Are you OK?" she asks me.

I flex a few more times, just to be sure. The growing darkness outside takes my sin-spots and makes it look like my arm is invisible. "Yes. Oya, I'm fine."

I was worried I'd shown up at the wrong time. She'd written the numbers in the dirt with a twig, and I'm nowhere near as good with numbers as I've gotten with letters. But she's here, so I must have been at least close to right.

She sidles up next to me, and we both stand there, facing the sins written on the Wall. "Mages once lived in the Forum," she says at last. There's an edge in her voice I've never heard before. It's almost as though she's a different person. "They used to shop in the marketplace. They used to go from stall to stall in the souk and buy jewelry—"

"What's going on?" The attack of numbness in my arm has made me edgy.

She's quiet for a long time. I have no idea what she's thinking, but then she looks up and I know she's looking past the Wall. "What I'm trying to say is that the Mages weren't always this powerful." She lets out a sigh. "We used to read poetry. And preach, if we attained the necessary training. Whenever a Baptism is announced, it's not King Kolade who makes that decision. Not Princess Karima. Not Prince Haris. No one in the royal family decides what dahia will be Baptized and when. Izu makes that decision. Izu chooses who will lead the call to prayer. Izu himself decides if and where new temples will be built." She turns, first to me, then facing the direction of the camps. "Izu is behind all of this."

"I know this already. I'm here so he doesn't Baptize another dahia." I absently flex my left hand. "This isn't news."

"But you don't know, Taj."

Which, for some reason, stops me.

"For some time, there has been talk of liberalization, of changing the way things are done. Making things different. But Izu stands in the way."

I remember Princess Karima's words. The way she looked at me and held my arm and wished things were different. The way she spoke about me. Is Princess Karima serious about changing things? Is this what Aliya is talking about? Then the night terror. The snake and the lion. It all means something. At the center of it is Princess Karima.

"Taj? Taj."

I realize where I am. "Why did Izu all of a sudden decide to send me out here? What is he trying to do?" Thinking about Karima again has me all worked up. For so long, I'd been able to forget about her and about the way her fingers would glide along the ridges of my sin-spots and the way she would breathe kindness into my ear. The time she held my arm as we walked down the corridors in front of kanselo and other royals like I was one of them.

"Taj, calm down." She waits for me to catch my breath. "What I'm going to tell you is very important. If it is repeated anywhere, here or in Kos, we will both be hanged." She takes a breath. "The kanselo must be destroyed."

My head is on fire with questions. I can't get any of them to sit still. "I don't understand." I put my hands to my head, hoping I can squeeze some sense into it. "Why am I here?"

"Izu knows what you can do." She takes a step closer to me. "He knows what you did to that sin-dragon. He sent you out here to Eat sins. To Eat—"

"Until I couldn't anymore." This doesn't make things any clearer. "But why me? Why not just throw me in jail or make something up to have me hanged?"

"Because you are training his army."

"The aki." It's coming together. Whatever Izu has planned, it involves all of the aki I've been training. Is he trying to take over Kos? What have I done? I remember what Zainab said to me about using the aki to destroy Kos. "How do we stop this?"

"Don't worry." She's smiling now. The call to prayer sounds, faint in the distance on the other side of the Wall that separates us from the city where I was born and raised—the city that will soon be overrun by an army of aki I've been training. And here she is telling me not to worry.

"I need to leave. The Mages are expecting me for evening breakfast." She darts off toward the forest.

"Aliya, you have to tell me."

She turns, and even though she doesn't raise her voice, I can hear her. "You're not training his army. You're training ours.

"The Wall," she goes on. "Tomorrow night. Watch the Wall." Then she's gone.

What is she talking about?

By now, it's getting so dark I can barely see the colors of the inisisa painted on the Wall. Falcons, sparrows, griffins, bears, dragons, snakes. I look a little closer and see the writing underneath each animal, the Kosian script that I now know how to read. Zainab. I scramble closer and smush my face up to the Wall, and that's when I see it. The names of the sins . . . someone changed their lettering. They're different words now.

My eyes widen in shock. This is it. This is why she's been teaching the aki to read. This is why she was teaching me how to read. By the Unnamed . . .

These are directions.

Chapter 27

Since Zainab's gone, there's no more Catcher.

None of the Mages have given any official word on who the next Catcher is supposed to be, but I figure it's what I'm here for if Aliya is right about Izu. This was what Zainab tried to warn me about. I wonder if there were others before Zainab, and how many. These camps must have been here for some time, but most of the aki I know learned how to do it on their own, or they got sent to me and Bo and some of the others by Auntie Nawal and Auntie Sania. We were supposed to be their older brothers. But to think that there has been this whole arrangement this entire time, my fists tremble at my sides. How many aki are buried underneath our feet right now? The more I think about it, the stronger my resolve to stop Izu. I look out onto this circle of aki now, and I see kids who will hopefully end up saving Kos. From what, I don't even know. When Aliya first cornered me and Bo at Zoe's, she spoke of Balance, of how necessary aki were. And so did Princess Karima. They knew something. And it's something Mages like Izu don't want us to hear. They want us to keep thinking we're disposable, like when there's no more room to write on a piece of parchment so you set it aside and grab another sheet. Or you throw that old one in the rubbish bin. But no. We matter.

It's morning now, and I think everybody can tell that training is almost over. There's more and more chatter about the Festival of Reunification, and some of the more observant aki have begun preparing for it the way they remember their parents doing. Some of them have begun fasting but don't complain when I run them down with drills. Whenever the call to prayer sounds, so faint you can barely hear it from this part of the forest, a bunch of them gather, and even though they don't have prayer rugs, they line up facing the city and they pray.

Most of the other aki don't really say anything to them about it. They just sort of let them do their thing in peace, even though I know some of them think it's stupid or a waste of time. But if they're cynical about it, they don't show those other little aki who are always brushing dirt off their knees and foreheads when they come back from prayer in the mornings and afternoons and evenings.

I don't know what to tell the aki who still expect to be reunited with their families when they go back into Kos and begin their new lives as tools for the Mages. Am I supposed to tell them about how cramped their rooms are going to be? How they're gonna have to practically sleep on top of one another? Am I supposed to tell them about how Costa's always messing with the rates so you can never get paid decent money for what you Eat? Do I warn them about the Palace guards and how they'll bust your head first and figure out a reason later? I don't know.

Maybe I'll tell them about the view from the shanties and how much of Kos you can see from up that hill. Maybe I'll tell them about how there are so few lights at night that you can actually see the stars. You can see how very many of them there are and how impossible it is to count them all. Maybe I'll tell them about what it's like to learn Kos, to really, really learn it. Its streets, its alleyways. To learn it like the newsboys. To see Scribes paint the Wall. Yeah, I think I'll tell them that.

The one at the center of the circle, her name is Noor.

She has a number of small sins running up and down her bare arms. Snakes coiled around each other. Mages stand behind the other aki gathered, an outer circle. Me, I'm perched on a rock, watching the whole thing from a grassy ledge. I need this view. And I'm close enough to Catch the sin if Noor isn't able to beat it.

I don't want to bury another aki.

A rustle of clothes behind me, and I can tell it's a Mage. I squint. Aliya's already down there.

"If the sin-beast escapes, try not to rush in too swiftly. Exercise caution." It's Ishaq. And he's really telling me to let the inisisa consume Noor before I go in to Catch it.

"I'll go in when I feel it's necessary to go in, Mage."

He bristles at my tone; I can feel it behind me. He wants to say something or do something, anything to assert his power over me, but he can't. This one is probably with Izu. They're all of the same breed. But things will change. Soon. We aki are necessary, I want to tell him. And I want to watch his brown irises flicker, knowing that any secrets he thinks he has aren't secrets anymore. But for now, I say nothing else. I just watch.

A Mage with silver braids running down her neck stands before Ras, chooses him, then brings him to the center of the circle. A pattern has been crudely etched into the dirt, like what was painted on King Kolade's floor when his sin was called forth. By now, tattoos circle Ras's wrists, ankles, and forearms. It's too far away for me to see clearly, but I know something large has been branded into his back. That's what the Mage is going to call.

When they get to the center of the pattern, the Mage has Ras come to his knees. Ras undoes his shirt and lets it fall past his shoulders, revealing what I can now see is a griffin.

The incantations from the Mage's mouth are whispers on the wind from where I'm sitting, but now I can sound out the words. It's not just noise anymore. It's a prayer.

Then there's no sound. Not even wind. I can't hear the incantation anymore. Ras bends over on all fours and vomits onto the ground. Black bile, thick, solid. His back spasms with each convulsion, and several seconds in, he can barely hold himself up. No one here is seeing this for the first time. The younger aki used to cry or shake with fear. Some would stare in sheer terror. Now they watch the same way they'd scan the sky for a monsoon.

Finally, Ras spits out the last of the sin. Aki dart into the circle and help him to his feet, then bring him back to the others.

Noor hasn't moved. She has her daga in her hands and her legs shoulder-width apart in her fighting stance. In a moment, it's just her in the circle with the boiling pool of sin.

The wings sprout first, instantly at full spread, then the rest of its back. It raises its neck out of the pool, and shadows drip from its beak. It crows soundlessly, then leaps into the air, leaving a thin trail of dark that evaporates once the griffin gets high enough in the sky.

Each flap of its wings raises dust and twigs. The circle spreads.

I scan the tree line and note which branches are where and how easily one can get to the tops of those trees. Which branches are thin, which would support my weight. What the inisisa wants is below, but if it ends up trying to fly away, I have to figure out how best to Catch it. We're far enough away from the Wall that it shouldn't be able to scent anyone in Kos, no matter how hard the wind blows from there.

The griffin circles.

Everyone, aki and Mages, has their breath held tight in their chests. Aliya, who had been taking notes this entire time on her parchment, now just stares, unmoving. Some follow the griffin's flight. Others keep their eyes trained on Noor. She is the only one moving. And just barely. Slow, easy breaths.

Just like I taught her.

One flap of the griffin's massive wings and everyone's arms go up to shield their eyes from the twigs and dust and leaves blown our way.

The griffin dives straight for Noor.

She rolls to the side, avoids the pass. The inisisa circles, drifting upward, wafting on a gust of air. It turns, then swoops.

Noor catches its talons with her daga, slices, and the thing flaps backward. Sand and twigs blow straight for her. The circle spreads wider. The griffin steadies itself. Leaps into the air, then dives again. She's not able to bring her daga up in time. Claws tear through her shoulder. She throws herself to the ground. The griffin soars with nothing in its talons while Noor drags herself along the ground. The claws have cut her strap. We all see the griffin turn, and I flick my daga into my hand. She doesn't have enough time to get to hers. She gets her feet underneath her, staggers into a run. The beast heads straight toward her. Its claws are ready to tear through her back.

She falls. The griffin misses her. On her feet again, she darts for her daga. Grabs it just as the beast whirls around. It pecks at her with its beak. She has the daga in her good hand, bats away each strike with one of her own. Left. Right. Right. Left. Left. Right.

End it soon, Noor. You're getting tired.

It flaps at her again. Fallen branches and dirt go everywhere.

Noor snatches a broken branch out of the air and, with her good hand, wields it like a staff. That stance . . .

Her torn arm lies limp, but in her good arm is the staff.

Each time the griffin reaches for her, she smacks it away. Again. Again. Spinning to add power to each strike.

It lunges for her, beak wide open. And grabs her staff.

I get ready to leap off the ledge and Catch, but Noor holds on. Swings herself onto the griffin's back using the staff. Her knees wrap around the griffin's neck. She flicks her daga upside-down in her fist and stabs the sin-beast in the nape of its neck.

The griffin's back arches. Noor holds tight.

Then it dissolves beneath her, and she lands on her feet. Her knees buckle, but a moment later, she's upright.

When she goes to sheathe her daga, she misses a few times, then gets it in the armband. And she does it with her bad arm.

The griffin has turned back into a puddle of ink. Noor turns to face it. The sin arcs up in the air like water from a fountain, then lands in her open mouth. Her legs almost give out beneath the weight of it. But it's not till she swallows all of it that she falls to her knees. Immediately, the others rush to her aid. One of them has already torn off a piece of his shirt to make a sling.

I can't believe she did it. I've already seen a couple of my students Eat, but this was the biggest sin-beast, and Noor was among the youngest aki. It's her greatest sin so far. From the way they're carrying her, she has already passed out from the pain of the branding.

That's today's big event, so the aki'll have nothing else to do until they break fast. Ishaq is gone, so it's just me on the ledge.

Which makes me relieved, because it means he's not here to watch me try to bring feeling back into the left side of my body.

By the time I make it back to my cave, both my legs fail me and I have to crawl. It's never been this bad before. Now when part of me gets numb, pain flashes in my brain, then everything becomes gray. Everything turns into shapes, and then when I close my eyes, the vision returns. Karima surrounded by the lion and the snake. When it's not that, it's the memory of Zainab Eating my mother's sin. I manage to get my hand to my face. I open my eyes and see that her stone still shines around my wrist.

It's getting harder and harder to sit through these. I thought I had more time. I can't Cross yet. The sins I've Eaten are catching up to me. If I Eat any more sins, it may be too much. I'll never make it back to Kos. To Karima.

A stray cat ambles by, turns to look at me, then moves on. That's right. Nothing to see here.

Images swim in my head. Guilt swims in my stomach.

But it will pass, I tell myself, as I try to sleep. Just a few hours of rest, and it will pass.

Chapter 28

The camp is deserted when night falls.

It's only a few more days until the Festival of Reunification, and some of the aki have started to realize that their return to Kos might coincide with al-Jabr, the Day of Reunification. I guess it makes sense. If we're supposed to be celebrating the Reunification of Broken Things, why make it just about being reunited with the Unnamed and being purified for a night? Why can't it mean something more literal? Why can't it be these children seeing their families again?

I take my time walking through their quarters. It's so quiet. I hear crickets chirping and night birds chatting with one another. Animals scurry up trees, but I'm the only person I can hear. I walk by the bathing area, now with a few stalls and a bucket for each. I can't believe how good it feels just to be able to walk again.

The griffin Noor defeated takes up most of the space in my brain. I'm replaying her moves, the whole course of the battle, when I almost trip over something. I look down, and it's her staff. Rather, it's the random tree branch she turned into her staff.

In my hands, it's an awkward thing. I try to swing it around, to hold it like she did, and I can't get out of my own way. I'm probably still recovering from the earlier numbness. It's almost like I have to relearn how to use my arms and legs. It's a mystery to me how Noor did what she did. I put down the staff before I break my own nose with it.

These aki have shared so much. Living quarters, food, sins.

With a start, I remember that their sin-spots will fade with time while mine won't. I look at my hands, my arms. In the darkness, they're hidden from me. When my limbs aren't numb, I spend almost all my time thinking about when next they'll go numb. It takes every inch of willpower to stop myself from shaking. After several minutes, I've caught my breath again. Now I feel like I can join them. Follow the noise. The music and the conversation. The candlelight. The closer we get to al-Jabr, the Day of Reunification, the looser things get here. The old rules and hierarchies start to rust and fall apart. Maybe we're all just getting tired.

The soft glow just over the ridge throbs like a heartbeat.

I crest the small hill, and it all spreads out before me. In the Mages' quarters, tables have been arranged in a line along the main path, and seats have been crafted out of tree trunks, large boulders, unused thatch crates, and anything else that could be found in the forest or among the supplies. Aki seven years of age eat next to Mages who have seen seven decades. The Mages with the different stripes denoting rank are scattered throughout, and I can tell which aki have classes with which Mage because of how they joke with one another and how some Mages can't keep from practicing lessons with the little ones even at the evening breakfast. Aliya's there too. Some of the older aki crowd next to Noor and help her with her food, her bad arm in a sling. She still looks weary, but she's smiling. And enjoying the attention and respect the others now throw her way. The tables are laden with bowls, and I can't imagine where and when all this food was made. But they're all eating it, so it can't be that bad. Maybe they're all just that hungry.

Each place setting has its own glass, and pots of tea dot the tables at regular intervals. At one point, several Mages retreat into one large tent and reemerge with massive dishes of meat and vegetables. The aki cheer.

Some of them swing their legs because their feet can't touch the ground from where they sit. I don't know why I can't bring myself to join them. The Unnamed knows how hungry I am, chai!

Maybe it's because I know there's a fight waiting for them, one they don't know they're a part of. And, if I'm being honest, maybe it's because I can't bring myself to sit next to a Mage. No matter what Aliya says, a Mage is always going to be someone who shorts me on my payments, who stalks the city during Baptisms, pointing out aki to be snatched up and brought to camps like this. And now, after she's told me that the kanselo must be destroyed, I don't know if I can trust any of them. Forever, I'll be wondering, with each Mage I walk past, whether they're a friend or enemy, whether they want to save Kos or hand it over to Izu. Or maybe it's because something might happen to me, and the aki will have to figure out what to do when I'm not around, and I don't know how to prepare them for that.

So I turn back and head to the Wall.

Moonlight illuminates enough of the Wall for me to read the Kosian script running like a band underneath the colored paintings of inisisa. I'm lucky the words are simple enough for me to follow.

Eventually, I get to a dip in the ground running along the Wall. My hands reach out all around me, and I figure out I'm in a tunnel. No light to guide me. The recent rain has my feet sloshing through mud, but hearing the sound gives me a little bit of comfort. I don't have to feel like I'm sneaking up on someone. According to Aliya, I'm supposed to be among friends.

When I do find the glow of candlelight, I still have to make sure to stay along the right tunnels. In some places, it reflects off into spaces that don't exist. But soon enough, the tunnel narrows into a small passage that I have to crawl through.

Suddenly, I'm in a room twice as big as our whole shanty. In it, several Mages gather around a table. Others rush back and forth, while others still are huddled in corners, whispering quietly to themselves.

Aliya looks up from where she stands at the table. How did she get here so quickly from the breakfast?

"Oh, Taj, you made it." She hurries over to me, grabs me by the arms, and looks me up and down, as if to make sure it's really me. "I can't say how happy I am you received our message."

Another Mage walks up to me, silver braids coming down her neck. The one who'd called Ras's sin for Noor to fight. "To you and your people, aki."

I look down, and her hand is out. It's the smallest of moments before I slide my hand over hers, but everyone notices my hesitation. "To you and yours, Mage."

She turns to Aliya. "So this is the aki you spoke of."

Aliya puts her hand to my shoulder. "Taj, this is Miri. She's the leader of our faction. She and Amadi first brought us together." She nods to another Mage, this one by a separate wall. He has a red stripe on his shoulder.

"We are nearing the end of our plans," Aliya says to me, "so it's imperative that we catch you up. You are an integral part." She looks around. "We are only now waiting for our agent to return with the map."

"The map?"

Before I can get an answer, a gate swings open at another entrance, and someone calmly steps through. Soft boots. Cotton leggings. Leathers.

"Arzu?"

She turns at the sound of my voice, as shocked to see me as I am to see her.

"You're their agent?" I cough out a laugh and run to her, practically tackling her in a hug. She tenses in my arms, and I realize that me being like this is probably stranger for her than it is for me. I let go and hold her at arm's length, give her a chance to see how much her habit of dress has influenced mine, give her a chance to see how happy I am to see her.

The reunification of broken things.

"Taj." Aliya again.

I let go of Arzu and see that she has rolled-up parchment under her arm.

"I have finished mapping the tunnels beneath Kos," Arzu says, then she and Aliya hurry to the table, where a map is spread out, and they pore over it, heads bowed together.

Miri looks me over.

"Am I the only aki here?" I ask her.

"Aliya speaks highly of you," she replies, not really answering my question. "She says you want change, like all of us."

"Yeah. I do. And I'm ready to do whatever needs to be done."

"Good." She smiles. "In three days' time, during al-Jabr, we will kidnap King Kolade."

I was ready to hear some real lahala from these Mages. I was not ready to hear this.

Chapter 29

I'm a kid again. A little aki. My eyes have just started to change, and I can feel in my bones that I'm becoming something different. But it still looks like I'm a normal child. And Mama can just call it a "trick of the light." She has my hand in a soft grip. Light shines through the small windows of the stone temple she and Baba take me to every Blessday morning. The temple is simple. Stone and adobe. Most people can't tell it apart from the nearby homes in the Khamsa dahia. There's no room for a balcony, so those who can't fit inside the sanctuary are forced to stand or sit around it and listen to our temple's Ozi, who speaks softly but whose voice is amplified by the Unnamed, whose power courses through him, according to Mama.

In these early mornings, she walks me down the aisle between the pews, and other mothers grab at my cheeks and fawn over me and praise Mama for having made such a beautiful, curly haired jewel. And Mama hefts me up into her arms to show me off, as though I'm her blessing. And Baba stands dutifully while the women fuss with my hair, and there's so much light shining into our tiny space. And even though I'm a child and can't speak the words, I know I can feel joy pulsing in the air. And I know that were I to ask Mama where it came from, this joy, she'd say it came from the Unnamed, who lives in all things. And I'm standing on the pew, because I'm not yet tall enough to sit down and see over the heads of the adults sitting in front of me. But even as a child, I know I'm supposed to keep quiet. I'm not supposed to ask for my blocks or wail to be picked up or let Mama know how hungry I am, even though we've eaten just before leaving and a Blessday meal is waiting for me at home when we finish.

The same light gilds the temple Ozi as the congregation sings the Otuto, the praise song, and there is always one point we reach, when we're all singing, everybody inside and outside, and I always smile at this part. Always. Because I can't imagine any other reaction.

Another memory: Mama in her nightgown at her bedside, elbows propped onto sheets, fingers clasped before her face, whispering one half of a conversation I can't hear. Her head is bowed, and I know not to disturb her, even though I'm a needy child. I know I'm witnessing something special. Her arm is healed, no longer sick and limp with guilt-poison from a sin. When she finishes, she prepares her prayer mat for sitting, and the memory ends.

Then I'm in darkness. Complete and utter darkness.

A bright-white glow. I feel it on my back before I turn around to face it. So bright I have to shield my eyes. The glow dims, and I see someone standing at the center. Not again. Princess Karima. Already, I know to look for the inisisa, silhouetted against the night by the greater thickness of their own murk.

No. Princess.

It's like the night around me has wrapped itself around my arms and legs. I can't move. Even as the sin-snake and the lion circle. Even as they prepare to strike.

No.

When I wake up, I'm in a room. Alone. It's so dark in here that I must still be in the dream. Until I hear footsteps, then see an orb of light getting closer. It's Aliya. She stands in the doorway to my room, really just a space carved into the side of a tunnel.

There's that concerned look on her face again.

"Don't worry. Bad dreams." I don't know how much she knows about Princess Karima or how it all ties together. I don't know if they're just going to go after Izu or if kidnapping King Kolade is a means to protect Princess Karima. If not, I may have to take care of that myself. Whatever it takes. "What's going on?" I can't tell whether the fog in my mind is a remnant of the night terror or confusion as to what exactly I'm doing here. "Why are we kidnapping King Kolade?"

Aliya picks something up off the ground next to the lamp she put down, and I realize, just as she's handing it to me, that it's a bowl of pepper soup. "You didn't break fast with the rest of us. You must be hungry." Then she hands me a bowl of fufu.

At first, I'm slow to eat. I scoop up a fistful of fufu, dip and scoop into the pepper soup, but once the mashed yams and soup touch my tongue, then slide down my throat, I can't stop. Before I know it, I'm using the last of the fufu to scrape up the bottom of the bowl. I get my fist up to my mouth just in time to stifle the burp.

Uhlah, that felt good.

"In one day's time, we'll be ready to enter the palace." Even crouched, she straightens her back, and it looks like she's turning from scholar to soldier. Back when I last saw her, she had the look of a military commander, marking positions on a map and dictating troop movements. She'd sounded like a warrior straight out of the ancient stories. "The movements of the Palace guards have been easy enough to track."

"How?"

"We've had scouts monitor the movement of Palace guards along the Wall."

I suddenly remember the aki who would climb trees during breaks in their training, seeing how high they could get. I remember climbing up to watch the Palace guards myself. Had the aki been told to do the same?

"Yes," Aliya answers, as though I'd spoken the question out loud. "The problem is that once we move, the other Mages will have to reveal themselves. All of them. Right now, we are fairly certain of our number among the rebels. But there are too many whose allegiances we don't yet know, and for this reason, we've had to keep them at a distance."

"I still don't know what I'm here for."

Someone darkens my doorway. It's Miri. "You will be our shield. If we should need to call forth a sin-beast, you will keep us safe."

"What? By waving my hands and distracting it?"

Miri is unfazed. "No. By commanding it. Like you did with the sin-dragon."

What? I look to Aliya. "I've only done it once," I hiss. "And after the dragon, I could barely stand." The way my limbs randomly go numb, I can barely stand even now.

Before Aliya can reply, Miri speaks again. "What we're going to do is very important. You must understand that. Izu intends to have King Kolade appoint him as chief advisor. We've learned that the announcement is planned for al-Jabr. The opening ceremony is when it will most likely be made. We will capture the king and force him to denounce Izu and his agenda before all of Kos."

"But why would King Kolade agree to appoint Izu as his advisor?"

It's Miri who finally breaks the silence. "He is threatening to unleash an army of inisisa on the city unless Kolade continues to keep him in power. This allows him to strengthen his agenda of moral purity and tighten his grip on Kos." She frowns. "That means uncleansed sins will be subject to greater punishments. Aki will be run ragged. It will be impossible to train them fast enough. Ultimately, you all may be eliminated. And Izu will silently rule over Kos."

Aliya jumps in. "Unleashing the inisisa in such great numbers would attract the arashi. They are drawn to uncleansed sins, and if there are enough of them, they will come and burn all of Kos to the ground. That is how the dahia were made. Before the aki were made into servants of the Mages' kanselo, the dahia would fill with uncleansed sins, and it would draw the arashi. During al-Jabr, all of Kos will be out in the streets. If there is an arashi attack, all of Kos will be killed. No one will be left standing. That's why the threat is so powerful."

It's finally coming together. Some parts of it I'm hearing for the first time, but even though I have heard parts of it before, it all still stuns me into silence. If any of this were spoken inside the Wall, everyone in the room would be hanged. A Mage threatening to unleash sins and destroy Kos. Aki as tools to keep Kos safe and not untouchables and slaves. I keep expecting someone to speak up and denounce the plan. But no one does. They're serious.

"You want me to help you kidnap the king," I say again. It comes out like a question, but it's really just me trying to get used to the idea. Maybe if I say it enough times, it'll sink in.

I want to ask about Princess Karima. Aliya told me in the camps that Karima was in danger, but I don't see her role in all of this. And no one brings her up. So maybe it's best I keep quiet. If whatever plans they have don't include keeping her safe, then I'll have to figure things out on my own. Best if the Mages in front of me aren't able to get in my way.

"You should rest," Miri tells me. Her voice is deep with authority. "We will be moving soon, and we need you at full strength." With a flourish of her robes, she's gone, and it's just me and Aliya left.

She sits down and doesn't seem to mind dirtying her robes. It's as though, with Miri gone, she's back to being the excited scholar. She slouches, lets her hands lie in her lap, fiddles with a small stone she picked up from the ground.

"What are you thinking about?" I ask her.

For a long time, she doesn't look up. "Since I was a child, I've dreamed of joining the Scriptors." At the question in my eyes, she clarifies: "They're scholars, a special class of Mage that studies with the algebraists. They immerse themselves in the Proofing. Their entire lives are spent learning the applications of algebraic geometry and trigonometric functions. They use math to study the stars. They use it to discover new medicine. Together, they carry knowledge of the entire history of Kos. In the Ulo Amamihe, the Great House of Ideas, they . . ." She doesn't finish.

I think of the books Mama used to collect from her sisters. Any time they would visit, they would bring whole crates with them. I have no idea what was in those books, never did. But Mama would glow at the sight of them. I think of the look of joy and peace on Baba's face when he saw Mama like that. Mama and Aliya would've gotten along well.

"In my village, we held contests. All the surrounding villages took part. And they would gather the schoolchildren who had begun to study rudimentary mathematics. *Poetry* contests, but what we were supposed to do was write proofs. Each dahia puts forward the children who will try to write out the most elegant mathematical proof they can. If you're a child who shows promise, your parents will spend an entire year grooming you for the poetry contest. That's your ticket to the Palace competition. Do well enough at home and you just may get to meet the Kaya family. My baba, he once saw me after I came home with a mark of 98 on my assignment. He told me to go out and find the other two points, then come back home."

That makes me chuckle, and Aliya chuckles too, although hers holds a tremble.

"You remember the poetry contest Princess Karima held in the Palace? It's a way for the Palace and the algebraists to spot early talent. And if you're chosen, your family is afforded a lot of prestige. It's a very high honor. And you're celebrated in the whole entire dahia. You represent them now."

"Did you win during your year?"

She snorts, but I hear sorrow in it. "I would have. I *should* have. But they said I had skipped too many steps in my proof. One of the judges said I had lost points because what he saw was intuition and not real work, as though the Word from the Unnamed is supposed to come to us in sentences we can understand. As though the Unnamed doesn't force us to intuit its message. Idiots." She takes a second to calm herself. "It was beautiful, that proof. And I keep a copy of it in my notebook. But I wasn't chosen by the algebraists that year."

"And you can't do that anymore? Join the Scriptors?"

She laughs, and there's nothing but sadness in it. "I'm a rebel. They would never let me become a Scriptor. Learning the art of reunification, really studying the meaning of al-Jabr, piecing together the entire grand philosophy." She uncouples her glasses and pushes the lenses back into her hair so that she can wipe the tears from her eyes. "All because I decided I needed to do what was right."

"If you're saving Kos, you're saving the Great House of Ideas too. Right?"

She snorts. "Sure." She sniffs, wipes her sleeve across her nose, her face. "What does it matter? Seeing all of this, how the aki truly live, the way the kanselo rules everything . . . I'd spent so long apart from the real lives of the people of Kos. I don't know if I can go back." Another chuckle. "Early on in my training, Izu would take me through the catacombs, past the prison cells. I was so immersed in my studies and my notes that I didn't even hear the young aki whimper all around me. The children who had been captured in the last Baptism? I'd walk right past them, because I was too busy memorizing sura."

Silence falls between us.

With the stone, she etches patterns into the dirt.

"That doesn't mean you have to give it up," I say at last.

She looks up.

"I don't know. Maybe knowing how people live their lives will make you a better scholar, you know? You will know what it all looks like when you read the texts. You can put faces and names to it all. It all becomes fuller. Myths and legends, they all come from people. You'll know better than most what it all looks like. I don't know—I'm probably not making any sense."

She smiles but doesn't look up at me. Almost like she's become shy. "You know, in the Before, the Prophets could speak directly to the inisisa. I mean, they weren't sin-beasts, because this was the time before sin. But they could talk to them. The Unnamed would use them as messengers. It was a way of communicating with the natural world. To be able to do that, to speak directly to the Unnamed, to hear its voice! They must have been truly holy."

"So you're saying I'm supposed to be a Prophet?"

She starts. "What? Oh, no. Not that. Just. I don't know, really. We'll see."

"I gotta stay alive, right?"

A wry smirk from her. "That helps. Yes."

"You think the Prophets ever flirted with gear-heads?"

"What?"

"Just asking." I raise my hands in defense. "In case, well, in case I ever want to use that line. About me being a Prophet."

"I don't think there were gear-heads back then." She glares.

I laugh, and before long, she's laughing too. It feels good to see her happy like this. Warm. If I ever see Omar again, I'll tell him about this. About what it feels like to care for someone.

"Why do they call you Sky-Fist?" she asks.

No one's ever asked me that question. Everyone just accepted it as fact. All the new aki would hear it, and it would stick. "Some stupid poem. A song, really. You kill enough inisisa and live, then people start saying all sorts of things about you. You're an untouchable in the streets, but you get this power. And they make you into a legend." I relax against the wall of my room. "Sin-beasts are shadows, beasts made of night. And an aki is like a ray of sunlight that comes down from the sky and shatters the sin, kills the shadows."

I'm using my hands to gesture, to imitate light falling from the sky like a fist. "Aki are like that fist coming down from the sky, and that's how you get rid of the darkness. Or some stupid thing like that. I forget how the song goes exactly." But I can hear the song in my head. Clearly. Jameelah is singing it. Dilif is humming the melody. "Somebody's father might've been a poet or a crier; maybe he wrote the song." Maybe no one did, and it just came to them. Came to us. I can see them singing it. Right in this room.

I notice Aliya staring at me. Smiling. She gets to her feet, and I rise with her.

She sticks her hand out, palm up. "To you and your people, Sky-Fist." The way she says it, she's halfway between rebel commander and friend. A friend . . .

I step close to her and slide my palm onto hers. I bring my lips to her ears. "To you and yours, Aliya."

Her hair brushes my cheek, my ears. I close my eyes, flushed from the feel of her against me. I could stay like this forever.

She steps away. "We should get some sleep. Tomorrow's going to be an important day for us. For Kos."

"Yes," I say quietly. And I watch her go. I can tell from the way she hurries away that she doesn't want to risk looking back.

I can't fault her for that.

CHAPTER 30

THEY TELL ME it's morning, but I have no way of telling underground.

Arzu's with us again. With Aliya, we head into the tunnels. They're supposed to lead us into the catacombs, and from there, to the Palace grounds. My legs are still working.

Miri warns us, before we leave, that recent reports suggest the Palace guards have increased their patrols in advance of al-Jabr. We'll have to use a different route than initially planned.

So it's not long before the underground cavern starts to echo with the sound of footsteps that aren't ours. I try to keep up and step gingerly at the same time. Arzu and Aliya had elected not to use a lamp, for obvious reasons, but it turns out they know these tunnels way better than I do. The way the sound bounces off the walls once we get to the dank catacombs makes it more and more difficult to find them. But then we reach a part of the tunnels where lamps cast golden light.

I miss Bo. I wish he could see all of this. I wish he knew. Sometimes, I hate the way he seems automatically like some authority figure, how his word often goes unchallenged, how people automatically defer to him even though I'm the more skilled aki. Bo's sins fade with time, just like everyone else's. I realize now that Zainab and I had that in common. She was covered head-to-toe in sin-spots, and all of them looked deep and new. They had all stuck with her, and she'd been driven mad by it. The others, if they don't Eat too often, can walk around like any other Forum-dweller. Maybe this is why the aki in the shanties revered me but always felt more comfortable around Bo. He was more like them than I could ever be.

He could fight, though. He could fight-oh! He once killed a sin-lion while he had a broken foot. Another time, he popped out a shoulder while battling a sin-bear. And he once left a fight with a large sin-snake while holding his ribs together in barely disguised pain. Always, though, in a few moments, he was upright and laughing and in charge again. And he'd have no trouble haggling with the foodsellers for our dinner meal's ingredients later that day. Sometimes, I would see him wake up in the mornings if I rose early enough. I can only guess at what aches and pains took him over when he struggled to dress himself. His body probably screams at him every morning. But he's always grinning. Like it's only a matter of time before you're in on the joke too. Hopefully, I will see him again.

I want to ask Aliya how much Zainab knew. If Zainab worked with Aliya to paint directions on the Wall, maybe she was part of the rebellion. I mean, with Arzu on our side, I have no idea who stands where. What I do know is that the sin-snake and the sin-lion that circle Princess Karima in my night terrors have something to do with all of this.

Ever since waking up this morning, the princess's face has appeared in front of me, like an inyo. And I get scared that I've already missed my chance. I feel like that's what I'm running after. And whenever I close my eyes to shake away the vision, I see King Kolade and the princeling Haris and the menace in the way they walk. Then the vision goes away, leaving silver spots. Then those clear, and I hear the boot-steps of Palace guards splashing through puddles behind us.

Voices up ahead.

Aliya glides to our right, and I follow her into a small enclosure. Arzu disappears into the shadows, her knife clasped close to her chest.

Soft footsteps and the swishing of cloaks announce a small group of Mages. They amble past. Mumbles and murmurs in a language I can't understand, then one of them chuckles. When the light catches the space beneath their hoods, their eyes glint silver. Then they're gone.

Aliya peeks around the corner. Arzu steps out and looks both ways, then beckons the both of us, and we turn down another pathway.

A broken gate blocks our path.

We crouch for a moment and look around before Arzu's and Aliya's gazes settle on me.

"Taj," Aliya says. "I'm going to need you to do what you did with the sin-dragon."

"What?"

"I'm going to call forth a sin from Arzu. I'm going to need you to command it through this gate."

I try to act calm, but I can't keep the shake out of my voice. "Won't that weaken her?" I whisper.

"We can't go back and use a different path, Taj." This time from Arzu. "This is the only way through." She sheathes her knife and kneels before Aliya. "I'm ready."

There's nothing I can do as Aliya puts her hands to Arzu's face and begins the prayer. The way Aliya does it I've never seen before. She presses her forehead against Arzu's. And there's almost a pleading sound in her voice. As though she's not so much calling forth a sin as asking the Unnamed for a blessing.

Arzu retches.

Aliya continues the incantation.

Spasms rock Arzu, and she falls forward. Her knife clatters in a puddle.

Aliya speaks in more fervent whispers now. There's pain in her voice. Syllables cascade like a waterfall out from her lips.

I crouch into a fighting pose. I might not be able to control the inisisa when it appears, and I'll need to be able to beat it quickly.

Arzu bucks. Her back arches. Just as she's about to scream,

ink chokes the sound in her throat. Her mouth fills with it, and it spills in one vicious torrent from her.

Aliya continues her prayer as if in a trance.

The sin bubbles up from Arzu's throat like a fountain. As soon as it hits the tunnel floor, it arcs in all directions until legs come down all around us. They dig into the stone of the enclosure, the floor, the walls, the ceiling. Arzu falls to the ground, and I find myself looking up into the eyes of a sin-spider. Its face and body are one single sphere with shadowy wisps peeling off and dissolving into the air. Aliya has grown completely still, frozen at the sight of the inisisa. It turns its eye to consider her. I remember the knife in my hands.

Something, maybe courage, pushes me to my feet. A familiar feeling seeps into me. It warms me and beats away the chill of the cavern we stand in. I no longer hear the sewer water running over our feet or the steady drip from the ceiling. I stand to my full height so that my face is only inches from the sin-spider's.

Before I can think of what to tell it, it turns to study the broken gate, then squeezes its body through it. Once its torso pokes through the other end, its legs wrap around the gate and pull it away. It screeches. Our hands go to our ears at the sound. The sin-spider scrabbles onward with its free legs to where the corridor dips.

Water slides beneath our feet right over the lip of our passageway to form a small waterfall landing right in the midst of three Palace guards. One of them sneezes. Another complains about the cold and how it cuts straight through their armor. Aliya and I take Arzu in our arms and carry her forward, then gently lower her onto the chilly ground. My feet are numb from the sewer water. I lean forward and see the guards, several meters below us, strolling in tiny circles, their hands on the hilts of their swords. The first one sneezes into his gauntlet again, then lifts his face to the arched ceiling. I scurry back at a crouch and look to Aliya as if to say, *What now?*

Her eyes cast about for a plan, when all of a sudden swords slide out of their sheaths. The air fills with shouts. The clanging of steel against steel, a swirl of bodies being flung about the small enclosure. Aliya and I lie down in the water to hide. The chaos goes on for almost a minute before silence cuts off all noise. Part of me hopes, when I look over the ledge of the opening, that there won't be anything there. I hope the soldiers will have gotten away. No comatose bodies. No innocent men devoured by Arzu's renegade sin. Then I catch myself. Are they really innocent? Suddenly, I realize where the guilt is coming from. It's not mine. It belongs to the sins I've Eaten. The sins I've been forced to Eat. I will never be rid of the guilt of others. Thinking of this, it becomes easier to hate Haris the princeling, easier to despise King Kolade.

There's only empty space below. Relief. I look around just to make sure, then swing over the edge and try to find purchase with my feet. But I slip on the slick stones and fall with a crack in the shallow water. I come up with my daga at the ready in case anything, sin-beast or otherwise, comes back for me.

"We're clear," I whisper.

"Help me get her down," Aliya says from above.

After a moment, I sheathe my daga and turn back to the opening to try to figure out a way to get Arzu's body down. Her boots poke out over the ledge, then slowly, her legs come down. I put my hands up to her and try to keep her close to the wall so that if she falls, she falls on me.

"She's slipping."

Aliya loses her grip, and I have my arms out, ready to catch Arzu, but she hits me hard, and we're both in the water. My back aches. Arzu stirs against me, then climbs off, but she still can't get to her feet. She coughs, then spits droplets of sin into the sewer water.

Meanwhile, as Aliya clings to the wall, her robe is a tangled mess, with her legs spread awkwardly trying to find two poorly placed footholds. She looks like a spider herself.

"Some help please!"

Her arms shake with the effort it takes to keep from tumbling.

Pain throbs in my lower back, but I'm up and with my arms out again. Aliya won't let up on her grip until I assure her for the third time that I'm ready. She lets herself go, as gracefully as her robe allows, right into my arms. Holding her, I do my best to school my face into an expressionless calm, but I know she sees through it. She fights her way out of my arms, and I nearly drop her.

By now, Arzu is up again and moving just fine. Her shoulders slump a little bit, but she's able to stand and, I guess, able to run.

When Aliya stands upright again, she makes a show of brushing the dust from her robes, then strides past me and Arzu to stare down two tunnels running perpendicular to each other. "This way," she says, with purpose.

By the time we surface from the catacombs, dusk cuts purple and golden arrows across the sky. I come out of the passageway last, after Aliya and Arzu. Grunting, I grip the stone slab Arzu had moved and slide it back over the hole out of which we crawled. With my foot, I move brush and twigs till it looks like any other patch of shrubbery. Right now, we're toward the portion of the Forum that abuts the hill. It's quiet, and when I venture out into the main thoroughfare, I can see the tallest gilded dome of the Palace, an eye looking in all directions at once. The smaller estates are aglow with light. Princes and princesses ready themselves for what I realize is going to be King Kolade's grand announcement. It's only now that I notice the Kosian script splashed in paint across all the walls. Every storefront, every home. Even in crude markings on the daises criers and poets and preachers stand on.

"We have to make it to King Kolade's private chambers." Aliya stands between me and Arzu in the empty street. "The gardens will be almost empty. People are likely gathering for the announcement."

"How much time do we have?" I ask.

Arzu casts her eye at the darkening sky. "Not much."

"We have to get to him before the announcement," Aliya says.

We hurry through Kos's side streets, and I realize only once we arrive at the side gate what route we're taking. It feels weird and appropriate to retrace this path, to do it in reverse. The last time I crossed this boundary between the Forum and the Palace estates, I'd been running from the guards, afraid that I'd be thrown in jail and worried that they had already chained Bo in a dark cell.

Even though my clothing resembles Arzu's outfit, my presence would raise too many questions. So, instead of just walking through like a Mage and her charges, we have to sneak. But eventually, we make it to the burbling stream; then, crouching, we hurry up the rolling green pasture until we get to a wall that I recognize. Draped in banners, that wall with a tower on top offers a view of Kos that I begin to remember. A view I remember I hate.

Arzu takes Aliya on her back, and we all scale the wall, using the banners for purchase. My former sicario makes it up first and, with a few swift motions of her knife, pops the window open.

When I climb through, the room is shrouded in darkness. It looks almost exactly how I left it. But when I wander to the closet, none of my clothes hang from the wires. It's completely empty.

"Come on," Aliya hisses. "Taj, let's go."

She and Arzu are already ahead, and I hurry after them. Arzu leads the way. I rush down corridors and around corners where I used to saunter. I hurry past portraits I used to stare at, of the Prophets, of the royal family. I hide where, before, I could walk freely.

The murmur of the crowd grows louder, muffled by the walls separating us.

We're almost there.

So close to King Kolade, to getting him and forcing him to denounce Izu in front of the whole Forum. So close to saving Karima and changing Kos.

Arzu tests the door.

It's not until she closes it behind us that I realize what's wrong. No Palace guards. Why wouldn't there be Palace guards protecting the king?

Something massive rolls its wheels against stone outside. The cannon to signal the beginning of al-Jabr.

King Kolade is nowhere to be found.

Moonlight has replaced sunlight and casts glowing squares and stripes across the room. The chairs are empty. He's not here.

Soft footsteps click against the tiles. A face passes into the moonlight. Even with his hood up, I know it's Izu. And he's smiling.

"I was afraid you wouldn't make it in time," Izu murmurs.

Aliya steps forward, past the rest of us. "Where's the king?"

"He's safe." Izu inclines his head, as though listening for something. "Before long, Palace guards will arrive. You three will be brought into custody, and it will be the king's decision as to whether you will be quietly executed or publicly tried and hanged for plotting to overthrow His Majesty and do unspeakable harm to the royal family." The sound of prayer beads clicking fills the room. "Whether or not you three are hanged outside the gates, the Mages who have chosen rebellion will most assuredly be tried publicly. And they will be disgraced. Their families will suffer, and every trace that they had ever existed will be wiped from this city."

Arzu and Aliya glance at each other, then look around the room, trying to figure out what to do. I smell it first before I see it. Like fire and metal charring my nostrils. The shadows bend along the floor, and that's when I realize they're legs.

Spider legs.

Out of the darkness, the sin-spider's torso emerges, hovering just over Izu's head.

He freezes. I know he feels it too. Without even having to see it. Maybe he can smell it as well. Or maybe the inky tendrils that swirl out of the sin-spider's head brush against his hood. It raises two legs, hooks them into Izu's hood and pulls it back, so that his head, his face, all of it is in full view.

"Now, Taj!"

I snap out of it and see Aliya pointing.

"Now! Command it to consume him."

"It'll kill him." It's like she hit me in my chest. "I can't."

"Taj! Do it!"

Izu chuckles. "You won't kill me. You won't do it, because if you do kill me, you will kill everyone else in this city."

The Mage sees the question in my eyes. A grin twists his lips. "Before my body is cold, the sins of everyone within the Wall will be called forth. And this army of sins will swim through the streets until no home, no shelter, no corner is untouched." His smile disappears. "Aliya." He says nothing more, just shakes his head. It's as though the sin-spider isn't even there.

He's lying, I know it. There's no way he could do what he's claiming. Even still, I can't do it. This is different. This isn't letting a sin-beast go. This is commanding it to kill someone.

What would that do to me? I want to. I want to so badly. Images flash in my mind of dahia in the aftermath of Baptisms, of Mages sweeping through and snatching children from their families, pulling them out from under the wreckages of their old homes. I see Costa and the sacks full of money he refuses to give us. Palace guards with their short canes in hand, ready to beat us bloody. Then I remember Izu's threat. If I had refused him, if I had chosen not to go out into the camps, he would have an entire dahia destroyed. If he's gone, he can't issue that edict. It'll be safe. But Kos.

Suddenly, I realize I've been staring at my hands. I look up just in time to see a blur of white, then a stream of red. Someone's cry is cut short. Princess Karima. I run to her. She turns her face to me, then turns back. Absolute serenity. If Izu hurts her, I don't care what the consequences are; I will cut him. The Mage trembles before the princess and coughs. Red splashes onto Karima's white dress. Izu crumples at her feet.

"Karima," I gasp. I reach to turn her around to see if she's hurt, and that's when I see the knife in her hands, glinting in the moonlight. "What have you done?"

Chapter 31

She's shaking. Even as I hold her, she's shaking. "I couldn't do it, Taj. You were going to Eat that sin to save him, and I couldn't bear to watch you consume another sin. I won't allow it." She raises her head from my shoulder and looks at me, eyes as clear as fresh river water. The air around the princess curls with sin. "I want to bear this. I want to know what it feels like. To carry this inside of me. Sin, Taj, it must be borne. It cannot be wished away. Its taking cannot be purchased. It is our own lot to bear." She looks past me, and I see that she's staring straight at Arzu. She must know what this means, that Arzu has betrayed her.

"It is our lot to bear," Karima repeats. "I won't become a monster like my brother. Utterly and completely ignorant of the burden of sin."

A single step back, and she stands before me, a small trail of blood running down the front of her gown. Then she turns her face toward that of the sin-spider. She doesn't tremble. She doesn't gape. "So this is a sin," she says in a voice caught between wonder and curiosity. She reaches up to touch it.

"Princess, no!" The words burst out of my mouth, and just as Karima's fingers brush the sin-spider, the beast dissolves into a puddle that splashes against the ground, then rushes into my mouth.

My body seizes, and I can feel Arzu's guilt coursing through me. I can feel her relationship with Princess Karima, its entire history, all the different sides and edges and facets of it pass through me. The affection Arzu felt for Karima, the gratefulness in having had a companion as a child, the resentfulness as they grew up into separate castes, the bitterness with which Arzu watched the royal family treat her mother, the sweltering rage that filled her upon hearing her mother's punishment, the stoic determination Arzu felt as she continued her service to the princess.

Then it's all gone. Feelings of guilt climb up my spine and into my brain. Their tendrils latch on to my heart, but I push them away. Arzu's guilt. Not mine.

Palace guards are coming.

Aliya grabs my arm and pulls me to the window. "Taj, we have to go. Now!"

But I can't. I won't. "No."

Her eyes widen in shock. "Taj. What are you doing?"

My head is swimming. Sins float through it, over and under one another, forming into different beasts battling between my ears and behind my eyes. Everywhere I look, I see sin-beasts forming, bears bending out from the drapes, rodents emerging from the tiles. Everyone's sins. Everywhere. I see nothing but sin. But Princess Karima is the clearest thing in my mind. She glows. Everything is darkness, but she glows.

I think I'm Crossing.

"Taj." Tears hang in Aliya's eyes. "Taj," she says softly. "Please."

The footsteps grow louder. Aliya glares at me, then heads to the window. Princess Karima wears a look of gratefulness on her face. The doors creak on their hinges, and I stumble into the shadows, just as King Kolade and a phalanx of Palace guards spill into the room.

"Sister, what have you done?" The king breaks away from the Palace guards and races to the princess. Izu's blood pools at his feet and soaks the hem of Karima's gown. Questions form on the king's lips, but all he can do is step back to avoid the puddle. The red, like a finger, points to me. A dragon's scaled tail rises out of it. "Are you hurt?"

"No, brother," Princess Karima replies softly, reassuringly.

"There were reports of trouble in my chambers. I had gone to pray before the grand announcement and—" His words run together.

"Please, brother. The Unnamed watches over all of us. I am safe now." She gestures to Izu. "He tried to attack me. Arzu was able to fend him off, but it fell upon me to strike him down." She collapses into her brother's arms. The knife clatters on the tiles.

From where I hide, I can see the look on Arzu's face, all the different emotions battling themselves. It's a single moment of clarity, before the world blurs again. I keep fighting the darkness, but with each second it gets harder and harder. Whenever I look for Karima, though, or listen for her voice, the light shines a little brighter. The darkness becomes a little less.

Karima puts a hand to her brother's face, steps close to him. Envy stirs in my chest. Someone else's envy, I tell myself. "Brother, there has already been too much chaos. I know you worry about what you will say to the people. The Unnamed will guide you. For now, seek its counsel." Her smile deepens. "Pray, my brother. Pray." She holds her hand out, palm up. "To you and your people, brother."

"To you and yours, Princess," Kolade says, returning the smile. He turns his gaze to Izu's body and stares for several silent seconds. To the Palace guards, he says, "Attend to this," and together they lift Izu's body and carry him away, a red streak marking his path.

The retinue, with the king at its head, leaves the room. The clank of their armor and the slip of their boots grow fainter until there's nothing but the sound of us breathing. Princess Karima glides to the doors and barely touches them, but they close.

Before she comes to me, I take one step out, and she holds me, and I can't think of anything else but the warmth that suddenly bleeds into me, a light that pushes out every bit of darkness. It fills every crack inside me, flooding me, so that were I to open my mouth, light would shine from it. The only thing that stood between us, the Mage Izu, is now gone. Then her lips are on mine.

I feel . . .

I feel forgiven.

Chapter 32

It's easier now to imagine a life with her. If Karima accepts me, perhaps it's only a matter of time before the others can. I can wear clothes to hide my sin-spots. I can learn the rules, how to behave, how to walk, how to wear my hair. I will never have to worry about when and how I will eat. I may never need to Eat again. I have earned this.

"Princess," I whisper. My heart-mate.

"Taj," she breathes, and it is the most wondrous sound in the world. It is music.

I can't remember the last time I wanted something so badly, the last time I *dared* to want something so badly. I am holding a dream in my hands, and I squeeze tighter, because if I don't, maybe it will escape me. But Karima doesn't push away. Instead, she leans farther into my embrace. If I never moved an inch again, it would be worth it.

Screams. From outside.

Arzu's already at the window looking over. I still hold on to Karima. I don't want to let her go just yet.

A griffin crashes through the windows, spraying shards of glass everywhere. Arzu falls backward. When she tries to get back up, her arms are bloody from where she has skid. The inisisa flaps massive wings. My feet slide against the tiles. A trail of blood marks their path. Izu's blood.

Arzu struggles up onto her knees.

I feel fearless. Calmly, I guide Karima behind me and walk to the griffin, which swings its head back and forth as though in pain. The crowd below us keeps getting louder. Maybe they saw this inisisa and are simply scared. I stand before it. "Enough," I say, and it stops moving. Docile, it lowers its head. The nape of its neck meets my eye. I unsheathe my daga, and in one slice, the griffin's head falls away.

This must be what power feels like. To command these things and have them obey. My fear is gone. No sin-beast can kill me. My head is aflame with them. I see them everywhere. They turn the world into a whirlwind of shadow and light, but I can move. I can feel myself walking and using my daga and turning to face the princess, my heart-mate.

The smile fades from my face when I see how Karima stares at me. Arzu, too, is frozen where she stands. I hold my hands out into the moonlight. My sin-spots are shifting. The tattoos are morphing. Bits of black rise from the skin of my arms and legs. My sin-spots, they're leaving me. Suddenly, I can see my skin beneath them. Smooth. Unblemished. Beautifully brown.

Pain like I've never felt before lances my stomach. Everything hurts. Every single part of me, ripped apart. My legs collapse beneath me, and I can't feel them anymore. I try to get to my knees, but I can't move. My body seizes, then my limbs thrash. A scream comes out of my mouth. I've lost control of my arms. My breath catches in my lungs.

By the Unnamed. I'm Crossing.

Bile spills out of my mouth, black, as black as dreamless sleep. My mouth fills with it, but more of it pours out, a fountain of darkness. It streams down the side of my face and pools on the floor, leaking into my hair, my clothes. I gag, and more comes out. It feels like every sin I've ever Eaten is leaving me. When it ends, I can't move. Pain blinds me. But when the world comes back into focus, I see that my arm, stretched out in front of me, is clean. My skin. I can see my skin.

Then, as suddenly as it had come, the hurt is gone. In an instant, I can stand. I can feel my limbs. When I look up, I can't believe what I'm seeing. The entire room is filled with inisisa. Snakes, large and small, slither on the ground. Griffins hang in the corners of the room while a sin-dragon scrapes its claws against the tiles. Bears roar at us, and lions slink back and forth, eyeing us hungrily. Above the rest, the torso of a sin-spider hangs, its legs arcing over the heads of the beasts. Everywhere I look, inisisa.

All at once, they tense. They'll kill us all.

"Stop!" I hold my hands out, and the creatures all still. It worked. I can't believe it.

It worked.

Karima's eyes change. "Your power." She talks as though there's no more air in her lungs. And she strides toward me slowly, hesitating. She wants something, but she's slightly frightened to take it.

"I've saved you, Princess." When I talk, she stops where she stands, and the fear returns to her eyes. "Izu and Prince Haris, they were going to kill you, and I saw your cousin's sin before he could commit it. Izu is gone. It is nothing for us to wipe the rest of them out of the city."

She puts her hands to my chest, looks me in my face, and says, "Yes."

Then, from somewhere in the distance but getting louder, the sound of screams. Like a wave, rushing up on us until the noise is unmistakable. Then I remember Izu's threat, and my heart chills.

I break away from Karima and step to the window to see inisisa spilling like oil through the streets of Kos, inky black filling every alley and side street, leaving comatose Kosians in their wake. Then I see it. Bo, his shirt torn, daga in hand, at the center of a circle of sin-wolves. Without thinking, I leap over the edge and onto the stone steps of the Palace.

Chapter 33

I HIT THE ground and roll down the stone steps, then come to my feet and sprint straight toward where Bo was standing. I turn down one of the narrow alleyways, but a puddle of blackness appears. It spills toward me and rises up off the ground, morphing into a sin-bear. As it rears on its hind legs, it growls, showing sharp black teeth. I jump out of the way as it slams its paws down, narrowly missing me. I lunge for it, slicing straight through the nape of its shadowy neck. Before it even fully evaporates, I'm off again. Sin-snakes coil and spring at me, and I slice and slice and swing my daga and spin, cutting a path straight through them.

A window crashes open in a home overhead, and a sin-wolf grips an aki in its claws as it crashes to the ground. Other aki run along rooftops, shouting to one another, teaming up on inisisa together. I look up again and see Omar darting from one balcony to another, swinging himself off of ledges and leaping over bannisters. He moves with a quickness and grace I never could have taught him. A sin-leopard chases him, nipping at his ankles. In one swift turn, he attacks, plunging his daga between the beast's eyes, driving it all the way back into the nape of its neck. The inisisa explodes into a tendril of blackness.

Panicked Kosians dart in every direction, and I can barely keep on my feet. Something smacks me in the back of the head, and then I turn around to see a spear of black ink rush toward my mouth. The inisisa I killed—I can't escape those sins. The bile from the snakes and the bear slides down my throat, and I choke, but a moment later, it's all gone, and all that's left is some dizziness. I rock back and forth but manage to still myself. Noises soften, and the world blurs, but I put my arm out in front of me, and sin-spots appear. Four sin-snakes wrapped around my left forearm. A bear running down my right. It hurts my heart to see them back, these sin-spots. The last time I'd been able to see the skin of my arms so unspotted, I was a child. And then, with Karima, to see again what it looked like to be a regular Forum-dweller, only now to have that taken away.

My face is wet with tears, but I can't stop.

A sin-griffin swoops low overhead, and I chase after it. Kosians cower in corners, scurry down alleyways, barricade themselves in vendor stalls. Inisisa tackle the Kosians who couldn't find shelter in time and devour the ones who can't get away. I can't save them.

I cut into a small alley and vault onto a rubbish pile, scrambling up to the roof of a home. The griffin flaps its wings in the distance and circles the teeming masses of Kosians trampling one another in a stampeding herd below. It dives down and reemerges with comatose bodies in its talons, then arcs through the street again.

My body aches, but I force myself to continue. I jump from rooftop to rooftop, just like when the guards were chasing me. Just as I did before any of this happened.

As I run through laundry hanging on clotheslines and around rooftop gardens, I angle myself toward the main thoroughfare and time my leap so that I hurl myself through the air just as the griffin is about to pass beneath me.

I fall on the griffin's back, and we spiral down into the street, crashing hard onto the ground.

Already, the Eaten litter the streets while inisisa pick over them, then move on to other Kosians. Furniture lies on the ground in the Forum as the sin-beasts tear into homes, looking for their victims. Storefronts and stalls are toppled over with their wares scattered all around me.

Just as I turn, the griffin, now turned into bile, jets down my throat. This one dizzies me. I take a few steps forward, then stumble. I can feel inisisa circling me. They make no noise except for the sound of paws and feet crunching in the dry dirt. I come to my feet. My head is still swimming. They've cornered me. I hold up my daga and get into fighting stance, but I know it will be no use. The beasts come closer and closer. I close my eyes. I'm shaking, but if this is how I'm going to go, by the Unnamed, let me die fighting.

"Eh-eh!" I hear from above. When I open my eyes, Ifeoma,

Tolu, Emeka, and Sade jump down from a balcony above. Just in time.

They each take one on, and I jump in. Together we fight them off, our dagas moving at lightning speed. We choke down the sins, and a moment later, it's over.

"So," Ifeoma says, strutting forward. "The city of Kos is needing us now? They better write songs about us."

Sade laughs and loosens the strap for her daga, holding it out into the light and doing an elaborate bow. "You see, I am keeping track of all the inisisa I kill tonight. So that when I tell the Mages, they will call me diligent." She is smiling when she says all of this, and her teeth glow pearly in the night.

Emeka comes forward and slides his arm out. "To you and yours, Taj."

I smile. "To you and yours, Emeka." I face the rest of the group. "Bo?"

"He didn't find you?" Tolu asks.

"No," I tell him. "He was looking for me?"

Sade puts her strap back in place. "Yes, he said it was urgent. Acted like fire ants had crawled into his pants."

Then I remember seeing him surrounded by that pack of sin-wolves. "Bo." I set off at a dash, having to hurdle over the broken remains of shop stalls and dodge crumbling balconies. The others follow close behind me. Each protecting a side, they bat back any inisisa that chase behind us.

The circle, when I see it, has grown smaller. There are fewer sin-wolves, but Bo is down on one knee. His chest heaves. His shoulders have slumped.

"Bo!" I call out, and the inisisa turn.

The wolves rush toward us, and Sade and the others scatter.

The first wolf leaps for me. Emeka tackles it, and the two roll. When they come to their feet, they lunge for each other, but Emeka stabs the beast through its torso. Sade has already attracted the attention of another, while Tolu steps in front of me to draw even more. Ifeoma and I rush to Bo. But just as we reach him, a lion leaps out of the shadows and barrels into Ifeoma. She cries out in pain. A scream catches in my throat. Fury builds in my chest. I stalk over to the inisisa she's fending off, and my daga catches the light from overturned lamps. Ifeoma has her own daga in the lion's chest, and I run up to it and bring my daga down swift, straight through its neck.

Blood is pumping through my veins, and I can't catch my breath. I feel powerless. All around me, inisisa stalk. Bodies everywhere. Motionless. Glass-eyed. Eaten.

Aki still battle the remaining inisisa, but the sins they've Eaten slow their movements too much. Some are Crossing over. There's not enough skin on my body to Eat them all. There's not enough skin on all of our bodies to Eat them all. I fall to my knees next to Ifeoma, whose eyes have begun to glass over. Inky teeth marks show where on her shoulder the sin-lion has bitten her. She blinks at me, and for a second, her white-pupiled eyes return, and she fumbles for my wrist, and I give it to her.

Her legs shake, and I know she's lost feeling in them. Her mouth is now frozen, and no words escape. She's Crossing. Her arms go limp, and her hand falls out of mine.

The aki from the forest stand on rooftops or crowd windows, slashing at sin-falcons, climbing onto the backs of bears and stabbing at the napes of their necks. It's war. And they're dying. So many of them are dying.

Air fills my lungs. And I scream.

"STOP!"

It stops. The rampage, the carnage, it all stops. All of Kos is silent. My voice wasn't my own when I said that word. It felt like someone, something, was speaking through me. Passing through my body and out of my mouth. Something Unnamed.

Every face in Kos turns my way.

I stand.

The inisisa, as one, bow their heads.

Chapter 34

It stills my breath to see them like this.

The noise has ceased. There isn't even any weeping for those just consumed or those trampled underfoot. There is complete and utter silence. And all around me are sin-beasts.

That's when the realization hits me. I am the most powerful man in Kos.

Behind me, the other sin-beasts walk, crawl, slither, and climb over the balcony so that they fill out the steps around me. An army of shadows.

At the top of the stone steps stands Princess Karima. A lightning bolt of red stains her white dress. Izu's blood. Other than that, she is pristine. She glows. Like a beacon of light, she draws me to her. When she stands at my side, she seems to draw all the light in Kos into her. The flame in every candle bends her way. The two of us. I have the power to control inisisa. She now has the power to rule. We are Kos's protectors. We will change this place. We will fix it. Remake it. Together.

There's commotion down below. Aliya pushes through the crowd to stand near the bottom of the steps. Other Mages flank her, filling out the bottom row. The rebels.

"Taj!" Aliya's voice steadies me. "Taj! I knew it was you. Ever since that night at Zoe's, I knew you were special." Her voice carries. It turns the massive distance between us into nothing. "I knew it, Taj. I swear to the Unnamed, as soon as I saw you, I knew you were different. In the prophecy. The Paroles of the Seventh Prophet. He speaks of aki who can command and control sin-beasts. Your coming was foretold! Join us." She waves her hands wide to indicate the Mages on both sides of her. "Call off this army of inisisa."

I don't move. I can't.

"Taj. Please." She takes a step closer, daring me to do something. "From the moment you sat at my table, Taj. When you kicked your feet up and ate my date, I knew." Her lips curl into a smile.

"Aliya." The night at Zoe's. The shisha smoke. The smell of her hair as we leaned against each other in that underground cave, palms pressed together. The sound of shovels digging into loose earth, rain falling all around us while we buried Zainab. Flashes. Like light shining on shattered panes of glass. I blink it all away. I can feel my fists clenching at my sides. "I'm not just a tool."

"Taj, I—"

"A Mage is a Mage is a Mage. Whether it's to Eat someone

else's sins or bring about someone else's prophecy, we're all just tools, aren't we?"

She takes a step closer. A sin-dragon leaps over the balcony overhead and lands between me and Aliya. It takes one step forward and growls at her. "Taj! It's me! Aliya!"

Karima is at my side. She wraps her arms around mine and pulls herself close. "I knew you were different, Taj," Karima says, as she brings her free hand to my face. "It's you. You're the one who will help me change everything."

Karima turns to the devastated city. "City of Kos, the face of evil is not something to be found solely in the Word. It is not the inyo that haunt your streets. It is not the guilt of your sins. It is this man. Kolade"—she points to her brother, who kneels at the bottom of the stairs, surrounded by Mages, his clothes rumpled, dirt smudging his brow—"who would carelessly cast the burden of his sins upon others. Who could not be *bothered* to live with his own guilt. Who would order the destruction of dahia merely to find others upon which he could paint his sins." She leans down to meet his eyes. "Who would order the murder of his own sister."

She turns to me, shining like something sent from the sky. "Taj. Join me. Rule by my side." She points out over the heads of the crowd at the sin-beasts that hover in the air and stand on rooftops and crowd the streets among the Forum-dwellers. "Look at the army you command. No longer shall the wealthy use the poor to absolve themselves of their guilt. No longer shall people be forced to bear the guilt of others because of where and how they are born. With this army, we can overturn the order. Whether you live in the dahia or on the Palace estates, no one should be immune from bearing the weight of their sin." She steps toward me. "Let us smash the old Kos until it is unrecognizable. From the ashes, we'll build a new Kos."

She takes my hand in hers, and together, we mount the steps. I feel intoxicated by her, by her vision of this new Kos.

"Taj!" Aliya calls from the bottom of the steps. "Don't." Her voice breaks when she speaks. "Taj, this isn't you. Already, the power is changing you, Taj. It will corrupt you if you let it. Taj, please, don't go." She struggles to speak. "Balance, Taj. In the prophecy. You have a responsibility!"

Karima urges me forward. "Think of your family," she whispers in my ear. "You can give them any room in the Palace. They will never want for anything. All the money they could ever need." She squeezes my hand. "They will forget hunger."

"You feel it, Taj." Aliya doesn't sound like a rebel commander anymore. She doesn't sound like a scholar. She sounds like the girl who slid her hand beneath mine and wished peace upon me and my people. "You wonder. With every single thing you do, you wonder if the guilt is yours or theirs. But you can't keep telling yourself it's all theirs. Sometimes the remorse you feel is your own. The guilt is your own. You know this, Taj. If you go that way, you will forget this. You'll think you're above blame, above guilt. You'll become just like King Kolade." She takes two steps. The sin-dragon growls, but she walks past it as if she doesn't see it.

"Taj, listen to me. If you walk back into that Palace, you will forget all of this." When she spreads her arm to indicate Kos, I know what she means. I know she means wandering the Forum and trying not to trip over newsboys scurrying through.

Listening to people trade and drink and fight in Zoe's. I know she means the comatose aki who have Crossed and whose limbs have betrayed them, out in front of temples with bowls for begging. I know she means sleeping in shanties with a family of aki, a family we make for ourselves.

Suddenly, the dirt and the smell and the stifling heat, all of it makes me close my eyes. When I open them again, everyone is still there, waiting for me.

"She knows nothing of your world, Taj." Karima's voice still soothes tension from my shoulders.

Distant thunder crackles. Everyone falls silent as it happens again. A booming that rumbles closer and closer. The sky goes red and purple over dahia to the north. I look southward, where the same is happening. It's getting closer; then a sound so sharp rips through the air, and I fall to my knees, hands over my ears. It sounds as though the very sky is tearing itself apart. I grit my teeth. People all around us begin moaning, writhing on the ground in pain.

Another boom. This one is so close it shakes the Palace.

"By the Unnamed," Aliya whispers.

We look up, and a hole opens amid the swirling clouds. Black wings that span the entire Palace grounds emerge, dark and shimmering like polished coal in the night. Then come talons and feet and legs as tall as the statue of Malek in the Arbaa dahia. Then finally, a face, bent into a rictus snarl. It feels like the city of Kos is holding its collective breath.

"An arashi," Aliya breathes.

By the Unnamed. They're real.

Chapter 35

The sin-beasts . . . the pieces slam together in my head . . . Izu knew this would happen. He summoned all the sins in Kos. This many sin-beasts all together, it must have drawn the arashi from the sky. The verses are true. The arashi have come to cleanse the city.

The biggest sin I've ever Eaten is no bigger than this thing's smallest talon.

The arashi rears its head back, and there is that ear-splitting roar again.

Forks of lightning snap down in the dahia. One hits the Forum directly, and the ground quakes. Cracks thread through the main street. Storefronts burst into flames. Then, suddenly, it's chaos. Everyone runs in every different direction. People are praying, shouting orders, crying for their families to stay together. I can't stop staring at the thing that has come to burn Kos to the ground.

Karima smiles at my side.

Seeing her this way breaks me from my trance and returns me to the present. "Princess, we have to leave. The arashi will attack!"

She turns to me with a haunting expression. Her face has paled, but her eyes are alight. She looks mad. "No, Taj. This is it. This is exactly what is supposed to happen."

"What?"

Her smile widens. "The arashi will raze Kos to the ground, and we will build it anew." She moves closer, so close I can feel her breath on my cheek. "I knew Izu's plan all along. The camps. Everything. He had hoped the king would give in easily and that he would live to become the chief kanselo. And I was prepared to kill him. You see, Taj, he was the key. He would unleash enough inisisa to draw the arashi at last. I could not have planned this more perfectly—"

"How could you!" My head spins, and I clench my hands into fists at my side. She's the one. Of all the Kayas, she's the most dangerous, the one who would destroy our homes and not bat an eye. "You're going to kill us all!"

"Stay with me and be spared."

"TAJ!"

I turn, and there's Aliya at the bottom of the stairs. Arzu stands next to her.

"Run!"

Fire burns in the north, a red-and-orange line blazing along the horizon. The Kosians shouting and weeping and running through the Forum can barely stand from the wind created by each flap of the arashi's wings. Towers and homes explode with each crack of lightning.

"Princess, stop this." I don't know how she would, but I need to say it.

Her face hardens. "Leave, and you will know nothing but pain."

"TAJ—" Aliya again, but an earthquaking roar cuts her off.

I turn to go, and that's when I see Bo rushing up the stairs. My heart rises. Bo and I—we'll fight this together.

"Bo, we have to g—"

He lunges at me with his daga, and I leap away just in time to keep him from gutting me. "Bo, what are you doing?"

He flips his daga in his hands and charges at me again.

I catch his daga with my own. He kicks his leg out, and I fall hard onto the steps. I feel something in my back snap and cry out. My arms tremble, trying to keep Bo's daga out of my eye.

"Bo," I plead. "What are you doing?"

"I can't let you leave."

"What? Why?" Dizziness hits me. The sin-spots on Bo's arms start to swirl. Another explosion in the sky brings me back to reality, and I flip over onto Bo. "Bo, stop this."

"Karima will restore us." He's stronger than me, and he pushes me back. Hard.

I scramble up, and he swipes at my shoulder. Then again at my stomach.

"Bo, she's trying to kill us!" I wave my arm to indicate the city falling around us. Aki and inisisa cluster at the bottom of the stairs, watching us.

Another boom.

Bo loosens his strap and flings his daga at me. I move just in time to keep it from slashing me, but a cut opens up on my cheek. Bo snaps it back, then flings it loose again.

"Bo, can't you see what's happening?" I try to dodge, but I'm getting slower. This time, he cuts my arm. Pain blossoms. Red starts to leak down my sin-spots. "What are you doing?"

Bo's daga returns to him. "We were supposed to do this together."

"What?"

"When the moneychanger purchased my freedom, I was offered a choice. Remain aki forever or change this city. A Mage approached me, and I was granted an audience with the princess. She told me of her intentions. And she told me that you would be joining us. I was ready. I was ready to fight alongside you to repair our city." He grits his teeth. "No more aki need die. No more aki need hide in the shadows, rejected by the rest of this city. We both have the power, Taj. I too can control the inisisa."

The fires spread. More explosions rip through Kos. This is all too much to believe.

"No more of my people need die in the mines, finding gemstones for the unworthy who live on the hill. Isn't this what you wanted?"

"Not like this, Bo. Not like this."

"Fine." He whips his daga out toward me.

Just as I raise my left arm, it goes numb, and the blade slices through my forearm. The strap wraps around my wrist and cuts through my bracelet. Zainab's stone falls at my feet.

With both hands, Bo tugs me forward.

I stumble but throw my fist out just in time to catch him on his cheek. We both fall so hard his strap breaks.

The sins I Ate roar in my head. Numbness creeps through my limbs. I can't go on much longer.

The Palace shivers with each new explosion.

I reach my hand up to wipe a gash on my temple, and Zainab's stone catches my eye. Its glow fades. A shadow darkens the stone, and I have only enough energy to look up and see Bo standing over me. He has his daga in his hand. Blood trickles down the side of his chin.

"You were supposed to join us." He raises his daga, and I close my eyes. "I'm sorry."

Suddenly, someone tackles him from behind.

Arzu. She pins him down on the cracked stone steps.

Palace guards and Mages run in all directions, some trying to bring order to the chaos, some swarming to protect the princess, some trying to save their own lives. I feel steady hands tuck under my arms.

"Taj," Aliya says softly in my ear, as she gathers me up in her arms. "Let's go."

"But Arzu," I murmur, barely able to stand.

I look back one last time and see Arzu and Bo struggling as Palace guards rush to them.

More holes open in the sky as giant arashi pour forth. By the morning, there will be nothing left of Kos.

Aliya takes my arm, and we charge through the crowd. I can feel my legs again. I'm able to run. We dash down the thoroughfare, past aki, past temples and foodsellers' shops, past jewelers' stalls, past dimming candlelight glowing in abandoned homes, past shattered dahia, past even the sins painted by Scribes on the Wall. Inyo swim down our throats, choking us.

My eyes burn at the thought of Arzu and what will happen to her. Fear and anger and guilt clench my heart at the thought of Bo's betrayal.

Fire roars throughout the city.

I don't stop running until I get to a part of the forest I don't recognize. Aliya is beside me. Other rebel Mages have gathered. Noor and Ras and others who escaped, they fill the space too. I have no idea how much time and distance separate us from Princess Karima and the city overflowing with inisisa.

Guilt. So much guilt. I left them behind. All of them.

And pain. I collapse. This time, it feels real. I'm Crossing. Liar. Thief. Sinner. Adulterer. Thief. Killer. Braggart. Brawler.

Liar. Thief. Betrayer.

My head in my hands, I scream. Then it comes. Like a river, the sin gushes out of my mouth.

Then it stops.

"Taj?"

I look up at the sound of Aliya's voice. An inisisa hovers over me. A massive sin-bull whose horns twirl from out of its head. Somehow, slowly, I find the strength to stand. "My sin,"

I whisper. My betrayal. My not choosing Karima. Leaving her behind. Choosing to rebel. Fighting Bo. "Aliya, did you call this from me?" I put my hand to its forehead. Slowly, it's darkness begins to fade, revealing coarse tawny fur. The beast glows.

Aliya walks to me, catching her breath. "No, Taj. You called forth this inisisa yourself."

"But only Mages can do that. I'm not a Mage. I couldn't have called forth my own sin."

"I always knew you were special, Taj." I can see her small grin in the darkness. I remember Arzu and her story of the tastahlik, the healers in her homeland who also Eat sin. Could they call forth sins as well as Eat them? Am I one of them?

But before she can say anything else, we hear something rustle from far away. I almost collapse, but Aliya gets her hands under my arms just in time, struggling to hold me up. I can barely see a thing.

A small form comes crashing through the brush. The girl pulls down her mask, and it's Noor. No fear in her eyes. None whatsoever.

"They're coming," she says.

And that's when we hear the stampede.

The arashi's cry is a memory now, as are the pleadings and prayers of the people of Kos. I pray Mama and Baba are still alive. Omar and Ifeoma and Sade and Tolu and Emeka. So many others. I can't let myself believe they didn't make it out of Kos alive. The hooves and feet of sin-beasts draw near. Bo is likely leading them.

Fireflies flit between tree branches. Otherwise, the only light that illuminates us—Mages, aki, me—is the lightning that ripples beneath the flesh of the bull walking silently like a sentinel among us. This beast made of light. But we hear the stampeding. Hooves thundering not far from here, brush swishing against what can only be the shadowy flanks of inisisa.

They've sent their army after us.

Acknowledgments

A BOOK GETS written, and that's hardly the end of it.

I could not have asked for a more capable team than the folks at Razorbill. From the beginning, Ben, Casey, and my editor, Jess, believed in Taj and his story, and in the necessity of its telling. With the steadiest of hands, they guided me through the exciting and sometimes nerve-wracking process of launching a debut novel. And kept me from getting lost in the chaos of the Forum.

I'm also grateful to my agent, Noah Ballard, for being as wonderful and capable a companion in this endeavor as I could have asked for. I am a supremely lucky writer to have him at my side.

My eternal gratitude goes out to every writing teacher whose instruction has ever fallen upon my sometimes stubbornly blocked ears, whether or not your name appears on my transcripts. In particular, I must thank notably John Crowley, Ken Liu, and Elizabeth Bear, who have transformed from mythological beings to colleagues and friends, retaining their heroic qualities all the while.

Tiffany Liao saw Taj in the very beginning of his journey and saw me in the beginning of mine. And she believed. Without her, Kos and its wonders would never have made it to the page.

And, finally, I must thank Mom, who held Nigeria in her bosom while traversing an ocean and brought that place into our household. Mom, whose courage and wisdom have carried me my entire life and whose jollof rice is peerless.